"EVERYONE HERE HAS A MOTIVE FOR WANTING SHARKEY DEAD," TORY WHISPERED.

"That's ridiculous!" Dodge cried. "You mean, everyone except you and me, don't you? Or aren't you so sure about me anymore?"

"Oh, Dodge, of course I trust you!"

"Then don't accuse anyone here of murder, Tory. These people are my friends, and they were Sharkey's friends, too. As far as we know, Sharkey wasn't murdered—it was just an accident. I don't want to hear any more about it."

Tory gazed at him sadly. "Okay, Dodge. I'll forget all about it."

He held her gaze a moment longer. "I think we'd better go to bed now. Alone."

As she watched him leave, Tory prayed in angry silence, *Not you, Dodge. Don't let the murderer be you!*

CANDLELIGHT SUPREMES

CALLAHAN'S GOLD

Tate McKenna

A CANDLELIGHT SUPREME

Published by
Dell Publishing Co., Inc.
1 Dag Hammarskjold Plaza
New York, New York 10017

ISBN: 0-440-11076-9

Printed in the United States of America

June 1987

10 9 8 7 6 5 4 3 2 1

WFH

*Thanks to Tex and Janet for
introducing me to Tombstone Territory.*

*And to Johnnie Frederick and Linda Cox for
keeping romance alive in Clinton, Mississippi,
with heroes like Dodge Callahan.
Now he's all yours!*

To Our Readers:

We are pleased and excited by your overwhelmingly positive response to our Candlelight Supremes. Unlike all the other series, the Supremes are filled with more passion, adventure, and intrigue, and are obviously the stories you like best.

In months to come we will continue to publish books by many of your favorite authors as well as the very finest work from new authors of romantic fiction. As always, we are striving to present unique, absorbing love stories —the very best love has to offer.

Breathtaking and unforgettable, Supremes follow in the great romantic tradition you've come to expect *only* from Candlelight Romances.

Your suggestions and comments are always welcome. Please let us hear from you.

Sincerely,

The Editors
Candlelight Romances
1 Dag Hammarskjold Plaza
New York, New York 10017

CALLAHAN'S GOLD

PROLOGUE

Her most vivid memory of her father was the day he told her he was leaving. She was six years old. Over the years, his face had faded into an obscure vision, reinforced only by a few photos her mother had kept. She did remember his eyes, not just blue, but a deep, almost violet color. And when she looked into the mirror as a child, she'd remind herself she had eyes like her daddy.

And people claimed they had the same black hair, black as the night. It was small consolation to the child who barely remembered him. When Tory Carsen was a lonely teenager, caught between being a woman and a child, she sometimes wondered if this man who'd once been her father were still alive somewhere and if he still loved her. Her memory of him was foggy, consisting of fleeting glimpses. But one conversation, the last one, was distinct.

"Of course I love you, Tory darlin'," he had vowed the day he left. "You'll always be my little girl."

Being a child who didn't accept answers easily, Tory followed him down the sidewalk to the rickety old Ford. "Then *why* are you going away, Daddy?"

He tossed two beat-up suitcases into the backseat. "I know it's hard for you to understand, Tory darlin', but I have other worlds to explore. The city life just isn't for me. I have to seek the sun. Someday I'll come back to you, and we'll be rich, and you can have anything you want."

"A pony?"

"Yep. A whole corral full of ponies! And a room full of toys! And . . . anything you want!"

"But I don't want anything, Daddy. I just want you to stay here with me and Mommy."

"I can't, Tory. Your mom and I have grown-up problems."

"Then why can't I go with you?" she persisted stubbornly.

He shook his head and looked away. "It isn't a place for little girls."

"Maybe it isn't a place for daddies, either."

Gazing down at his tenacious daughter, Sharkey Carsen heaved a sigh. "Maybe not, darlin', but I have to find out." He lifted her up in his arms and kissed each chubby cheek. Then he set her down and walked out of her life forever.

Tory perched Indian-style on the sidewalk and watched her father drive away in that dingy yellow Ford.

He never returned. Never brought her that pony he promised. They were never rich. By the end of the month, she and her mother had to move out of the neat little house on Beale Street and into an incessant string of apartments on L.A.'s south side.

Her father had claimed he'd gone off to find the sun, and Tory grew to despise him for leaving them.

Twenty years later, when Tory Carsen Talbot received the certified letter informing her of Sharkey Carsen's death, she scanned the letter coldly, with no emotion. By now it didn't matter that they had the same deep blue eyes, the same blue black hair. He was like a total stranger to her, and she bore no grief for the man who had been her father.

But the second paragraph of the letter captured Tory's natural curiosity. She was named as an inheritor and was urged to attend the reading of the will. A melange of emotions swept through her—of hate and anger, of curiosity and indifference, of concern . . . but definitely not love.

Spontaneously, she decided to go, not stopping to determine if her decision were a reasonable and logical one. An inheritance . . . By God, he owed her that much.

Tory Talbot reached across a paper-cluttered desk and picked up the phone. Her ivory crepe sleeve brushed two unopened envelopes onto the floor, but she ignored them. They were only more bills.

"Megan, do you think you could handle the shop for a few days? Something's come up, and I need to go out of town. It's quite important. Could mean enough money to salvage *Tall and Terrific*. Incidentally, how do I fly to Tombstone, Arizona?"

CHAPTER ONE

The tall cowboy's spurs jangled as he ambled up to the bar, planted his boots wide, tipped his white Stetson back with his thumb, and drawled. "Can I buy you a drink, Miss Katie?"

"Why sure, Marshal. I'd be mighty pleased. Where've you been? Haven't seen you around the Short Branch Saloon lately."

"I've been out roundin' up that dirty, thievin', low-down Phoenix Gang. Got 'um all but the leaders, Buck and the Moondance Kid."

"Oh, Marshal," Miss Katie sighed, batting her long black artificial eyelashes, "I'm sure a great big hunk-of-a-man like you will get them, sooner or later."

"Jes' hope I get 'um afore they get me and take over the whole town of Tombstone." The tall marshal gazed down longingly at the pretty woman clinging to his arm. His square-jawed profile was shadowed beneath the curve-brimmed Stetson hat, and a craggy russet mustache occasionally caught glints from the sun.

Miss Katie smiled up at the handsome cowboy and tipped her amber-filled glass against his.

Golden ringlets dangled sexily across one creamy shoulder where crimson ruffles dipped to reveal a daring amount of cleavage. One side of her skirt was tucked up to expose a shapely stretch of thigh. The marshal clearly enjoyed the view.

A voice boomed out of nowhere: "Hey, Marshal, I hear tell yer callin' me 'n my brothers names!"

All eyes swung around to the four meanest-looking characters they'd ever seen. The intruders were dressed in black and wore wide-brimmed black hats.

"Why, if it isn't the dirty, thievin' leaders of the Phoenix Gang, Buck and the Moondance Kid, and Buck's two stupid brothers!" Miss Katie exclaimed loudly, wide-eyed with fright.

"You forgot 'low-down,' Miss Katie," the marshal growled.

"Nobody calls me 'n my brothers names, Marshal!"

The handsome marshal motioned to his shapely companion. "Clear out, Katie. This ain't no place for a lady."

"That ain't no lady, Marshal!"

"Them's fightin' words, Buck. Apologize to the lady!"

"I ain't apologizing to nobody," Buck snarled. "Prepare to die, Marshal!"

Tension mounted as the tall man with the tin star pinned to his chest squared around and faced his four enemies. His long legs spread apart, and curved hands poised near the six-guns strapped to

16

each hip. The sun sizzled overhead, almost audible in that terrible moment.

Suddenly, all hell broke loose in a barrage of gunfire and smoke. When the air cleared, four black-hatted men sprawled dead in the street. The marshal coolly blew smoke from the barrels of each six-gun, holstered them, turned back to the bar, and calmly finished his drink. Miss Katie hung admiringly on his arm.

"You saved the whole town, Marshal! You're our hero."

He touched the brim of his white Stetson with a reverent caress. "Jes' doin' my duty, Miss Katie. Now Tombstone will be safe for another day."

The crowd lining the old town of Tombstone's wooden sidewalks broke into polite applause, and the four bad guys hopped to their feet and bowed grandly to their appreciative audience. Then the actors began to mingle with the crowd, signing autographs.

Tory Talbot stood with the audience, engrossed in the unique street scene. For a few minutes it was easy to imagine she had stepped back in time, to the wild and wicked days when gunslingers were a way of life in this historic town of Tombstone, Arizona. To a time when the marshal indeed ruled with a six-gun.

Modern tourists, braving ninety-plus temperatures in shorts and T-shirts, were conspicuously out of style as they mingled with local townsfolk dressed in 1880s attire. Here was a chance to relive another era. This time, however, it was all done in fun, and the 'bad guys' weren't planted in Boot

Hill at the end of the day. Instead, they posed for photographs and let kids in the audience try on their black hats.

Yes, Tory decided, this make-believe rendition was far better than the real-life version. That is, if reliving the past was of interest. She preferred not to dwell on it, herself. It was too painful. The future held her only hope for happiness.

Like any June day a hundred years ago, this one was hot and dusty. Tory felt a trickle of perspiration travel down the middle of her back. Even with her shiny black hair clipped in the newest short-short style and wearing a casual blue silk dress, she was anything but cool. She dug into her leather purse for a tissue to dab at her temples and the back of her neck.

She couldn't help noticing that the town marshal, too, was showing the effects of the heat. He stood with his broad back to her, signing autographs, and she paused to admire the width of those masculine shoulders and the trim thrust of his hips. A large, dark oval of perspiration marked his western shirt between his shoulder blades and angled downward to the leather belted waistband and tight-fitting jeans. His legs were long, and on his feet were the scruffiest, most well-worn cowboy boots Tory had ever seen.

She wondered how he could have abused those boots so badly. Was he a *real* cowboy? He certainly looked lean and fit, just the way a cowboy should be.

Reminding herself of her reason for being in this remote "town too tough to die," Tory turned away

18

from assessing the marshal and pushed through the swinging doors of the Crystal Palace Saloon. She approached the bartender. He wore a black string tie and white apron over his ample belly and looked right out of 1880. He gave her a ready smile.

"Help you, ma'am? How about a sarsaparilla?"

"Something cold with ice. Perrier with lemon?"

"Coming right up."

She waited until he slid the drink across the bar. "I'm looking for a Mr. Cliff Snyder. I was supposed to meet him here."

The bartender's eyes swept appreciatively over Tory's tall but impressive form. She was obviously a tourist in town. "Why does Cliff get all the pretty ones? I'm sorry, but he isn't here right now. Maybe I can help you."

"I doubt it," Tory answered honestly, letting her gaze travel behind him to the massive mahogany arches that formed the antique bar. "We have some business to discuss. I understand Mr. Snyder's in charge of reading my father's will. I received a notarized letter from him requesting my presence at the Crystal Palace Saloon this afternoon."

"Reading of a will? Oh, you must mean the reading of ole' Sharkey Carsen's will." He wiped his hands on a white towel and tucked it into the string at his ample waist.

"Yes." Tory nodded, wishing fervently that the old saloon were air-conditioned or that she were somewhere—anywhere—else at this very minute. She took a grateful sip of the Perrier.

"You aren't Sharkey's little girl, are you?"

She nodded. "Sharkey Carsen's daughter."

He leaned forward, his elbows on the bar, and scrutinized every bit of her slender five feet nine inches. His smiling eyes settled curiously on her face as if she'd announced she were Annie Oakley, reincarnated. "Honest?"

Tory paused and rubbed the bridge of her nose. "It's been a long time since anyone's called me a 'little girl,' but yes, Sharkey Carsen was my father."

The bartender's chubby hand shot across the bar. "Heck Griffin, here. Your pa was a friend of mine. Fine man, ole' Sharkey. Pleased to make your acquaintance."

Tory took his hand. "Tory Talbot, Mr. Griffin."

"Call me Heck. Everybody around here does."

"Heck, then. Now, if you'd kindly direct me to this Cliff Snyder's law office, I'd appreciate it."

Heck straightened up with a proud smile. He motioned to the rear with his thumb. "Right back there. Last table in the corner. Cliff said to direct Sharkey's heirs to his spot, and he'll be here shortly. The last show'll be over soon. I think he had to break up a lynch mob."

She stiffened. "Did you say 'lynch mob'?"

"Yep. Most all the business folks around here play some part in the shows. Entertaining the tourists keeps this town alive. Take that last show, for instance. Miss Katie runs the Lucky Cuss restaurant, and the marshal is a college professor. One of the bad guys is the Presbyterian preacher."

"I see." Tory smiled politely, wondering how to

speed up this will-reading process. She could only think that she wanted to get out of here as soon as possible. The place had certain unpleasant—invisible—vibes. "You mean a lawyer does his business in here? A bar?"

"Yep. It isn't exactly a bar. It's an Old West saloon." Heck spoke with a certain pride. "There's a difference, you know. It isn't unusual for all kinds of business to be conducted here—everything from horse trading to assaying a bag of gold nuggets. We here in Tombstone have a tradition to uphold, you know."

"Yes, well, it may be usual for Tombstone, but it seems highly unorthodox to me. I'll be waiting for Mr. Snyder back here in his, er, office."

"Sure I can't get you something a little stronger to drink?"

"No, thank you." With her iced glass of Perrier in hand, Tory dutifully took a seat at the round gambling table in the rear of the room. Instinctively, she sat with her back to the wall, like the old gamblers used to do, and watched everyone who entered the saloon. Indeed, she felt very much like a gambler today. Only she was gambling on a future and daring to touch the past. Neither was her style.

The handsome marshal, surrounded by several admiring fans—mostly young and female—entered the saloon and sidled up to the bar. He moved with a certain air of dominion as he leaned one elbow casually on the bar. Perhaps this swagger of authority came with the badge and the role.

Curiously, Tory watched the man. His motions

21

seemed exaggerated and reminded her of the heroes in old western movies. Only this one was real, in an almost-real setting. He was a combination of John Wayne, Clint Eastwood, and Gary Cooper with a hint of Audi Murphy's devilish smile. He was at least six feet four, maybe taller, and when he removed the white Stetson, she admired the way his thick shock of dark brown hair curled damply around his crown.

The man was extremely masculine and intriguing. Tory had never been attracted to such a man, one so rough around the edges. But she was certainly fascinated with this one. The bartender leaned over the bar toward him and, as he spoke, motioned to the corner table where Tory sat.

The marshal eyed her for a moment, and Tory felt an aggravating tingle down her spine as their gazes clashed. After a few minutes, he ambled toward her, a beer in each hand. Tory caught her breath when he stopped beside her table. "Can I buy you a drink, Miss—?"

Tory's gaze traveled up his lean blue-jeaned length and she smiled. "That line sounds familiar, Marshal."

"It usually works." He grinned and shrugged angular shoulders. "I'm not the real marshal—just filling in today. Have a beer?"

She looked at his hands and noted long, sturdy fingers wrapped around the moist bottles. Lifting her violet gaze to meet his brown one, she nodded. "Thanks. Looks like I may need one before this day's over."

He set the bottles and a single glass on the table

and whirled a chair around backward before strad-
dling it. Giving her an all-over curious glance, he
introduced himself. "Dodge Callahan."

Tory reached for his outstretched hand, oddly
eager to touch him. When she pressed her palm to
his, it felt every bit as strong as she'd imagined, yet
vibrated with a certain warmth that created a sensation within her she hadn't expected. "Tory Talbot. Nice to meet you, Dodge. With a name like
that, I'd say you were certainly dressed appropri-
ately."

He gave her a sideways embarrassed grin. "My
mother thought a person ought to live up to his
name. I had three older brothers, and she figured
I'd need a name like this to get me through."

"Three older brothers? I'd bet you were a pretty
tough kid."

"Took me eighteen years to get taller than my
oldest brother. I spent a lot of time praying to
grow. And a lot more time dodging."

They laughed, and Tory liked the way his face
crinkled warmly around his almond-shaped brown
eyes. "Did you grow up around here?"

"Wyoming."

"What are you doing way down here?"

"Teaching part-time. And mining. I understand
you're Sharkey's little girl."

"Word travels fast," she replied dryly, tilting the
frosty glass and pouring the cold beer against the
side.

Dodge Callahan's presence was somewhat unnerving to Tory. Up close the man was even more
commanding than he had been in the middle of the

23

street firing make-believe bullets. His unruly brown hair bore amber streaks from being in the sun too much and curled low on his nape. His nose wasn't quite straight, nor was his grin. They were offset by a wonderfully bushy mustache with reddish highlights.

His eyes were bold brown, the color of mahogany, as he squinted his assessment of Tory.

"Did you know my father?" She tried to mask her feminine response to him.

"I just can't believe you're Sharkey's little girl," Dodge marveled with a nod, peering closer as if trying to discern a familiar gene or two.

"Actually, I'm nobody's 'little girl.' I'm not even little, unless you consider five nine short. Yes, Sharkey Carsen was, at one time, my father."

"This is such a pleasure to finally meet you." Dodge smiled warmly at her, and his sincerity was obvious. "Sharkey often talked about his little girl."

"Then you did know him?" Somehow, her inflection made it sound like an accusation.

"I'm one of his partners in the mining company. Was, that is. My God, I just can't get over it! Sharkey's daughter." He slapped his thigh with delight and took a long swig of beer from the bottle.

"I can't understand why you're so surprised, Dodge."

"Well, you aren't exactly what I expected."

"You probably thought I'd be older. You see, Sharkey was more than twenty years older than my mother."

"Actually, I expected . . ." Dodge rested his

muscular forearms on the chair's back and continued to appraise her with those deep-reaching brown eyes. "I thought you'd be much younger. The reason Sharkey talked about his 'little girl' so much was that he remembered you just the way you were the day he left."

"At age six? Figures. He never bothered to find out whether or not I grew up." There was an unmistakable tang to her words. "Nor did he contribute in any way to the process."

Dodge leaned forward and lowered his voice. "Sharkey wasn't perfect. But then, none of us are, are we?"

Tory backed off. No need to dredge up old feelings with this stranger. He had no idea of the hardships Sharkey had caused her and her mother. "I suppose not," she conceded.

"You know, Sharkey wasn't much of a looker, and I don't see much family resemblance—except maybe your eyes. You have beautiful eyes, you know. Bold and a little daring."

Tory's dark eyelashes fluttered to her cheeks at his compliment. "Yes, he gave me blue eyes and black hair. But that's about all he contributed."

Dodge ignored her acerbity. "I would hardly call your eyes blue. They remind me of wild violets. And 'black' doesn't do justice to your hair. It's more . . . like a shiny . . . jet that the Indians used for money. Sharkey's hair was snow white when we knew him. So was his beard. Nobody ever saw him clean shaven or knew what color his hair was."

"Yes, well, I'm sure my father spent many years

cultivating that distinctive old miner's appearance. About twenty to be exact."

"You say your name is Talbot, not Carsen? Then you're married?" Dodge's brown eyes classified her boldly, then dropped to her left hand, which was conspicuously bare.

"Divorced."

"Oh." There was a moment of silence, as if in tribute to the fact that she wasn't legally attached. "Funny that Sharkey never mentioned his daughter's being married. Or divorced."

"It isn't funny at all, Dodge. You see, Sharkey Carsen closed my mother and me out of his life many years ago. And we closed him out of ours. It was better for my mother to think of him as dead. So we did. He never knew, or cared, that I was married or that I was divorced two years ago. And he never knew that my mother was ill or that she died last year."

"Your mother died? I'm sorry. Did you try to notify Sharkey? I'm sure he would—"

"No, he wouldn't have wanted to know. It would have reminded him that he had us. And I'm sure he didn't want that." She faced him squarely. "But it didn't really matter what Sharkey thought. My mother didn't want him to be contacted, and I concurred with her wishes."

"Maybe you were ashamed of him," Dodge accused suddenly. "A grimy old miner, plodding along behind a mule loaded with a pick and six-month's worth of beans and flour."

"Frankly, I don't know this miner character you're talking about. This is the man I remember."

26

She dug into her purse and produced an old, faded photo.

Dodge looked at the wrinkled and faded snapshot of a younger man, dark haired and clean shaven, staring arrogantly at the camera. His arm was draped over the shoulders of a very attractive woman, definitely resembling the young woman who sat next to him.

"That's him with my mother about six months before he left. Does he look like a man about to walk out on his family?"

Dodge's eyes flickered, and his facial expression changed. Softened. "So this is old Sharkey in his younger days? Hell, he wasn't too bad looking. Still doesn't look much like you, though. Except the eyes." He lifted his gaze to meet her violet eyes, then back to the photo. "Yes, there's a touch of the same glint."

"You say you were Sharkey's partner, Dodge? In a mining company?" Tory changed the subject as she took the photo of her father from Dodge's large hand and slipped it back in her purse.

"I was one of his partners. Here comes the other one now. Rex Fierro. He's the money man, put up our initial capital."

Tory quickly assessed the man entering the saloon. Rex Fierro was slight of build, not as tall as Dodge, but energetic and dark haired. He moved rapidly across the plank flooring, greeting a few of the patrons and the bartender along the way.

"Rex wasn't an active partner in the actual mining," Dodge related before Rex arrived at the table. "Oh, he'd come up to the camp occasionally, but his heart wasn't in it. Sharkey never could understand him. He thought any man who put money into an endeavor should be enthusiastic about the project. Rex wasn't. He was only interested in the bottom line. Can't really blame him for that, though."

Rex approached the back table, moving fast and talking. "Dodge, *mi amigo!* How the hell are you? Damn shame about Sharkey, wasn't it?" Without waiting for an answer, he turned to Tory. "I don't think I've had the pleasure, senorita."

Dodge stood and introduced them. "Rex Fierro, this is Tory Talbot, Sharkey's little girl."

"Con mucho gusto, Miss Talbot. Accept my condolences, *por favor,* about your father's tragic accident. Sharkey was a fine man . . . A little bit strange, but aren't we all? Just a little?"

Tory couldn't help bristling. "To be honest, Mr. Fierro, I'm not in mourning any more than you are."

He paused shortly and nodded at her pointed correction, his black eyes dropping to her left hand, then lifting questioningly.

"She's divorced, Rex. But I think she's trying to tell you something. Tell us both, in fact." Dodge quirked an eyebrow.

"Maybe we can change her mind." Rex winked and turned quickly to the hefty bartender. "Hey, Heck, fix us a round of drinks over here, will you?"

"I'm fine, thanks." Tory shook her head and indicated her half-full glass of beer. "Don't we have business to conduct here? Where is Mr. Snyder, anyway?"

"Don't know about Cliff, but here comes Ramona."

Tory turned curiously toward the door. "Ramona? Who's that?"

"Sharkey's—uh—lady friend."

She glanced over the attractive jet-haired woman, then inclined her head toward Dodge. "His lover?"

"Well, yes," Dodge admitted with a quick nod. "I'm glad you're so understanding about this, Tory. It could be a little sticky."

" 'Tolerant' is a more correct term, Dodge." She paused to sigh impatiently. "Do I have to stay around for this whole charade? I really have no desire to sit around and listen to tributes to my father. Frankly, I just came out of curiosity."

"I thought you came to claim your inheritance," Dodge replied bluntly. His words were cryptic and his brown eyes accusing.

"Something like that," she countered with narrowed eyes. "Can you blame me for being interested in the bottom line?"

He turned his palms outward. "I'm not a judgmental man. This'll be over soon. It looks like everybody's here who should be."

"Except Cliff Snyder."

"Speak of the devil." Dodge motioned to the door, then rose to greet the lovely dark-eyed woman who approached their back table. "Hello, Ramona. I want you to meet Sharkey's little girl, Tory Talbot."

29

"Hello." Tory smiled politely and weakly shook Ramona's hand. Sharkey's lover. This wasn't going to be easy. She turned to Dodge and muttered for his ears only, "I am *not* a little girl and have never been Sharkey's. Not since I was six. I'd appreciate it if you'd stop referring to me as such."

"Yes, ma'am," he nodded solemnly, then winked one of those devil's brown eyes. "It just slipped out."

Tory bustled in her seat, straightened her shoulders squarely, and looked away. What nerve! She thought she'd made herself perfectly clear to both Sharkey's partners. Her father certainly had some strange associates.

"Here comes the lawyer."

Cliff Snyder, dressed like an 1880s banker complete with gold chain watch looped in his vest pocket, hurried up to the table, a thin manila folder in his left hand. His graying hair peeked from beneath a dark hat, and his thin, straight mustache was as white as snow. "Sorry I'm late, folks. This town is growing so much it's getting downright busy! I see we're all here." He nodded to each member around the table. "Dodge . . . Rex . . . Ramona . . . And you must be Sharkey's little girl." He smiled benevolently at Tory.

She drew up tight. If she heard "little girl" one more time, she thought she'd scream. "I'm Tory Talbot, Mr. Snyder. Sharkey Carsen was my father. I have my birth certificate for identification." She handed him the form, but he didn't even look at it.

"My, my, Sharkey sure would be pleased with the way you turned out."

"Thank you, Mr. Snyder, but if my father had wanted to know how I turned out, he would have handled things differently, I'm sure. Now, could we get on with this? I have a plane to catch in Tucson in a few hours."

"Certainly," he nodded, growing serious. "Are we ready to start this very unpleasant business, that of reading the last will and testament of Sharkey Carsen?" He looked up at the assembled group. "No, there's one more thing. Heck? Bring the pot, please."

Tory expected coffee, thinking it was damned hot for coffee, but it might keep this group sober. Heck ambled toward them, holding a rather large, brightly painted Indian pot that he set in the center of the old gambling table.

"Thank you, Heck. Now that we have Sharkey's remains—and his spirit here with us—we can begin the reading of the will."

Tory's eyes riveted to the gaily decorated Indian pot. "You mean"—she halted in a soft gasp—"he's . . . right there?"

"Yep," Cliff Snyder said proudly. "He's here with us, waiting for a proper burial."

"Why—why didn't you take care of that already?" she rasped.

"Because it's not my job. It's yours. All of yours." The lawyer smiled benevolently and opened the folder.

Tory took a deep, calming breath and slumped against the chair. It was like a dream out of the past. A nightmare coming true. Today she had stepped into a time warp to a town that still had gunfights in the streets, where the women wore hoop skirts and the men stuffed gold chain watches into black vests. Seated next to her was the handsome town marshal with a tin star pinned to his chest; around the table were the gamblers and the old miner's Indian lover. And in the center was a vessel containing the old miner's remains.

Tory kept reminding herself it *was* the twentieth century. But she couldn't prove it by looking around her there in Tombstone.

CHAPTER TWO

Tory stared in amazed disgust as Cliff Snyder fortified himself with a stiff shot of Scotch before he
began reading the last will and testament of one
Sharkey Carsen.

" 'I, Sharkey Carsen, being of sound mind and
body, do request a gathering of my friends for this
reading, including my little girl, Tory—something
I could never do during my lifetime.

" 'I was always an aimless sort, following the
wind, seeking the sun. Now maybe I can leave a
legacy of some worth to those people who stood by
me.' " Cliff paused and glanced at Ramona. She
dropped her eyes, and he went on. " 'I'm sure of a
treasure hidden in the Dragoon Mountains. I've
come mighty close to it. Now it's up to you to find
it, my friends. With my help. To my partner, Rex
Fierro . . .' " Cliff paused to look at Rex.

"Well, go on," Rex urged, impatiently tapping
his fingers on the table.

" 'Rex, you can have my lucky pick. It's a good
one, has dug its share of the glitter. Use it to dig
for that sparkly stuff, and you'll get rich. You always were a lucky cuss, anyway.' "

Rex squirmed in his seat, then swore. "I always thought that old coot was crazy. Now, here's proof! Who the hell would leave anybody a damned rusty pick? If I wanted a pick, I'd go down to the hardware store and buy one for twelve bucks!"

"But, Rex, it wouldn't be lucky," Dodge said, chuckling. "And it wouldn't have come from Sharkey."

Everyone laughed except Rex, who demanded of Cliff, "Is that all? All he left for me?"

Cliff's eyes dropped to the paper. "There'll be more later. Please, Rex, let's continue here." Cliff took another quick gulp of his drink. " 'To my partner, Dodge Callahan, I leave all my other mining tools. Use what you can, Dodge, and sell the rest. Or give them to some poor jackass prospector just starting out to seek the sun. You can have the trailer, to sell or use as you see fit. And I want you to keep an eye on the map.' " Cliff paused to take another drink of the Scotch and water before him.

"Map?" Rex asked anxiously. "What map?"

"I'm getting to that, Rex. Just be patient."

"Well, get on with it!"

Cliff started again. " 'To Ramona, the lovely lady who has provided love and laughter to my empty life, I leave my Jeep. Now, Ramona, you can hunt those Indian ruins wherever the four-by-four will take you.' "

"Oh, my God, Sharkey . . ." Ramona seemed to be moved by the practical gift and wiped a tear from the corner of each eye.

"You'd think," Rex mumbled, "he'd leave her

34

something valuable instead of that rusty hunk of tin."

Suddenly, Ramona stood and railed across the table. "What do you know of value, Rex Fierro? If it doesn't have a dollar sign on it, you think it's worthless! But you don't know anything about real worth! Watch what you say about Sharkey or I'll—"

Dodge rose immediately and stretched his long arm around Ramona's shoulder. "Come on now, you two, take it easy. Rex, you're being very insensitive here. And, Ramona, you're a little upset today. We all know this is unpleasant, but let's try to make the best of it."

Tory watched the drama unfolding before her, taking mental note of these unique acquaintances of her father's.

Ramona seemed sincere about her feelings for Sharkey, and Tory felt a natural curiosity about this woman who claimed to love her wayward father. Ramona appeared to be about fifty, was slender and attractive, and carried her Native American traits proudly. Her dark hair was pulled back severely into a knot, and her hands were unusually large for a woman. Her nails were blunt cut and not polished. This was obviously a woman who worked with her hands and didn't pamper them.

"Ladies and gentlemen," Cliff requested, "we must have some decorum here. After all, this is a solemn occasion. Are we ready to continue?" His gaze settled accusingly on Rex.

"Yeah, yeah, I'll be quiet." Rex leaned back and folded his arms.

35

Ramona and Dodge reseated themselves obediently, and there was a moment of silence during which Cliff fortified himself with Scotch again.

Tory felt that the only one at this so-called solemn occasion showing any concrete signs of grief was Ramona. That is, if one could believe her tears were real.

As Ramona resettled across the table from Tory, strain drew her mouth tight and her dark eyebrows into a wrinkled frown. If Tory cared a tinker's damn about any of this, she would have sworn the woman actually loved Sharkey.

However, considering the way he had treated her own mother, Tory could care less about Sharkey Carsen, his life and times, or the women who loved him along the way. This attractive one across the table, so neatly dabbing her nose and eyes, was probably just one of many.

Tory snapped to attention when she heard her name.

" 'And to my little girl, Tory, my only offspring, I leave my third of the Sun Seekers Mining Company.' "

"What?" The outburst came from Rex again. "Why would he do such a stupid thing? You'd think that at the very least he would divide his lousy third between his two working partners. Hell, Dodge and I have provided the work and money for the worthless mining company. Instead, he left it to an estranged daughter he hadn't seen in twenty years! I'll be damned!"

"I wasn't the estranged one," Tory said sourly. "He was. Anyway, I have no interest in owning

36

any part of this hopeless mining company. I'd be glad to split it between you two."

"That's more like it!"

She leaned forward and posed commandingly, "What's the going price for gold mines these days? This one's up for sale."

Rex's only response was a grunt.

"Please, could we continue here, folks?" Cliff took another quick drink.

"Sure, go ahead, Cliff," Dodge agreed, also taking a drink. "This is getting interesting."

Cliff cleared his throat and went back to the will. " 'But the greatest part of my fortune is still in the mountain. So I have drawn a map for my friends.' "

There was another interruption as a rumble rose from those gathered around the table.

"Treasure map? This is ridiculous!" Rex exclaimed above the rest.

"May I proceed?" Cliff gave them all a steel gaze that exacted immediate quiet. " 'Insofar as the map leads directly to the treasure of the Dragoons, it has been torn in two. The left part is here, at this time to be entrusted to my daughter.' " Cliff waved a small piece of paper containing strange markings. " 'The right side rests in a tin box beneath the skull *de la vaca* at the sight of the secret spring.' "

"What the hell is this?" Rex fumed. "What secret spring? Beneath a cow's skull? My God, there must be hundreds in that godforsaken area!"

Ramona turned on him angrily. "This should perk up your selfish ears, Rex. If it has to do with

37

money, you're always interested." Then she looked at Dodge. "I know where the secret spring is. It's an underground water supply beneath a hieroglyphic Sharkey and I found one time. It's completely protected by an overhanging rock. Because of its location, the original colors are vivid, and the drawings are unmarred by graffiti. In fact, you can only see it if you lie on your back and scoot under it. That's when you can hear the underground spring. Sharkey called it a secret spring. It probably sustained a small civilization in the area a thousand years ago and ran above ground."

"Could you find it again?" Dodge asked.

"Of course. I have it well documented. That was what I did while Sharkey hunted for gold. I hunted and documented lost Indian drawings in that area."

"Did you know about this map?"

She shook her head indifferently. "He never mentioned it."

"Then how do we know he's telling the truth about a treasure?" Rex countered.

"We don't," reasoned Dodge. "We'll have to find out for ourselves. By searching for it."

"Let's continue with the will, folks," Cliff said. " 'This map contains instructions for finding the treasure. Those of you who travel the trail past where Coronado's Peak can be clearly seen will share the wealth. The greatest reward of all rests at Pyramid. And that's where I want my ashes tossed to the sun.' " Cliff paused and looked up. "That's all, folks. The strange last words of Sharkey Carsen."

38

There was a moment of awkward silence, not particularly in reverence but from the tension created by the promise of Sharkey's will. *Gold!*

Cliff sighed. "I must admit, folks, I've read some unusual wills in my time. But this one ranks right up there with the lady who left her fortune to a monkey and the bequeathed macaw nobody in the family wanted. I ended up selling the damned thing myself. People get the craziest notions when they start making out wills. Do you know that one time a woman by the name of Lizzie wanted her ashes enshrined right behind this bar in a tin can so folks who came to Tombstone could have a drink and say hello to Lizzie in a tin?" He laughed raucously. "The owner of the bar refused because her tin can might rust."

"Cliff, please . . ." Dodge said uncomfortably.

"Does anyone know what all that stuff about the sun and the pyramid means?" Rex asked with a sneer.

"Well," Dodge motioned with one hand, "Sharkey always called people who searched for gold like himself sun seekers. He said it was a touch of the sun buried in the earth. So seeking the sun is looking for gold. And Pyramid is the name of a lost gold mining town. Supposedly, gold was found there several times over the last hundred years or so, but the mine claims were wiped out by Indians each time, and nobody ever found the actual town again. Or the gold."

"Do you think Sharkey really found it?" Ramona asked softly.

Dodge shrugged. "Don't know. We uncovered

an occasional vein of placer gold, but no mother lode. I've heard legends about this lost town of Pyramid, but who knows if they're true? Of course, Sharkey spent a lot of time in the mountains without me. I just went along when I had time."

"I think old Sharkey went crazy toward the end," Rex asserted. "I just can't believe he found gold and didn't tell us."

"Looks like we'll just have to follow the map and see for ourselves," Dodge proposed.

"That's ridiculous. A waste of time and money. Is that it, Cliff? If so, I'll take my lucky pick and go," Rex muttered sarcastically.

"One more thing," Cliff said. "A toast. Heck?"

The hefty bartender hurried over to refill everyone's glasses. The look on his face was pure delight. He'd been privy to a tale that would entertain tourists for years to come. It was just like the old days when claims of gold flew fast and furious across the old saloon's mahogany bar. Often people went to their graves with knowledge of secret locations. Oh, yes, he was sure of it!

"Sharkey wanted everyone to drink a toast to the fun and good times we all shared. Then, Dodge, you're in charge of the ashes until such time as they can be scattered properly." Cliff raised his glass to the gaily decorated Indian pot containing Sharkey's remains. "Here's to Sharkey Carsen, my friend and the best damn poker player in Cochise County."

The toasts went around the table. Dodge raised

his glass. "Here's to Sharkey, a good and trustworthy man who was forever seeking the sun."

Rex offered, "To Sharkey. And to finding the gold he left behind."

"To Sharkey," Ramona murmured softly, "my love."

They all looked at Tory, and she returned their glares with an upraised chin. Her contemporary hairdo curled riotously at her forehead, while the shorter, wispy edges clung damply to her nape. At the moment, she was only aware that it was damned hot and she had wasted her time and much-needed money in coming all the way from L.A. to Tombstone.

Mustering years of anger, she stood and lifted her glass. "The Sharkey Carsen you people remember was a man I never knew, a lousy father, and a disappointing husband to my mother. I think you're all lying!"

CHAPTER THREE

Rex broke the uneasy silence with a laugh. "I'll drink to that! I think old Sharkey would agree with her. We all know he was a regular hellion!"

There was a slight murmur of reluctant agreement from the group before they all turned up their glasses.

"I hope you'll change your mind about Sharkey before this is over, Tory," Dodge said quietly.

"The chances of that happening are pretty slim," Tory replied with finality. "I'd like to sell my share in this hapless company right now before I leave town tonight. I don't have any more time to waste here."

"That'd be sound logic if anyone around here had the money to buy you out. I, for one, couldn't even consider it." Dodge looked inquisitively at Rex, who shook his head.

"Every penny I intend to invest in this miserable fantasy of getting rich is already in it."

Tory turned hopelessly to Ramona, knowing even before the woman shook her head that she couldn't buy a nickel share in an ice cream store.

"Anyway," Dodge posed, "don't you think you

should go along to scatter the ashes? After all, he was your father."

"That biological fact hasn't enhanced my life up to this point," she retorted. "Why should I care about his ashes now? I have to get back to my business in L.A."

"Speaking of leaving," Cliff said, folding his papers together, "I'll be getting along. Now, I suggest you folks sit here in my, ahem, office awhile and discuss the, eh, sprinkling of Sharkey's ashes. And seeking this sun he kept talking about." Smiling officially, Cliff shook hands all around. "Rex, you may find this search worthwhile. I've heard for years that there's gold in those hills. It's up to you to find it. If not, this'll make a helluva story someday. Ramona, my condolences. Dodge, what about the map?"

He shrugged. "Give it to his daughter, like he said."

Cliff hesitated. "Do you think it's safe?"

"Sure. There's probably nothing to Sharkey's claim."

Cliff turned to Tory and gave her a folded yellow piece of paper. "Well, good luck. It was a genuine pleasure to meet Sharkey's little girl."

She gritted her teeth to keep from screaming: I'm *not* Sharkey's little girl! "Thank you, Mr. Snyder, for everything."

"Rememeber, if any of you need any legal work, like transferring the shares of the Sun Seekers Mining Company or anything like that, let me know. Sharkey . . ." Cliff tipped his hat to the brightly

43

painted jar on the table, then ambled across the plank floor of the saloon.

Rex watched him go, then heaved himself back down in the seat. "Wonder why he didn't tell Sharkey what absurd demands he was making in his will?"

Tory folded her arms, pressing the blue silk tightly across her breasts. "I can't believe I came all the way out to this remote place, only to be expected to go even further for a possible inheritance. And it's a remote possibility, at that."

Dodge braced his large hands on the table. "I think Sharkey wanted to share his wealth, or his possible wealth, with those he cared about. This was the only way he could do it."

Rex tapped his fingers impatiently on the table. "Obviously, he hadn't struck the mother lode yet."

Dodge nodded in agreement. "It's up to us to find it. It's probably in the vicinity of this map."

"Find it? Do you mean gold digging? Not me! Climbing around in those mountains is not my idea of acquiring an inheritance, thank you," Tory pronounced with disgust.

"I agree with Tory," Rex put in nodding. "This is crazy. It's a damned big risk, plus it might well be a waste of time and effort. You said yourself it was speculative."

"Regardless of the possibility of gold, that's where he wanted his ashes scattered," Dodge reminded them.

"I have no interest in going up there to do a crazy man's bidding," Rex vowed. "He was plain loco!"

44

"Nor I," Tory agreed.

"Then I'll do it," Ramona said softly. "I'll scatter Sharkey's ashes where he requested."

"You can't go alone, Ramona," Dodge countered. "It's too dangerous. I'll go with you." Then a slow grin spread across the angular planes of his face. "But if Ramona and I find Sharkey's gold in the process of this scattering, it's all ours. Legally, according to the will, the only ones who'll share the treasure are those who go along this bizarre trail to the sun."

"Oh, hell, Dodge," Rex fumed, "don't kid me. You'd have to split with your partners."

"Not legally. This is different, not under the jurisdiction of regulation mining operations. Sharkey's directing us to the spot. We have a specific map, remember? Frankly"—Dodge paused for emphasis—"I think ole' Sharkey was onto something."

"That isn't what you just told Cliff," Tory muttered.

Dodge just shrugged and gave her a devilish grin. His ragged mustache quivered, and she found it a little disconcerting.

"I know he uncovered a little gold," Ramona disclosed in a quiet, strained tone. "When Yazzie and I found him, he had gold dust under his nails."

"That's nothing new," Rex scoffed. "He came in with a few hundred dollars worth of gold every now and then."

"Who's Yazzie?" Tory questioned.

Dodge explained. "Yazzie lives in the mountains. Has a shack and a small corral of pack animals. We always rented his mules to go up to whatever mine we were working. When Sharkey was missing, Ramona became alarmed and went to Yazzie. They searched the mountains for Sharkey's body and brought it back to town."

"When we found him, he was holding these." Ramona fumbled nervously in her purse and rolled three gold nuggets on the table as if she were casting dice. They scattered into a triangle beside the Indian jar. "There were a couple of others, and I told Yazzie to keep them, for helping me with Sharkey."

"Pretty good pay, I'd say," Rex scowled, grabbing one of the nuggets and examining it closely.

Tory looked curiously at the dull, tarnished nuggets resting on the dark table. Only a trained eye would consider them valuable. *If*, in fact, they were. They certainly didn't look like she'd imagined gold nuggets to look.

"Have you had them assayed?" Dodge asked, also picking one up for scrutiny.

"Yes, they're twenty-grade."

Dodge rotated a nugget casually in his fingers. "It looks like Sharkey was onto something, all right."

"This is ridiculous," Tory protested. "I think it's a setup. How do we know she found these on his body? Or where they came from?"

"Are you calling me a liar?" Ramona's dark eyes narrowed threateningly.

Tory gave her an apologetic smile, thinking those sturdy hands of Ramona's might be tearing

46

at her hair if she didn't watch her mouth. After all, she was in a wild and wicked territory, where men were men and women were . . . well, strong. "No, of course not, Ramona. It's just that I've never seen crude gold before. If you say this is gold, and you found it with Sharkey, I believe you."

"I do." Ramona squared her shoulders and stared levelly at Tory. "I have no interest in the gold. I only want to go up there to scatter Sharkey's ashes."

"Me, too," Dodge agreed with a devilish gleam in his dark brown eyes. "Ramona and I have a job to do, and that's to fulfill Sharkey's request. If you folks want to go along and help us find the gold, you're welcome to share the wealth. If not . . ." He shrugged and smiled at Ramona.

"Then let's run up there tomorrow, scatter the ashes, and see what Sharkey was talking about," Tory offered briskly.

"Run up there?" Dodge hooted with laughter. "You don't understand, Tory. It takes two hours in a four-by-four just to get to Yazzie's cabin."

"What?"

"Then we have to load the mules and get ready for the trek into the Dragoons. They're pretty rugged mountains, even though they seem small in the distance."

"You're talking overnight?" She stared at him as if he'd just said to reach for the stars and pluck out a pot of gold.

"I'm talking about staying for at least a week. Maybe more."

"Oh, my God, I couldn't possibly do that. I have a business in L.A. I can't be gone that long."

"Then why don't you head back tonight, city lady?" Dodge countered sarcastically. "But don't expect someone to come looking you up again when we strike it rich on your daddy's gold."

"I don't expect anything of any of you!" Tory told him with a shaky voice. "Until a little over a week ago, Sharkey Carsen was just a memory—and a bad one, at that. Why I bothered to come all the way out here, I don't know. I guess the little girl in me dreamed that this rambler who was my father had an ounce of love for a child he abandoned years ago. I told myself he wanted to rectify all those painful years by leaving me something of value in his will. Some inheritance this is! A hot, miserable trek up a mountain, looking for an old man's dream! Well, count me out!" Tory fumbled with the map and stuffed it into her purse. Then, dramatically, she stormed out of the Crystal Palace Saloon.

It was nearly dark, and the air was surprisingly cool. She shivered in her thin silk dress. How could a place that was so hot in the daytime be so chilly at night? As her heels clunked on the wooden sidewalk, she thought of the real, honest-to-God cowboys who'd actually walked these streets, both heroes and outlaws, and the women who'd followed them.

Drifters. Entrepreneurs. Gamblers. Miners. Men like Sharkey Carsen. Her father was one of them in spirit, born a hundred years too late. She mulled over the unusual people she'd met today

48

and of the obligation of scattering Sharkey's ashes encased in that Indian jar.

She couldn't stop thinking about the handsome but enigmatic Dodge Callahan. Would he find the gold? *Her gold!*

Tory gritted her teeth and tried to convince herself there was no gold. But in the deep recesses of her mind was a doubt. And it would always be there unless she proved it wrong. Damn Sharkey Carsen, anyway! He probably knew this would happen. Gold fever!

"Some speech," Dodge observed dryly as Tory left. "Looks like Sharkey's little girl is just a little spoiled. I guess she wanted her inheritance handed to her in the form of a large check."

"Sounds good to me. Unfortunately, that's not the way we do things around here," Rex replied dourly.

"She'll be back," Ramona said quietly.

"You think so? She's pretty hot tempered. Sounded final to me." Dodge shook his head.

"I think she's like the rest of us and needs the money. I can tell by her eyes. Now here's a chance to get it easily and legally. All she has to do is follow his map up a mountain . . . It's the ultimate dream. Sharkey was a sun seeker and not ashamed to admit it. We're all sun seekers in our own way, pursuing a dream of getting rich quick."

"And you, Ramona?" Dodge leaned forward and caught her dark eyes with his. "Is that why you're here?"

She smiled sadly. "Sure. I won't deny I'd like to

find the gold. But I can tell you this. I cared more for Sharkey than that whole mountain full of gold."

"Looks like Tory's the only one who doesn't want the gold," Dodge drawled.

Ramona gave him a confident look. "She'll come around."

"Hope so, since she's got the damned map," Rex grumbled, then motioned to the Indian pot. "What are we going to do about this? Who keeps it until . . . *you* know?"

"I'll take care of it," Dodge offered.

"Thank you, Dodge," Ramona said with a soft glow in her jet eyes. "I don't think I could."

"Let's give Tory some time to change her mind." Dodge raked his large hand over his face, planning as he spoke. "That'll allow us time to pack for the mountain. How about going this weekend? You, too, Rex?"

The dark-eyed man sighed and glanced from Ramona to Dodge. "Looks like I have no choice if I'm going to share any of the treasure."

"You learn fast, Rex. We'll meet Friday afternoon at Yazzie's cabin. Around three or four?"

"Do you need a ride, Rex?" Ramona offered sardonically. "We can go together in that hunk of tin Sharkey left for me. Fortunately, it has four-wheel drive, and it'll make it just fine up the mountain."

"I don't know if I can trust you two not to scratch each other's eyes out," Dodge teased.

Rex heaved a sigh. "Just ignore what was said today, Ramona. We were all a little uptight."

"If that's an apology, I accept," she replied, smiling.

"Okay. Each of you pack just enough clothes to fit into the saddlebags on your mules," Dodge instructed them. "I'll be responsible for bringing the food and equipment we'll need. We'll meet at Yazzie's in plenty of time to get organized before dark. Then we'll get an early start on Saturday."

Ramona and Rex nodded in agreement to Dodge's directions.

"I'll pick you up around noon," Ramona told Rex.

"Now, look," Dodge posed, leaning forward with his elbows on the table, "I'm for inviting Yazzie to go along with us. He could be a great help on the trail."

"If he goes, that means he shares the loot, according to the terms of the will," Rex grumbled. "That is, if we find it. I don't know."

"Yazzie can be the cook, unless one of you wants to do it. Believe me, we'll need somebody to take care of the pack of mules we'll be taking along. He knows those mountains like the back of his hand. Anyway, if we find a mother lode, dividing it between one more won't matter that much."

"We might as well invite the whole damn town!" Rex retorted.

"There'll just be five of us, if Tory goes."

Ramona spoke softly, almost reluctantly. "Dodge, I don't like that man. Bad vibes."

"Yazzie?" Dodge shrugged her away with his hand. "Don't start with your Indian hocus-pocus,

Ramona. I don't believe in it. We may need this man."

She faced him seriously. "My feelings toward him have nothing to do with my being Indian. Or with hocus-pocus."

"What is it? Woman's intuition? He did help you find Sharkey, remember? Apparently, Sharkey trusted him. We always used his mules."

"Sharkey's intuition wasn't always as keen as it should have been," she countered with a faint smile. "Just look at this gathering of his so-called friends. Strange bunch. Okay, have it your way, Dodge. Invite Yazzie."

"I agree," Rex affirmed finally. "We may need someone like Yazzie who's entirely familiar with the mountain. If you don't trust the man, Ramona, at least we'll have him close so we can keep an eye on him."

"Okay, it's settled." Dodge scooted his chair back and stretched to his full six feet five. "You two ride up the mountain together in the Jeep. And I'll plan on bringing Tory, if your intuition's right about her, too, Ramona. If not, we'll have to figure out a way to get that map."

"Count on her." Ramona gathered the three gold nuggets, gave one to each of the men, and tucked one in her own pocket. "In case there isn't any more treasure, we each have a token from Sharkey."

Rex held the gold in his palm. "There'd better be more than this. I don't plan to waste a week chasing an invisible treasure in the Dragoon Mountains!"

"Plan on two weeks. And, Rex"—Dodge let his eyes flicker over Rex's expensive suit—"wear your jeans."

"I'll have to buy some."

Dodge laughed and picked up the Indian pot. He tucked it into the crook of his arm as if it were a prize pig. "See you Friday."

"See you," Ramona mumbled, gently touching the Indian pot as they left the Crystal Palace Saloon.

Tory Talbot entered the modest motel room at the edge of town, picked up the phone, and canceled her evening flight to L.A. For some reason the experiences of the day had left her exhausted. Maybe it was the heat. Anyway, spending the night would give her time to decide what to do.

She paced around the room. What was to decide? Of course she would head back to the real world tomorrow. Wouldn't she? *Wouldn't she?*

Sighing, she walked to the window and tried to sort out the strange events surrounding the reading of her father's will. She should just get out and never look back. That's what her reason told her to do. But somewhere deep within her heart, Tory felt a kinship with this unorthodox man, this father she never really knew.

In the saloon today she had been exposed to a fraction of Sharkey Carsen through his friends. First, there was Dodge Callahan. Even his name conjured a certain image, that of a western hero. But was he really a hero? She saw him as an enigma of a man with a marshal's badge on his chest, a contemporary man dressed for 1880. Dark hair and eyes, square shoulders—actually, he was a little too rugged to be called handsome. And yet Tory felt drawn to Dodge. He was strong and masculine. She found him both formidable and tempting.

Rex Fierro, Sharkey's other partner, was obviously a wheeler-dealer type. Was this a part of her father's nature, too? Rex was Hispanic, bright, educated, energetic, the man with the money. And out for more. He was quite different from Dodge, yet in some ways similar. Tough. Masculine. She wondered how her father had fitted into the partnership.

Then, there was Ramona—lovely, calm, intelligent. She wasn't exactly the kind of woman Tory pictured for Sharkey. If appearances meant anything, she loved Sharkey. That in itself was a mystery to Tory.

No, she wasn't being fair. Just because he'd been a lousy father and husband didn't mean he wasn't a loyal friend and good lover to others.

Tory scanned the purple-mountained horizon beyond Tombstone. The Dragoons. They were the same mountains her father had explored, had mined, had hoped would produce that elusive gold. She laughed to herself. Was it merely a dream? *A dream to seek the sun?*

She remembered him saying those words when she was just a child. He couldn't be tied down to family, to a real job. He had to seek the sun. Why? What was Sharkey Carsen really like? The answer lay with his friends, these strange people who had gathered today around the gambling table.

If she wanted to know more about Sharkey Carsen, she'd have to ask them. After all these years, the reasoning part of her objected stubbornly. Did she really want to know? Undeniably, she harbored twenty years of resentment because he'd abandoned her and her mother. That he never knew how her mother suffered without him.

In the next few quiet moments, her heart overruled her head and answered softly. Yes. Yes, find out all you can about this man who was your father. This is your only chance. Tears sprang to her eyes, and Tory quickly brushed them away. *Damn you, Sharkey Carsen!*

Tory didn't sleep well that night. When she awakened, she knew what she would do. What she *had* to do. The first thing was to place a long-distance phone call to L.A.

"Megan, I've decided to stay on for a few more days. Can you take care of the shop?" When she was convinced her associate could handle things, Tory dropped the phone into its cradle. After a thoughtful moment, she lifted it again and made several local calls. She had to find Dodge Callahan.

Following directions from the motel attendant, she drove her rented car through town and down a dirt road until she caught sight of an old pale green trailer. This rusty hunk of tin had been her father's home? She sighed. Whatever made her think he'd left her, or anybody else, an inheritance of value?

The door was open, and she could hear

55

whistling inside. For some reason, her heart pounded with anticipation as her fist knotted above the screen door.

"Hi."

Startled, Tory stared through the screen into the inquisitive dark eyes of Dodge Callahan. "Oh! Hi. I—I've been thinking about your offer, Dodge, and—"

"It isn't my offer. It's Sharkey's."

"Well, you *are* taking the group up the mountain, aren't you?"

"Yep. We're going to scatter Sharkey's ashes and look for the gold. Leaving Friday. Want to go?"

"Yes, that's why I'm here."

He pushed on the screen door. "Come on in, Tory. I've been expecting you. I wondered how long it would take you to get around to us."

She gave him a curious glance and mounted the steps into the small trailer. The first thing her eyes settled on was the audacious Indian pot containing Sharkey's remains perched in the middle of the kitchen table like a decorative centerpiece of flowers. Tory gulped and turned her face away.

CHAPTER FOUR

"Ramona said you'd admit it."

"Admit what?" Tory rubbed her arms and shivered involuntarily as she stepped inside. This was Sharkey's home,—still his resting place, in fact. And the whole feeling was eerie and unsettling. Yet Dodge looked as though he were quite at ease in the old miner's former abode. Never mind the fact that the Indian pot containing Sharkey's remains sat on the table.

"That you're a sun seeker," Dodge explained with a slightly crooked smile beneath that craggy mustache. "Sharkey claimed that gold was just rock that had captured a piece of the sun."

"Oh, yes. That's a little silly, don't you think?"

Dodge shrugged. Tory couldn't help noticing that his shoulders were broad and square inside his casual cotton sports shirt. Tiny curls crept alluringly along the vee of his open collar. "Maybe. Depends on how you feel about the gold."

"And if you believe it's there."

"Don't you?" He looked at her curiously, and when she didn't answer right away he asked, "Then why are you here?"

"Oh, I don't know. Inquisitive, I suppose. He *was* my father, and I'm curious about what he was doing in those mountains all those years." She tried to sound nonchalant, as if she didn't really care and hadn't lain awake most of the night puzzling over the strange life of Sharkey Carsen.

"Actually, he wasn't in the mountains all those years. Sharkey was my professor at the University of Arizona when we first met."

"Sharkey was a professor?" Her blue eyes registered shock. "He held a decent job?"

"For a little while." Dodge handed her coffee in a stout clay pottery mug and motioned to the small built-in table. "Have a seat, please."

Tory looked uneasily at the Indian pot centered on the table. "Could we move that?"

"Of course." Dodge exchanged his coffee mug for the clay pot and carried it to a back room. "Does it make you nervous?" he inquired on returning.

She slid onto the bench at the table. "Well, I prefer not to stare at the urn of my father's ashes while I have my morning coffee."

"I guess so, you being a city girl and all." Dodge squeezed in opposite her.

"You say that as if it's a shame."

"No, just a surprise that Sharkey's daughter would be so citified."

"Why a surprise? That's where he left me, in the city. That's where he left both my mother and me. And, life being the way it was in those days for a young woman with a child, that's where we stayed." She lifted her chin indignantly and let her eyes sweep over the ragged room. "But, believe me, where we lived was far better than this."

"I'm sure it was." His brown eyes flickered over her approvingly. "Of course, there's nothing wrong with the way you turned out. Nothing at all. Sharkey would be—"

"Look, I didn't come here for your approval. And certainly not for Sharkey's."

"What is it you want, Tory? Really want?"

She gazed at him levelly. "Just like all the rest. I want my share."

He grinned and white teeth reflected against his darkly tanned skin. "I thought so. At least you're willing to admit it. Nothing wrong with that, though. It's human nature. But I detect something else in your attitude. Something deeper. Maybe a little revenge?"

"Revenge?" She sipped her coffee and gazed thoughtfully at the Indian designs painted in pitch black on her mug. "Maybe you're right, Dodge. It's too late to help my mother, but I'm awfully resentful about the way Sharkey treated us. Especially her. She really struggled in her lifetime. And when I was old enough to realize why, I resented everything about my father."

"So now you're out to get what's coming to you," Dodge concluded.

"Do you blame me?"

"Nope. Guess not. Look, Tory, I don't excuse what Sharkey did to your mother and you, and I realize it must have been very difficult for her. Sharkey and I had been friends for the past five or six years, and while he was a bit strange—seeking

59

the gold with such a feverish passion—he was serious about some things. Believe it or not, he still cared about his family."

She knotted one fist on the table. "I find that hard to believe."

"Occasionally, he talked about the family he left behind. I think he sensed his time was running out and felt an urgency to accomplish his unachieved goals. He wanted to find the gold partly so he could send some of it back to your mother, as a sort of compensation. He felt remorse, I'm sure. He talked about hitting it big, about taking the devil's share. Unfortunately, the devil got him first."

"It wouldn't have done any good to send money," Tory muttered bitterly. "Even after my mother got sick, I doubt she would have taken a penny from him. But I would. I'm still paying her hospital bills."

"I knew there was some vindictiveness in your voice," Dodge chided softly. "Strangely enough, Sharkey thought you both were just the way he left you. He talked about how cute you were with your hair in pigtails."

"If he cared, really cared, why didn't he ever return?"

"He did, in the beginning. Tried to find you in L.A. a couple of times. But the addresses changed every few months, and he couldn't track your mother."

Tory's deep blue eyes narrowed. "That's because we were forced to move when we couldn't pay our rent. And my mother became very adept at covering her tracks so creditors couldn't find us."

"After a few years, Sharkey said he gave up. He figured your mother wouldn't want to see him after all that time."

"He figured right. She hated him more as the years passed." Tory's face softened. "But I would have liked to see him. Perhaps even to know him. I grew up with a dream of a father. Sometimes he was a devil, sometimes a saint. But never there. And it wasn't fair. As I became an adult, my impression of him was more like my mother's. I grew to hate him."

"And now?"

She shrugged and looked at Dodge honestly. "Nothing. No feeling. I didn't know him. I couldn't feel anything for him when I got the letter saying he'd died."

Dodge nodded solemnly. "That's too bad, but I think I can understand." He scooted out from the table and refilled their coffee mugs. "Care for some breakfast, Tory? I haven't eaten yet, and I'm starving."

She watched his tall figure move about the kitchen. He seemed to fill the room with his large physical presence as well as an indefinable strength. Tory suddenly decided that Dodge wasn't as forbidding as she originally thought. He even seemed like a reasonable man, and the fact that he was Sharkey's friend wasn't his fault. He had no idea what a rogue Sharkey was. Not until now. "Sure. Breakfast sounds great," she said, smiling.

"We can discuss details of the trip into the mountains." Dodge slapped some meat into a cast-iron skillet, and it started to sizzle.

Tory tried not to cringe visibly at the sound of frying meat. Obviously, this was not going to be her usual breakfast of yogurt, fruit, and nuts. "What's to discuss? Can't we go up there today? It's still early."

"We're leaving Friday. Meeting Rex and Ramona at Yazzie's cabin."

"Why Friday? Why not now?"

"We need time to get ready. Rex and Ramona have to make arrangements at their jobs. Then we need special supplies and the right clothes. You'll need something more appropriate than"—he motioned toward her—"silk or whatever you have on."

"Oh?" She looked down at her classy beige skirt and matching blouse. "What's wrong—"

"Nothing, if you're taking a plane to L.A. But for the mountains, you need some rugged clothes. Jeans, long-sleeved shirts, a jacket, and boots. You're going gold digging, Tory. And it's in the heart of some of the roughest terrain in this country. That's what keeps most folks out. Only the roughest and most determined make it."

She tapped her rose-polished nails on the table. "Well, you'll find I'm pretty determined. I'll make it."

"I have no doubts about that, city lady," he said as he gave her an approving grin. "But I couldn't help noticing you weren't very rough, so we have

62

some work to do gearing you up." He forked up the steak and plopped two eggs into the skillet.

Tory squeezed her eyes shut at the thought of all that cholesterol and oil. Oh, well, she wouldn't be there very long. Maybe a few days of the wrong foods wouldn't ruin her insides or her figure.

"Here. Maybe you'd like to see what Sharkey was really like." Dodge tossed an old, yellowed newspaper down on the table and went back to his eggs. "The Tucson paper did a story on gold mining a few years back and took this shot of Sharkey and his old desert canary. It's the only picture of him that I know of. Kind of captures the essense of him, though."

Tory tried to remain detached as she gazed at the yellowed photo of the grizzled, bearded old miner and his flop-eared mule. This was her father? It didn't seem possible. He didn't look anything like she imagined, or hoped. Of course, to expect a pin-striped–suited dandy wasn't reasonable, either.

Dodge slid a plate of steaming food under her nose. "Well, what do you think of your daddy?"

"Honestly, Dodge, I'm not impressed. Looks like a drifter to me." She shoved the paper away and tackled her steak with a knife. "Hmm, this looks great. I can't remember the last time I had a steak for breakfast."

He studied her silently for a moment, as if assessing her reaction. "It's beefalo steak. A fellow over at Sierra Vista, a town near here, breeds buffalo and cattle together. Pretty good steak, I'd say."

"B—buffalo?" She stared at the meat, then at Dodge. "We're eating buffalo meat?"

"Sure, why not? It constituted the mainstay of the old-timer's diet. Indians, too."

"I—I can't believe it. I thought they were extinct by now."

"Naw, they're coming back. Environmentalists, you know."

Tory nibbled her eggs, wondering if they were some near-extinct creature, too. When would she adjust to this . . . this time-warp place that seemed to be caught in a wedge of a hundred years ago?

Dodge paused. "What's wrong?"

"Nothing. It's just that this place is so strange. From the moment I arrived, I felt as though I'd stepped back in time. Like we're living in history in this distant corner of the world."

"That's the way we like it. It's why most of us are here, I suppose. Yep, I guess this is quite different from L.A." He finished off his steak. "You sure you want to go up the mountain with us?"

"Yes, of course. I'm not daunted yet. I was just making a comment on the social atmosphere. And if I need different clothes, I'll get them. Where would you suggest I go shopping?"

"I'd suggest Sierra Vista. I'll go with you."

"Oh, Dodge, you don't have to—"

He stopped her with an upraised hand. "I'd like it. I need to make sure you get the right equipment. Plus I have some shopping to do, too."

"Oh, sure." She hid a smile with her hand. "Sure you do, Dodge."

He leaned forward, and his dark brown eyes held a gleam. "Actually, it's just an excuse to spend a little more time with you. It isn't often that such a pretty lady comes to town, way out here. Plus, it's an honor to finally meet Sharkey's little girl."

"I'm not—"

"I know. You sure aren't, Tory. You're very much your own person."

"So was Sharkey, from the look of that photo," she claimed defiantly.

"Yep, Sharkey sure was. Guess you're your father's daughter, after all, Tory."

She leaned back in her seat and glared at the tall cowboy opposite her. Damned if he wasn't right.

Within the hour, they were rambling in his shiny black and red Blazer toward Sierra Vista. On every horizon loomed another range of blue purple mountains. To the west, the Huachuca Mountains; to the south, the Mules; behind them to the east, the Dragoons. Dodge stopped a couple of times to show her abandoned gold mines, now fenced off to protect the public.

He ambled frighteningly close to the open pits, standing with legs widespread. "Glory holes, they're called. Gold seekers thought these mines would bring them absolute happiness. Many lost their lives instead."

"Like Sharkey," Tory nodded solemnly. "Some of them look like simple holes in the ground, made by some animal, not a gold mine."

"They're deceiving. The wooden structures have

all rotted away over the years. Each hole usually leads to a labyrinth of tunnels deep into the earth. That's why they're so dangerous. Many an unsuspecting hiker has fallen to a horrible death by plunging down ten to a hundred feet. The government now requires fencing abandoned mines."

"Well, the place looks deceivingly barren and empty," Tory commented as she noticed the gathering of dark clouds in the distance.

"Monsoons," Dodge commented. "The heat draws moisture up from Mexico and gives us much-needed rain this time of year."

"Well, at least the heat's good for something," Tory mumbled as she wiped a strip of moisture beads from her brow.

They stopped again, this time to inspect a time-ravaged adobe structure used by miners seeking that elusive gold stuff.

"This cabin was built over a hundred years ago by a German mining engineer named Brunckow. He used this very fireplace to assay his ore before Tombstone was a town. But old Brunckow never got to enjoy his wealth because he and his men were murdered right here on this spot."

"Murdered *here?*" Tory looked around as if to find some clue to the crime. There was nothing, just the wind whistling through vacant window frames.

"It's rumored that as many as seventeen men were killed on this property over the years. That's why Brunckow's cabin is known as the bloodiest cabin massacre in Arizona. But the mine here produced enough gold to sustain and encourage those determined miners who came after him."

Tory looked at the worn walls of the forlorn building, and a chill ran through her. "Are you trying to scare me off, Dodge?"

"Not at all, Tory. But I want you to realize that this may be a dangerous mission into the mountains. When word gets around that there's gold to be found, you never know what can happen. It's just a fact, proved by history."

"I don't scare easily, Dodge."

"Good. Because only those who were determined enough to rough it out found their treasure."

"If it's there, I expect we'll find it."

He caught her eye. "You don't really think it's there, do you?"

"Not really," Tory admitted as she let her fingers trail over the gritty adobe bricks. "But I'm willing to go along with the game, just in case."

"Damn!" he muttered. "Craziest thing I've ever heard. This trip up the mountain won't be a picnic, Tory. I'll be hanged if I'd bother with it if I didn't know—for certain—there was gold waiting for me!"

"And you know for certain there's gold?"

He looked at her coolly for a moment. "Yes . . . I know it."

She gave him a smooth, easy smile. "Well, your confidence is enough for me, Dodge. Shall we go?"

He followed her to the Blazer, studying the young woman who was the offspring of Sharkey Carsen. Obviously, Tory Carsen Talbot had a mind of her own and was quite determined and opinionated. Like her father.

He had to give her credit for having enough spunk to leave her familiar life and travel to this godforsaken place. It seemed strange, though, that on something as important—and possibly dangerous—as trekking up the mountain after gold, she was willing to defer to him. She claimed she didn't believe there was any gold. But, Dodge wondered, maybe that's what she wanted him to believe.

At any rate, all this only made him want to know more about her.

Later that afternoon, loaded with enough jeans, shirts, and jackets to keep Tory warm and comfortable for at least a week in the mountains, they piled back into the Blazer.

"Tomorrow we'll get supplies. I'm in charge of bringing food," Dodge said as he shifted into gear. "But now, I'm starved, Tory. How about you?"

"After that huge breakfast, I thought I'd never want to eat again, but it sounds like a good idea." She smiled warmly at him and slumped back in the seat.

"I know a place near here that fixes great bison steaks."

"No more buffalo meat!" she cried, laughing. "Don't you know some place that serves regular food? You know, salads and vegetables?"

"You aren't a vegetarian, are you?"

"No, but I also don't think a person needs to eat red meat two or three times a day."

"Watching your weight?"

"Well, in my business, it helps to make a good appearance."

"What *is* your business, Tory?"

"I have a dress shop in L.A. that caters to tall women, called Tall and Terrific."

"A place for tall women, huh? Guess I never thought of them as being a market by themselves."

"Oh, yes, women over five feet seven or so can't just walk into any store and find clothes that fit properly. They have particular needs that aren't met by the average ready-to-wear garments."

"Do you?" His traitorous eyes scanned her length. "You're quite tall."

"Of course. My legs are very long, and it's hard to find slacks long enough."

One of his almond eyes squinted as he assessed her legs. "Yes, they're long. But very nice. And they're slim and, uh, have a good shape." He paused and cleared his throat. "Uh, the Lucky Cuss in Tombstone is a pretty good restaurant."

"The Lucky *what?*"

"The Lucky Cuss. It's named after a gold mine. The man who found gold in his diggings was a darned 'lucky cuss.' "

"Do you think we will, Dodge?"

He looked at her and nodded. "I sure do. Wouldn't bother with going if I didn't."

Tory glanced at the straight-lined profile of Dodge Callahan while he drove and realized that she trusted him even though she barely knew him. Maybe her father wasn't such a bad judge of character, after all.

* * *

Dinner at the Lucky Cuss was another step back in time. The place looked like a restaurant that could easily have served Wyatt Earp and his contemporaries a hundred years ago. And probably did!

"I feel as though I'm dressed inappropriately for this occasion," Tory said as they finished eating. "I should be wearing a hoop skirt with a bustle and carrying a parasol."

"Some of the ladies around here do. They even have an organization called The Vigilettes who do style shows and perform in various historical activities throughout the year." Dodge motioned to the waiter for coffee refills. "But that kind of outfit wouldn't be right for you."

"No? Why not?"

"All that material would hide your long legs. And they're too gorgeous to hide."

"That, Mr. Callahan, sounds like a sexist statement."

"I meant it as an honest statement, from an honest man admiring a beautiful woman."

She let the comment pass and sipped the strong coffee, then steered the conversation toward Dodge. He aroused more than a little of her curiosity. "What are you doing here, Dodge?" Tory looked at him thoughtfully. "Are you like the others? Do you enjoy this historical atmosphere, the feeling this time warp gives you?"

He scratched his chin. "I came here for one reason. To strike it rich."

She cocked her head. "You're admitting to being a gold digger?"

"Pure and simple." He shrugged with a devil-may-care attitude. "I'm a sun seeker of the first order."

"Somehow you just don't seem like the type to—"

"To want to make a fortune without working?"

"Well . . . yes."

"Why not? I tried the other route, and it backfired in my face."

"You mean you had a regular job? How did it backfire?"

"Oh, it was fine for a few years. I was a mineral geologist working for copper mines. Excuse me, I'm still a geologist, only now an unemployed, unemployable one. When the recession hit Arizona, the mines couldn't produce copper cheaply enough to compete with foreign markets. Many of them began closing and whole towns folded."

"Sounds awful." Tory's blue eyes grew soft and curious.

"For someone like me, with such a limited area of expertise, finding another job was practically impossible, unless I wanted to move to a foreign country. So I went back to college to upgrade my degree and get a teaching certificate."

"That's where you met my fa—er, Sharkey?"

Dodge nodded. "We hit it off right away. We both decided we knew enough about the minerals in the area to believe that gold, more than has already been found, is still in the earth. So we set out to find it."

71

"My God, it sounds like a fairy tale." She shook her head in disbelief at Dodge's story.

Dodge raised his hand and pledged comically, "Honest-to-God truth. Now I'll admit that Sharkey was more diligent about the whole thing than me. Occasionally, I took time out to earn a little money by teaching a semester or two at the local junior college."

"Obviously, not having any money didn't bother him a bit."

"Yeah. Or maybe he sensed he was running out of time and wanted to push for it."

Tory puzzled over Dodge's assessment. "Do you really think he sensed his death?"

"Not in the way you think," Dodge amended quickly. "I just meant that he was getting on in years and wanted to try and reach some unattained goals."

"He was nearly seventy." She sipped her coffee in silence and thought about a lonely old man seeking goals.

"Well, enough about the past." Dodge shoved his cup aside. "Ready to go, Tory?"

"Huh? Oh, yes, certainly." Something made her want to delay ending the evening, which was silly. They'd spent the entire day together, and it was time to go. "It's getting late and . . . Here, let me pay my share."

Dodge resolutely refused. "In old Tombstone, a lady is a lady and a gentleman pays."

With a gentle laugh, Tory decided to acquiesce this time. She took his offered arm, noting its muscled strength, and strolled across the wooden plank floor. "Do you mean that women's lib hasn't come to Tombstone, Dodge?"

He threw his head back and laughed. "There are armed guards at either end of the city to make sure she never arrives."

"Dodge Callahan, I think you're a holdover from the good old days."

"And you, Tory? What are you if not a product of one of those holdovers?"

"You think so?" She laughed inwardly. There was no way she was anything like he claimed. Tory Talbot was independent, her own person, completely in charge of her life. And she liked it that way.

They drove out to the old trailer, and she made a motion to open the car door. Reluctant to leave, she paused and gazed gratefully at him. "Thank you for helping me shop today, Dodge. And for everything—dinner tonight, even the beefalo steak this morning. Today has been . . . nice. Very nice."

He looked at her and smiled softly. His brown eyes were like chocolate, shining with pleasure, his lips slightly parted and appealing. The mustache shrouded his lips darkly. Oh, God, what was wrong with her? Suddenly, she found this man extremely attractive. No, he was more than that. He was alluring and downright irresistible.

She wanted to feel his lips on hers, to know the sweet caress of his breath on her cheek, to respond to the warmth of his masculinity. She wanted him close. She craved his kiss and leaned forward and

73

waited as his energy enfolded her and he edged closer . . .

The strength Tory had expected claimed her lips as his mouth melted over hers. There was no resistance to her invitation, for Dodge Callahan was a man to take advantage of every opportunity. And she had certainly offered that opportunity.

However, the warmth that radiated between them and engulfed her was more than she had anticipated. More than she had experienced in a long time. Suddenly, she felt like soft clay, ready and willing to be shaped and formed into whatever Dodge's hands chose to do with her.

Dodge was the first to pull back, although his eyes were hooded with desire and his lips smiling with the sweet taste of her. "Oh, yes, Tory, nice . . . ver–y nice."

"Dodge—"

"I know. You have to go. And you should."

"I—uh—don't intend for this to happen again." She looked down at her tightly clinched hands, suddenly shy and unsure.

"No? Now, that's a shame. Looks to me like we two matched up perfectly."

"No, we didn't. It was a spontaneous moment. I, uh, had better get my packages and go."

Silently, he helped her load her newly acquired clothes into her rented car. "I'll pick you up Friday, Tory, and we'll head up the mountain. Plan on staying about two weeks."

"Yes," she said, nodding weakly. "Friday."

He waved as she pulled away. When she disappeared from sight, Dodge felt strangely empty and alone. Damned curious woman, he thought. Maybe I was a fool to fall for her sex appeal. But she gave me that look, that damned feminine "come hither" invitation that said "It's okay this time." And, oh, God, I wanted to consume her with all my strength.

He ambled toward the trailer and felt an eerie glow, almost as if someone were there. He glanced around shakily, half expecting a form to appear around the corner of the old tin building. But *who?* "Sharkey? No, that's ridiculous," he scoffed aloud in a low mumble.

He sat on the doorstep and gazed skyward. The immense black bowl overhead was sprinkled with a million stars, glittering romantically as they had for millions of years. Even in the midst of such enormous grandeur, Dodge couldn't shake thoughts of Tory. She made him feel as he hadn't felt for many years. He was definitely attracted to her.

Today, in spite of her tough facade, she had seemed vulnerable, in need of help. Or a friend. Or both.

Dodge saw himself as her protector, her defender. Responsibility for this attractive young woman now rested on his shoulders—had been given to him by Sharkey. And he wanted to assume this responsibility with all his energy.

And undeniably, the man in him wanted to possess her completely with his body.

Tory was still thinking of Dodge's kiss when she arrived at her motel. With arms full of packages, she struggled to unlock the door to her lonely little room. Kicking the door open, she staggered inside and dumped her things on the floor.

But when she switched the light on, she drew back in horror.

Everything in the room had been turned upside down and inside out. Pillows, dresser drawers, bed covers, suitcases, and clothes lay in complete disarray. A cool breeze, deceptively peaceful, ruffled the curtain at the open window beside the bed.

Someone had broken into her room and searched every item there! She backed out the door. Could the intruder still be hiding in the bathroom?

CHAPTER FIVE

Tory was panic-stricken. One person should know about this; only one person in Tombstone could help her!

She pounded frantically on the rickety trailer door. "Dodge! Dodge? Are you in there? Please, help me!"

"Tory, what's wrong?" He threw open the door, filling the framed space with his half-clad body. His masculine muscular form was outlined in huge relief by a backlight from a small lamp somewhere behind him. "Are you all right? What happened?"

"Oh, God, Dodge, I'm scared. I wasn't scared, even with all the things you showed me today. The gold mines that left deep holes in the ground and how the Indians knocked everybody off . . . Nothing bothered me . . . until . . . until now—" She halted in her hysterical rambling and breathed heavily.

"Come on in and slow down. Calm down, Tory. Tell me what happened." He pulled her inside and closed the door. His large hands gripped her arms, and he looked at her intently. She was pale and her lips were thin and slightly purple from panting.

Those beautiful blue eyes were wide with outright fear. She needed help, needed *him*. His eyes implored her. "Tory? You all right?"

She nodded silently and drew in a sobbing breath. "You're right. I'm out of control."

When her frightened eyes reached his, he could resist her no longer and pulled her firmly against his chest. Wrapping his long arms around her shivering slender form, he murmured soothing words and held her close for a little while.

She buried her face against his bare chest, grateful for the warm strength she found in him. He was solid and strong, a fortress she could trust, a man who knew what to do in the face of a crisis. A man whose masculine body fragrance accosted her senses, whose soothing words rumbled through her. Oh, God, she was clinging to Dodge's bare torso, and she had to be the one to break this embrace.

When she shifted in his arms, Dodge realized she was calmer. Calm enough to stand alone without his arms wrapped securely around her. Reluctantly, he loosened his hold, releasing her at her own pace, which was wonderfully slow. Just being that close to her was sheer torture for him. But he could do nothing about that now. She needed his security, not his passion.

"Now, tell me what happened."

"My room . . . at the motel . . . has been wrecked. My things are everywhere, and the window—the window is open. Someone broke into my room! They're obviously looking for something, and they left the place in a terrible mess! I'm not even sure if they're gone!"

"You think they're still there?"

"I . . . don't know. Probably not."

"Was anything taken?"

"I don't know."

"Did you call the police? Or the motel management?"

She shook her head. "Didn't take time. I was too afraid. I wanted you to know first."

"Good." He turned away and raked a huge hand through his already disheveled hair. "I need to think this through. Let's decide what to do here. Whether to call the police or not. Whether to do anything. Decide what this relates to."

"The gold, of course."

He looked at her quickly. Then a slow smile spread across his angular face. "Yep. I think you're exactly right. We probably should go back and see if they took anything—"

"I don't think so," she answered levelly. "There was nothing to take. Oh, they made a mess of my clothes, but I had no jewelry, no money. Everything's with me."

His dark eyes narrowed. "The map?"

She nodded and patted her purse. "Right here. But if this is what they're after, I don't want the damned thing. Please take it." She opened her purse and lifted the folded piece of paper.

"You sure you want me to be responsible for this?"

"Positive."

"I'll be glad to take the responsibility away from you, especially if you'll feel better about it."

"I will. Definitely."

He grinned with renewed appreciation and took the map. "You're beginning to get the hang of this, city lady. I think you've got a smart head on your shoulders."

"Well, it stands to reason. Everybody at the table—and probably everybody in town by now—knew the map was given to me and that I walked off with it in my purse."

"You aren't assuming that the guilty party is someone around that table yesterday at the reading of the will?"

She shrugged. "Well, who else?"

Again he raked his hand through his hair. "Hell, I don't know, but I can't see any of them doing such a deed. Why, they're Sharkey's closest friends."

"You said yourself gold does funny things to people, Dodge. Maybe the prospects of finding it changed one of them. Maybe he—or she—wants it all."

"Oh, no!" Dodge's objection boomed loudly in the small confines of the trailer, and he began to pace. "I'm not prepared to believe that anyone at that table is guilty of ransacking your room or is entertaining the notion of getting all the gold for himself. And"—he halted and pointed a finger at Tory—"and I refuse to believe that Ramona had anything at all to do with this! She . . . why, Ramona was crazy in love with the old coot! Don't you think that means anything?"

Tory turned her head away. "It didn't mean anything to my father when my mother was crazy in love with him."

There was a moment of uneasy silence, and Dodge moved to her. "Oh, God, Tory, I'm sorry. I didn't mean—oh, hell. I keep forgetting . . ."

Her lips pressed together firmly. "I can't forget the past, Dodge. Sharkey may have been something close to a saint in the last few years of his life, but he wasn't anything like that to us. And I have a few doubts about some of his friends, too."

"Oh?" He arched an eyebrow and gave her a quizzical glance.

"Not you, of course, Dodge. You—you're different."

"Of course," he murmured, sighing heavily. "Let's drop the speculations now, while we're still speaking to each other, Tory. I think we should go over to your motel room and pick up the pieces."

"Do we have to go back there?"

He glanced at her and watched the fear return to her blue eyes. "Yes, we do," he repeated firmly. "I'll go with you and help you get your clothes. You can come back here for the rest of the night until we decide what to do next. Obviously, you don't feel safe enough to spend the night there again. And I don't want you to. If they could get in once, they can get in again."

"Where . . ." She halted and swallowed heavily.

"Right here." He aimed a thumb toward the back room. "You can sleep in there. I can bunk down on the sofa."

"Oh, Dodge, I hate to take your bed."

He grinned. "No, you don't. Because you know you'll be safe here with me, Tory. I won't let anything happen to you."

She gave him a shaky smile. "Thanks, Dodge. I appreciate your generosity."

"Generosity has nothing to do with it. Sharkey's ghost would haunt me forever if I let anything happen to his little girl."

She stiffened. "So it's for Sharkey? I should have known."

"It's a joint effort," he conceded with a devilish grin. "But I couldn't let you spend a terror-filled night all alone back at that motel. I'll get a shirt, and we'll go survey the damage and gather your things."

As Dodge ambled into the back room, Tory noticed that he was barefooted. No cowboy boots. No shirt. Just hip-hugging jeans on his lean male figure. And darned sexy, too. Was she crazy, agreeing to come back here for the night? Could she trust this man—this man she didn't know worth beans? But he was Sharkey's trusted friend and partner. Didn't that mean anything? Since she couldn't depend on Sharkey, what made her think she could trust his right-hand man?

When Dodge appeared again, he wore a blue plaid western-cut shirt tucked into those skin-tight jeans and no belt. But he'd put on his boots. He looked quite trustworthy . . . and ruggedly masculine.

"Ready to go?"

Tory nodded and knew immediately that she

could trust the man. She didn't understand how she knew that, but she did. And she slid confidently beside him onto the Blazer's front seat.

Dodge searched through the ransacked motel room, picking up items at random, stepping over piles of clothes. Tory stood in the corner, rubbing her arms with a feeling of foreboding she'd never before experienced. Dodge finally turned to her. "Let's get your stuff together here, Tory. Looks like a routine pilfering. Yep, he was looking for something, all right. And he didn't find it."

They worked quietly, Tory neatly folding blouses and slacks, Dodge crushing filmy panties and lacy bras into the corner of the suitcase. He tried not to think of her donning such frilly items. Curiously, he lifted a small hand barbell. "This yours?" he quizzed with a twinkle in his eyes.

"Yes," she answered defensively. "Helps keep me toned while I travel."

"Oh. Is that what does it?"

"Well, I don't have a chance to go to the spa and work out when I'm away from home."

"I see," he observed, tucking the barbell into her suitcase. "No wonder you're so well toned."

She gave him a sideways glance and continued packing without comment.

When they reached Sharkey's old trailer, Dodge hauled the suitcases into the back bedroom. Tory slumped on the sofa in the living room, staring off into space. "I can't believe this is happening to me," she muttered.

Dodge went into the kitchen and she heard glasses clinking. Then he was beside her, his arm

83

extended. "Here, Tory. This'll help. A little Scotch."

She accepted the small glass with a weak smile. "Thanks, Dodge. You know, I'm not usually such a wimp. It just caught me off guard, and I got real scared all of a sudden."

"We just have to be careful in the future."

"I guess . . ."

When they finished the drinks, he showed her the bathroom, hung up clean towels, and handed her a set of clean sheets. "This should be enough for tonight."

"It's more than enough, Dodge. And I promise not to be a bother again. Tomorrow I'll—"

"No, you won't. You're staying with me until this is over."

She drew up sharply. "Now listen here—"

"No argument, Tory. I feel responsible."

"To whom? Not to me! Why you never saw me before yesterday, so how could you feel responsible for me?"

"I'm responsible to Sharkey," he said, winking. "I told you, if I let anything happen to you, he'll haunt me forever. Don't worry, Tory. I'll take care of any intruders. You just go to sleep and try to forget everything that's happened." With that, Dodge wheeled around and turned his attention to fixing his bed on the sofa.

She prepared to launch another protest, but when he peeled off his boots and shirt and unsnapped his jeans, Tory thought better of the idea. Shoving the bedroom door shut, she decided she could wait until tomorrow for any further objections.

As she began to unbutton her blouse, she realized that Dodge was in complete charge of the situation and she had put him there. He was making her decisions for her, directing her next move. It had been a damn long time since a man had made *her* decisions, and she intended to get back in control again. First thing in the morning.

Quickly, she began stripping the bed to apply clean sheets. In the pale light, she noticed a small dark object beneath the head of the mattress and reached for it.

To her horror, Tory drew out a heavy black revolver. Inlaid on the wooden handle was a turquoise star. Distinctive, yet frightening. "Dodge!"

Instantly, he burst through the door and stood beside her, dressed only in his briefs. "What is it? Did you hear something?"

She turned to face him and lifted the trembling hand holding the ominous weapon. "Is—is this how you would take care of any intruders?" At the moment, she was too alarmed to notice his state of dress. Or undress.

His large hand closed briefly on hers as he casually removed the gun from her hand. "Oh, yes, my thirty-eight. Forgot to get it." He turned his back and took a step.

"Dodge?"

He turned back around, and this time she noticed how he was dressed. He wore only a pair of dark-colored briefs. Navy. Oh, dear heavens, navy briefs with certain areas outlined in white seam binding. And all the areas were bulging!

She tore her eyes away from his body and tried to pretend it didn't matter. Why, she saw men in similar attire at the spa all the time. So what made this cowboy different from any other well-formed, muscular, virile, tanned . . . man? Oh, dear, he *was* different. And the things he did to her insides were disastrous!

Dodge gazed at her levelly. "Yes, Tory, that's how I would handle any intruder, if I had my weapon within my reach. Obviously, it would do no good in here with you?"

"Y—you would *shoot* someone?" She stared at him incredulously, forcing her eyes on his. They were brown and warm and amazingly sexy.

She shook herself. It was just because those gorgeous eyes were attached to a gorgeous male body and she was extremely weak.

"I'm a crack shot, Tory. I'd aim for the leg."

"Oh, my God!" She sank down on the edge of the unmade bed and covered her face with her hands. "Oh, dear, Dodge! What—what kind of place is this? Have I stepped back in time to the old wild West? I don't think I belong here."

"Don't be alarmed by our old West attitudes. Let me worry about that. You just . . . go to sleep, and I'll take care of anything else that happens tonight."

"But, Dodge, I don't want any shooting."

"Look, Tory, do you mind if we discuss this in the morning, when I have a clearer head and more clothes on?"

86

"Oh! Yes, of course!" She blushed for the first time in years and waved one hand. "Yes, please, go. It's very disconcerting to see you standing there like that."

"Disconcerting? Does that mean there's a real woman beneath that haughty exterior?"

Her mouth twitched as she was torn between laughing hysterically and snapping his head off with another caustic retort. Then her emotions took over, and she responded quite unexpectedly. Large tears formed in her blue eyes as she said in a low voice, "Undoubtedly, I'm more real than most people around here realize or expect. And I'm damned upset by everything that's happened in the last two days. And now I'm damned scared." She turned her face away and quickly swiped at the tears coursing down her cheeks.

Dodge sat down beside her and tucked a long arm around her shoulders. "I guess all this has been somewhat traumatic for you, Tory."

She sniffled and leaned back against his shoulder. "This is stupid. Please, go on to bed, Dodge. Forget this ever happened. I—I'm just tired tonight. I'll be all right tomorrow."

He pressed her against his rock-hard shoulder for another moment. "I'll be okay tomorrow, too, but damned if I'll forget the way I feel right now." A quick squeeze-hug, and he was gone.

She sat on the bed's edge for a long time, thinking not of the break-in at her motel room or her father's strange friends or even the pending trek up the mountain for the gold. She could only think of Dodge Callahan and what he did to her libido and how being near him nearly wrecked her emotions. Crazily, she even marveled that a cowboy-type like Dodge would wear colored briefs and how good he looked in them. And, oh, how he filled them out.

The man had responded to her, too. She was close enough—and aware enough—to realize he had reacted physically to her. And that thought sent a feminine thrill radiating through her.

Although mentally and physically exhausted, Tory tossed and turned for hours. She wrestled with the mattress that Dodge's large frame had dented only a few hours before. She couldn't stop thinking about him and wondering what it would be like to make love to the man.

With a shudder, she remembered the gun he'd so easily claimed. He could be a dangerous, violent man. How could she consider letting him touch her when those same hands had eagerly wrapped around the handle of a deadly weapon?

But she did.

The next day, both Tory and Dodge made conscious efforts to regain control of their sudden hot attraction and keep their relationship on a business level. Over breakfast, they were subdued and relatively quiet. She didn't mention the dreaded gun and neither did he.

Between sips of steaming black coffee, he muttered, "You didn't sleep much last night. I heard you rolling around. Wasn't the bed comfortable?"

"The bed was fine. It wasn't that. Too much going on inside my head, I guess." Or in my body!

"Sorry I kept you awake. That's another reason I think I should get another motel room."

"Absolutely not. Much too risky. We don't want to take a chance on this happening again and you possibly being around next time."

"Then how about a small apartment for a few weeks?"

"This is a small town, Tory. There aren't any short-term apartments available. It isn't proper."

"And staying here with you is?"

"No one will know. I want to keep your presence here as quiet as possible, now that we know someone is causing trouble."

"I'm sure everyone knows about me after the will reading in the saloon."

"If you check out of the motel today, maybe they'll think you've left town."

"Is that necessary?" she asked.

"Well, we'll be leaving for the mountains in a couple of days, and you won't need that or any other room for a couple of weeks. It might fit in with our plans if they think you've left town completely."

"Will we be safer in the mountains?"

"I hope so." He rubbed his hand raggedly over his face.

"Dodge, I'm sorry I caused you so much trouble. It was a rough night."

"Couldn't be helped," he said tightly as he poured more coffee. There was a tension between them that would not go away. They tried to be polite, pretended to ignore the mounting electricity. But something existed that made them both aware of the other's every move.

When Dodge suggested they go shopping for supplies and groceries for the trip, Tory readily agreed to help him with the chore. That would keep them busy and in the public for hours. And Lord knows, that's what they needed until this rush of physical attraction subsided.

They were gone all day. First, Tory checked out of the motel, then drove down the highway several miles and circled back to the trailer on a back road. Dodge was waiting for her.

Then the two of them scouted the stores in Sierra Vista and filled the rear of the Blazer with items needed for the trip. Tory double-checked the lists Dodge had made and helped him organize everything into small boxes that could be easily transferred to pack mules and saddlebags.

Before returning to the tiny trailer for the night, they stopped in Sierra Vista for dinner.

Dodge rested his forearms on the table. "You tired?"

"Exhausted," she admitted. "I won't have any trouble sleeping tonight."

"Good. Me, either. Ready to go?"

Tory accompanied him out, congratulating herself on a day well spent and, soon, an uneventful night. Maybe they had conquered their sexual magnetism, after all.

Dodge unlocked the trailer door, and before she could step inside, he uttered a stream of expletives and bolted inside.

Tory followed him and looked around at the mess. "Oh, no, not again!"

CHAPTER SIX

Stunned, Tory gazed around. Every item in the entire trailer had been turned over—and tossed. The place was a wreck, and Dodge was acting like a crazed man.

Furious, he plowed through the rubble, throwing things, cursing. His long arms flailed in frustration, his fists impotently thrashed the air. "Damn it! Look at this mess! Just look at it! How dare he break in here? This is Sharkey's place!"

Last night Dodge had calmed her fears with his strength and self-assurance. And when she'd stayed with him, he'd kept her safe all night. Now was her chance to give him the same reassurance he'd given her.

"Dodge, please, you're making it worse." Tory reached out to him, but he wouldn't stand still and slipped from her grasp.

"What the hell does he think he's doing, disrupting everything like this? The map isn't his! It's ours." He flipped on the hall light and gazed angrily into the bedroom. "He has no right to it—no right to do this! No right to invade our lives. Why, I'll—"

"Maybe we should call the police." She followed him, picking her footsteps between the canned goods and skillets and overturned chairs.

"The police?" he repeated derisively, shaking his head. "Do you want everyone in Cochise County to know what we're up to?"

"No, but I don't want anyone hurt, either," she said. "Especially us."

Dodge gave her a speculative glance, squinting one brown eye. "He's after the map, Tory. Don't you see that?"

"*If* it's a he." She nodded bleakly. "The map— where is it? Do you still have it?"

He clapped his left hand over his heart, and she heard paper crinkling. "Safe right here."

Sighing, her shoulders slumped with relief that she'd given it over to him. "Good." She moved closer to him and barely resisted the urge to reach up and touch the spot on his shirt he'd patted. Oh, God, he was alluring. Damned appealing, even now in his anger. Maybe more so because he exuded so much power. And masculinity. "Right. It's safe with you, Dodge."

She looked up at him, her blue eyes sincere and warm. There was no fear in them, not even the deep resentment she'd exhibited in the past few days. Confidence and admiration replaced everything else.

He was momentarily caught in her gaze. Breathing in deeply, he tried to displace his frustration. "I wish I could say the same about us, Tory, that we're completely safe."

"I feel very safe with you, Dodge."

"Even after this?" He gestured over the mess.

"Yes. He—or whoever—is obviously after the map and waited in both cases until no one was home. He isn't out to harm us, only to steal the key to the gold. Anyway, you've got the gun."

"That doesn't scare you?"

"Yes, but I trust you. For some crazy reason, I trust my feelings about you, Dodge." She smiled breathlessly. They stood exceedingly close, not touching but exuding a strength of attraction that was nearly tangible. And strongly magnetic.

"Maybe you trust these feelings," he said softly, running a single tanned rough finger over her smooth cheek, "but I don't. They're dangerous. And exciting . . ."

She breathed through slightly parted lips as he moved slowly to take her in his arms. One hand reached around her neck, long fingers splayed in the wispy blue black hair at her nape. His other hand closed over her shoulder, then eased down the stretch of her back. The chasm between them narrowed until their breathing intermingled and his lips descended to hers. His mustache was like a feather, brushing and teasing her skin while his lips melded with hers. Gingerly, he sipped as if she tasted of sweet wine.

Tory poured herself out to him, giving and at the same time receiving. She opened her lips to take the strength of his tongue, symbol of his masculine life and power.

She needed his rugged kind of power, needed a man like Dodge to take her in his arms and bring her to the brink of her passion. She swayed eagerly against his lean hardness and thrilled as his hand caressed the length of her back, ever pressing her to him, tracing the gentle curves of her hips.

Suddenly, his hold on her gentled, and the hand at her waist pushed them apart. "Tory, I—"

"Don't apologize. I . . . it was me, too, Dodge."

Her eyes had darkened to the color of thunder clouds, and he found her exciting and vital. His response to her had been immediate and intense, and he knew he wanted her in a purely sexual way. But she didn't belong to him, wasn't his type. And obviously, he wasn't hers. "I'd like to say this won't happen again, but when I look into your eyes, I seem to lose control," Dodge admitted honestly, his smile slightly askew. "I'll have to work on that."

"We'll both have to work on it," she said softly. She couldn't help admiring his honesty and knew in her heart she didn't regret the incident one bit.

"Your eyes are a beautiful shade of blue," he continued as if in a momentary trance. "Deep blue. They remind me of Sharkey's. They were trusting eyes, maybe too much so. Do you trust too easily, Tory?"

"Probably."

"You should be careful who you trust."

Dodge's hands were still on her, and she felt the strength and magnetism of the man. Her mind whirled at his words, her body ached with desire, and she tried to think straight. "Does that include you, Dodge?"

"Yes."

"I find that hard to believe. My father trusted you and I guess I want to, also. Right now, though, I only see you and me together. And what's happening to us. And I'm afraid it's happening too fast."

He nodded briskly and let his hands drop to his sides. "You're right, Tory. This is crazy . . ."

Suddenly, she smiled with a twinkle in those intent blue eyes. "According to what was said the other day at the saloon, we don't even like each other."

He chuckled. "Yeah. You aren't my type, city lady."

"Nor you, mine, cowboy." She tapped the front of his shirt, then self-consciously dropped her hand before she could succumb to touching him more. "Well, that's over. So much for lust."

"And now I know how you kiss."

She nodded and affirmed, "I hope our basic curiosity has been satisfied."

His brown almond eyes squinted at her, and she couldn't tell if he were serious or teasing. "I don't know about your curiosity, city lady, but this cowboy isn't content with just a little sniff of the brandy."

She smiled sweetly. "But too much brandy gives you heartburn."

"I'm burning all over just thinking about it. Maybe if we took it slow and easy, we'd get used to the heat."

"Maybe . . ." She tore her gaze from his, feeling the same burning inside her. Desperate to change the subject, Tory surveyed the wrecked room. "Whoever did this didn't take it slow and easy. He went berserk."

"Yep."

They picked their way into the bedroom amid the upturned suitcases, the disarray of her clothes mingled with the overturned bedside lamp and corner chair. Even the sheets had been stripped off and the mattress scooted awry.

"My thirty-eight!" Dodge yelled suddenly and dashed back into the living room where he'd hidden the weapon. "Dammit, it's gone! He took my gun!"

She looked at Dodge mildly. "I'm not surprised."

"I'll damn sure report *this* to the police," he muttered furiously.

"Oh? You won't report two break-ins, but you will report your gun being taken? That's crazy logic, Dodge."

"When something's taken, it's burglary. This is serious. That thirty-eight was made specially for me," he fumed.

"Well, should we go now and not touch a thing until the police have completed their investigation? We might mess up the fingerprints or something."

"Oh, I won't tell them about all this. It'll only point out we might have something to hide and alert them to the fact that you're still in town. They'll want to know details of our trek up the mountain, all about the gold, who we're going with, and what we're going for." He shoved his Stetson back on his head and propped his hands on his hips. Standing with legs apart, he surveyed the room. "No, I'll stop by the station tomorrow and report it missing."

Tory looked at him curiously for a moment, then decided to let him handle the security problem. She turned back to the mess before her. Shaking her head, she muttered, "My clothes will never be the same. But these hardy things made it fine." She lifted a new stiff pair of jeans with tags still attached.

Dodge rejoined her in the bedroom. "We need to wash those about a dozen times to soften them up and make them fit comfortably."

"Soft? Is it possible for these jeans to ever get soft?"

"Sure." He rubbed the thigh of his well-worn jeans. "Mine are."

Her eyes dropped to his thigh and the large hand stroking it, and she tried not to think about that hand . . . and that thigh . . . and how they would feel. Certainly not soft. "Yes, but you live in yours. I only intend to wear mine for the duration of this trip. After that, it's—"

"Back to your silks and the big city?"

She nodded. "Yes." When he didn't respond right away, she added, "In my business, I can't very well appear in well-worn jeans."

"Fancy business, huh?"

"Well, not fancy, but . . . nice. It's a rather selective shop. Jeans do not have panache."

"Panache? Does that mean they aren't fancy pants?"

"Fanc— No! It means stylish. The latest vogue."

"Stylish, huh?" He looked down her length, taking purposeful notice of her slender hips and long legs. "You're that, all right. But you're a fancy pants, too." Then he grinned and picked up a pair of lace panties and dangled them. "See? Ve–ry fancy."

She snatched the meager item from his large hand. "You should talk about fancy pants! You, with your navy blue briefs!"

"Oh? You noticed?"

She turned an immediate shade of rose blush. "I —I couldn't help but notice when you barged in like that."

"I was only trying to help a lady in distress." He grabbed the small barbell and flexed his arm with the weight a couple of times before giving it to her. "Better not let yourself get out of shape while you're here. You might need your strength."

She took the barbell from him and tossed it into the empty suitcase. "I don't plan to let myself get out of shape."

"Riding those mules up the mountain should keep some parts of you well toned," he muttered as he bent to straighten the mattress. "Guess we'd better get some of this cleaned up so you can go to bed."

She sighed. "After everything that's happened, I'm wide awake. What if he comes back? Do you think he's gone for good, Dodge?" Suddenly, she wanted his reassurance again.

"And you don't have your gun anymore." Strangely, she felt a pang of regret.

"But I have these." He knotted both hands into

large fists and thrust them toward her. "I'll take care of you. Don't worry, Tory."

Instinctively, she reached out and grasped one huge-knuckled fist. She couldn't get her slender fingers all the way around the fist he'd made. "I have no doubt you'll be able to take care of me. And him. If you know he's here."

"I'll know."

"Only if you're close enough."

He took a step. "How close is enough?"

Her hand traveled up his sinewy forearm, over the bulging bicep, to his sturdy shoulder. She shouldn't be so impressed by mere muscles, but this brawny physique was attached to a man who illicited a reponse in her that went beyond reason. Beyond reasonable control. And she was rapidly losing hers. "This . . . this is probably close enough. In the next room."

"Not for me, Tory." His chest expanded as he took a slow, heated breath, and she could hear and feel the rise and fall of the powerful expanse beneath her fingertips. "Oh, God, Tory. Can't you tell that I want you . . . as close as possible?"

Her hand moved up his shirted flesh to the bare spot at the base of his neck where his collar opened and his pulse throbbed. Her fingers tingled at the sensuous touch. "As close as possible . . ." she repeated in a breathy whisper.

Renewed by her response to his desire, Dodge pulled them together again, clamping his lips over hers with a vigorous fervor. The timid gentleness was gone this time, replaced by strength of yearning. They clung to each other, grasping and clutching as the throes of gutsy desire took over. Now it was a man and a woman, giving in to feelings and lust, two firebrands seeking the heart of the flame that aroused them.

He kissed her lips, her face, her cheeks. His lips tasted her long, creamy neck, then traveled deeper, lower. With crazed hands, he practically ripped the blouse from her back and the lacy bra that embraced her firm white breasts. His lips descended to those prominent globes, setting them aglow with his fiery kisses. Achingly, she raised them to meet his feather-brushed kisses. Each nipple perked up and turned dusky rose as he alternated between them.

Her fingers hurried to unbutton his shirt and open it to reveal the expanse of masculine chest that she craved to touch . . . and kiss. And she did, until he moaned softly and pulled her close to kiss her lips again.

"Tory . . . Tory . . ." he murmured softly.

His hands caressed her bare back, and she fervently arched against him, crushing her creamy breasts to the carved muscles of his chest. His hands encased her buttocks and lifted her to press against the male hardness at his groin. "We belong together, Tory."

"Yes, Dodge. Yes, I believe it!" She moved seductively against him, her silk slacks rasping against the roughness of his jeans, her hips undulating with the basic need in her that he had aroused so quickly.

"Tory, my little fancy pants, I want you." Still, he made no move, except to hold her close.

"I want you, too, Dodge," she whispered, and wriggled loose from his embrace. "Come on," she encouraged, guiding him to the wrecked bed. With one bold sweep of her hand, she made room for them by pushing away the contents of her suitcases. Boldly, she slipped off her shoes and lay back on the bare mattress. She was topless but still wore her beige silk slacks.

Her breasts heaved as she tried to temper her breathing, but their swollen tips were rosy reminders that his lips had teased them to this tempting state of erection.

With exaggerated, purposeful movements, she gripped the beige waistband, unbuttoning and slowly unzipping the slacks. Then, with gently undulating hips, she scooted her slacks and sheer panty hose over the curve of her hips and down the long length of her shapely legs.

Dodge gulped and stood watching her, spellbound and rooted to the spot at the edge of the bed.

She smiled tentatively. "Well . . . ?"

"Oh, God . . ." Feverishly, he tugged at his boots, finally tossing them into the mess around them. His broad hands tore at the oversized belt buckle and strong zipper of his jeans.

Like Tory, Dodge was aroused and ready. His manhood proudly sprang forward as he discarded his jeans and briefs. He paused only momentarily, then he was beside her, one leg draped over hers, kissing her until both of them were oblivious of anything except their desire for one another.

He had given her a brief but tantalizing look at

101

his beautiful male body, the form that Tory had known all along was there but until now had remained hidden beneath jeans and western shirts. Last night had been a temptation when he'd stood there in those navy briefs. She'd wanted him then. Now she wanted him buried deep inside her, wanted his complete satisfaction.

She returned his kisses, plunging her tongue to meet his, letting them tease and dance together, finally giving in to his strength. It was only an overture, an example of what was to come. And they both anticipated the culmination with raging eagerness.

Finally, with a low rumble in his chest, Dodge moved over her, raising and trapping her arms on either side of her head. Hovering, he murmured, "You're beautiful, Tory. You do things to me, more than you could know." Kissing the insides of her arms, his lips lighted a hot trail all the way down to her already-heated breasts, then back to the sensitive areas of her arms.

She arched upward as his lips circled the gentle mounds of her breasts and closed over each tight, aching nipple. "Ohh, Dodge . . . ohh . . ."

His legs wedged between hers, forcing them apart. "Tory, you're soft and . . . ready for me. I . . . can't wait any longer."

"I . . . can't either," she said hesitantly. "I want you, too, Dodge." She felt the hard pressure of him against her belly, then a firm, sure probing against the most feminine part of her. Eagerly, she rose to meet the throbbing heat, seeking to satisfy her own intense burning deep inside.

"Tory, ahh, To–ry," he sighed as he glided steadily into her moist, welcome body.

With a small cry, she accepted the force of his male thrusting, and they merged, completely and thoroughly. When he heard her muffled sound, he stopped moving and lay very still.

She could feel him growing inside her, and she welcomed him fully, murmuring, "It's all right, Dodge."

"You sure? Tory, I can't hold back . . ."

"Then, don't." She rocked beneath him, urging him, stroking his taut hips with eager hands.

"Come with me, Tory."

She allowed her spirit to flow free, allowed herself the ultimate pleasure Dodge promised her. She was like a bird, suddenly freed from a passionless cage.

Seeking the rhythm, creating a wild, hot friction, they undulated in unison, spinning and whirling out of control. Together they ascended to the summit of a frantically created desire. Both thrusting, both crying out, both grasping as if never to let go.

"Don't stop! Don't—"

"Tory! Tory!"

Then they both were quiet and still, and only the sounds of crickets outside could be heard.

Just as they'd ridden to love's pinnacle together, they clung together for the slow journey down. Timeless floating, dozing, caressing, holding. Hours later, they woke in each other's arms.

Sometime in the middle of the night, she stirred

and found herself pinioned. "Dodge, your arm's heavy."

"Hmm? Oh, yeah. Sorry." He moaned as he struggled for consciousness and rolled to her side. "You okay, Tory?"

"Yes, fine," she mumbled, scooting off the bed. "I just have to go to the bathroom." She stumbled over the mess and remembered . . . Oh, how could she forget? In a moment, she returned and surveyed the wrecked room in the semidarkness. "Dodge, we have a terrible mess to clean up."

"Not now. In the morning."

"Don't you want to fix the sheets on the bed?"

"No. I only want you here with me."

She clicked off the small hall light and, grabbing a sheet for cover, rejoined him.

"It'll be okay, Tory. Come here." He reached for her.

"I guess I should be worried," she said, snuggling against him, "but I'm not. I trust you, Dodge. I trust you to take care of me."

"I will, my beautiful fancy pants. Trust me."

He turned her back to his chest and wrapped his huge arms around her. They lay curled together like two spoons. Two warm, very-much-alive spoons. His hand nestled between her legs, stroking gently, irregularly. She found sleep no insulation to her response to him as a heated path began to form deep inside her.

With some relief, she felt him grow hot and hard against her back, and she arched against his hand.

"Tory . . ."

"Yes?"

"Lie very still and I'll . . ."

She held her breath as he again sought her warmth. His manhood was a fiery shaft inside her, and she began to breathe rapidly as they started another erotic climb, this time with slow leisure. And again, they reached an ecstasy-filled climax.

His lips nibbled at her earlobe. "You're wonderful, fancy pants."

She smiled in the darkness. "Dodge, can I make a confession?"

"Depends."

"It's about you. Us."

"Well, okay." His tongue made a trail around her neck.

She paused, hesitant now. Embarrassed, even in the darkness.

"So, confess!" he urged.

She reached for him, turning in his arms. "Never better," she mumbled with a little laugh.

He chuckled roughly. "Aw, Tory. You were married. I know—"

Pressing a finger to his lips, she followed with her own kiss. "Believe me," she whispered, "never better."

"I want to believe you," he admitted softly, kissing her again. "Feeds my ego. But you had something to do with this, too. About half, I'd say. And you're great."

"Hold me, Dodge. Hold me close."

And he did. The rest of the night.

Morning came, and with it the natural light that revealed the full extent of the wrecked room. Tory lay awake and watched Dodge sleeping. It was a very quiet, private time, a time to speculate over what had happened to them last night. And why.

Why had she lost control like that? And seduced him? Admittedly, she had encouraged what happened. For all his faults, Dodge was a gentleman and would never have imposed himself on her if she hadn't consented. But she had done more than consent. She had enticed.

Did she regret it?

She gazed at the boldly masculine figure next to her on the bed. His proud head was thrown back on the pillow, his aquiline profile straight and strong. His chest was broad and covered with a sprinkling of sandy hair, curly and cushiony. The wrinkled sheet met his flat belly halfway, covering rock-hard thighs and the exciting form of his manhood. How could she ever regret making love to this man?

She didn't.

In fact, she reveled in the joy he'd given her last night. More than sex, what they had experienced had been both gratifying and complete. Somehow, they seemed to reach each other on another plane than simply sexual. They had been drawn to each other from the start, attracted and needing each other. And wanting. So what was wrong with that?

Deep inside, Tory knew. She and Dodge were two very different people from two diverse pasts, heading for opposite futures. Dodge was not the kind of man she wanted to be attracted to. Her mother had proved how disastrous that could be, and she wanted no part of a life like that. She'd already had it and it was not good.

So, when this was all over, she'd head back to L.A. and forget Dodge Callahan, her handsome cowboy. And he could forget her intrusion into his wild, western world.

He stirred and opened his brown eyes to find her staring. Unsmiling, he reached for her, his huge hand catching her behind the neck and hauling her to him. "Morning."

Immediately, she forgot all her clever in-depth analysis about why they'd made love and relented to her feminine desires to snuggle against his chest. "Morning, Dodge. We have a huge mess to clean up in here."

"Hmm. And I have to report my gun missing." His hand traveled down her back and settled on the smooth, gentle curve of her hips. He continued to stroke the silky feminine skin, obviously relishing the way she felt beneath his rough hand.

"And finish getting supplies for the trip."

"And wash your jeans forty-seven times so they'll fit you well." He caressed her rear affectionately. "To make them soft and comfy, Miss Fancy Pants."

"I need to call home and see how things are at the shop."

He kissed her rumpled blue black hair. "All to be finished in the next twenty-four hours in time to head up the mountain and meet the others by three in the afternoon." He rolled back and pulled her over him, kissing her soundly. "But all of that can wait."

"Dodge!" she gasped as her body felt his boldness. And responded to it.

"First, us," he promised with a chuckle low in his chest, kissing her again.

"Dodge . . ." she gasped, giggling.

"Yes, Tory." He rolled her over and murmured between kisses, "I've never seen anyone like you, fancy pants. Never had anyone like you. Maybe you're my type, after all."

"Maybe I'll reconsider, too," she said breathlessly. "I confess I always did like cowboys." Then she showed him once again exactly how much she liked this cowboy—from the tips of his toes to his earlobes, and everywhere in between.

CHAPTER SEVEN

Feeling especially lighthearted, Tory and Dodge spent the day doing what was required before their trip up the mountain tomorrow. But they had fun, behaving like two kids, teasing and laughing their way through each chore, sharing the jobs and the fun. For lunch, they munched foot-long hotdogs and double-dip chocolate fudge ice cream cones.

"If I gain weight eating all this junk," she warned, pausing to flick a large chocolate chip into her mouth with her tongue, "I'll never forgive you!"

"Don't worry," he told her. "We'll work it off with exercises of passion. But if *that* doesn't do the trick, there're always your barbells! You can exercise while I watch and count!"

"Oh, *you!*" She pinched his waist, but all she grabbed was a handful of lean, trim masculinity. Tory had never felt younger and happier than she did with Dodge. He allowed her to laugh and have fun and forget her responsibilities for a little while. And she loved the freedom.

While Dodge went to report his missing

weapon, Tory called home from a nearby phone booth.

"Megan, how are things going?"

"Tory! I can't wait until you get here! When are you coming home?"

"What's wrong?"

"Nothing much. I have the shop under control. It's, well, you know, the creditors. Mr. Koch, of Delta Products Unlimited, called to say if we didn't pay for that line of coordinated sportswear soon, his lawyer would be in touch."

"Now, Megan, don't despair," Tory said soothingly. "I explained everything to him before I left. He'll just have to wait."

"Well, he's not the only one, Tory."

"Who else?" Tory sighed.

"You know those fake leather pants . . ."

"How well are they selling, Megan?"

"Not very. I haven't sold a one in ten days."

"Okay, send the whole shipment back."

"But, Tory—"

"Do as I say," Tory instructed firmly. "Explain the situation. Tell them to accept the returns or lose money. Remind them they can't get blood out of a turnip!"

"Okay." Megan's voice quivered tentatively. "When *are* you coming back, Tory?"

"Looks like it'll be a while, Megan." Tory paused and thought of her night with Dodge and wished—suddenly—that she never had to go back. But, of course, she did. "Maybe in a few weeks."

"Weeks?" Megan repeated shrilly.

"Now, hold on," Tory cautioned. "When I return, we'll be able to pay off everybody. Plus a bonus for you, Megan."

"What? You mean the gold has panned out, so to speak?"

"I think it's going to."

"You *think*? Don't you *know*? What are you up to, Tory?"

"Can't tell you everything, Megan. I'll be back in touch, so don't bother calling the motel number I gave you. I'm not there anymore."

"Then where are you staying?"

"I can't be reached by phone. But I'll call you next chance I get."

"Tory, this isn't like you at all. You're sounding a little strange."

"Don't worry about me, Megan. Everything's fine." Tory spotted Dodge and waved. "Got to go now. Keep up the good job. You're doing just great, Megan. Bye."

"Tory, wait—" The phone went dead.

Tory hung the phone up and hurried back to the Blazer to wait for Dodge.

By noon the next day, Dodge's gleaming red and black Blazer was tackling the rugged route into the heart of the Dragoon Mountains. They rode in relaxed silence as Dodge concentrated on driving the rutted unpaved road.

Tory thought about how extremely happy and relaxed she felt, whether in Dodge's arms, like during the last two nights, or merely sitting beside him on the way to an unusual adventure. Just being with him set her heart soaring and her spirits aglow.

Furthest from her mind was going back home to the shop in L.A. Right now, she didn't want to think of it and all the debts and problems with the business she'd have to face when she arrived. She couldn't imagine saying good-bye to Dodge. Why, they'd just begun. And it was heaven! She smiled contentedly to herself. She felt like a girl with a first crush . . . in love. Oh, no, not really love . . . Couldn't be this soon.

"Can I interrupt?"

"Of course," she said softly, smiling across at him.

"You seemed a million miles away."

"Not quite."

"Thinking about home?"

She nodded, and strangely, he didn't respond.

"I thought you might like to see Coronado's route into America in the sixteenth century." Dodge pulled the Blazer to a halt and pointed out a marvelous vista that seemed to stretch forever. "Coronado's conquistadors marched up through this valley looking for the Seven Cities of Cibola. When they reached the Zuñi Indian village, up in New Mexico, they thought they'd found their treasure. Of course, the Indians had different ideas about the matter, and a major battle ensued."

"And I figured the old-time miners were the only ones who dared enter this wilderness."

"Far from it. Ancient Indians called Mimbres—and of course, Apaches like Geronimo and Cochise—used these mountains as their strong-

112

holds. The American miners came in the last hundred years or so looking for gold. Their stories fill volumes with tales of violence and bloody battles and hard-won success."

"My, my, I'm impressed. You're a regular history buff," she said teasingly.

He jerked the vehicle back into gear and they proceeded. "I don't often have such a captive audience."

"And one so ignorant of local history?"

"I'm trying to teach you about the real West, Miss Fancy Pants. Since you're Sharkey Carsen's daughter, you have quite a legacy to learn. He was a regular legend in his own time."

"What about you, Dodge? Are you a legend?"

"Naw," he said, grinning. "I'm just a simple old sun seeker, like dozens of men before me."

"Just men? No women sun seekers?"

"Oh, a few, I guess. But they usually came because of some man."

She settled back against the seat and studied the changes in foliage as they climbed deeper into the mountain's heart. "I guess I am, too," she admitted softly, "if you consider Sharkey."

Dodge smiled at her. "Because of him, you come by gold fever naturally. It's in your blood."

Tory pondered what Dodge had said about the bloody history in the search for gold. "From all the old tales, it seems that many—and we'll never know how many unknown ones—lost their lives searching for gold around here."

"You're right. We don't have records of them all. Sad, isn't it, to think of someone coming West to seek his fortune and never being heard from again?"

"Kind of like Sharkey," she mused. "How . . . how did my father die, Dodge?"

"Accident. He fell off his mule and plunged to the bottom of a slate cliff. They found him there."

"How could he just fall off the mule he was riding?"

"Who knows? He was alone. But the mule he'd rented from Yazzie wandered back down the mountain and ended up unharmed back at the corral."

"You sure it was an accident?"

Dodge nodded tightly. "There wasn't much of an investigation. It was assumed that he suffered a heart attack and couldn't prevent the fall."

"Assumed, huh? Nothing proved?"

"What are you getting at, Tory?"

"Is it possible that my father was killed since he knew about this gold?"

Dodge sighed heavily. "Anything's possible out here, Tory. But I doubt it. Look, don't get started on something so nebulous. Sharkey's cause of death has been settled by the coroner's report. You probably received a copy."

"Was it settled to everyone's satisfaction?"

"Yes."

"To yours, Dodge?"

"Yes! Now, please, Tory—"

The subject of the conversation and Dodge's tight-lipped reaction put a damper on the light mood between them, and they continued in strained silence.

An hour and a half later, Dodge pulled off the road and stopped in a small clearing near some pines. "Well, we're here."

They had traveled from the cactus-growing desert floor of Tombstone through scrub brush to sparse pines. Yazzie's cabin was a rough-hewn building, half rock, half logs, in a small stand of pines. Behind it was an ocotillo fence corralling a dozen or so mules.

"Now, who is Yazzie, exactly?" Tory asked as she mentally noted the rugged terrain. "And why are we meeting the others here?"

"Yazzie's a man of the mountain, has always lived here, as far as I know. This is a good starting place, where trekkers usually converge for food and drink. Plus, we'll rent our mules from him and take him along as guide and cook."

Tory frowned. "Do we have to go with him?"

"If you're worried about sharing the diggings with him, don't be. We need his expertise. There have been whole teams of people lost forever in these mountains. Believe me, he'll be worth every cent we have to share with him."

"Sharing is not my worry, Dodge."

"Then what?"

"I don't know. Just a feeling, I guess. You were the one wanting to keep this excursion quiet in Tombstone, and now you're including a stranger. I don't understand."

He clasped her hand and squeezed. "It'll be okay, Tory. Yazzie has always been a part of these mountains. Sharkey and I always rented our mules from him. He isn't exactly a stranger."

"Did you and Sharkey always take him along with you?"

He smiled at her perception. "Nope. But this is different. We have a group of people who are unfamiliar with conditions on the mountain, including you, my dear. Also, there's Rex. Even though he put money into the mining company, he's hardly ever been up here. Plus, we're searching for specific landmarks that I figure only Yazzie knows."

She nodded in silent agreement and looked over Yazzie's small, dilapidated spread. "What does he do up here? Just rent mules? How does he live?"

"Well, obviously it doesn't take much for him. I think he occasionally brings in a little gold dust or a few turquoise stones in exchange for bread and bacon."

"And he lives up here all alone?"

"Yep. Had an Indian wife, but she died years ago. According to Sharkey, Yazzie's mother was an Apache woman who ran off with a miner from Yuma. Because of his split heritage, Yazzie never really belonged anywhere. He's been here as long as anyone can remember."

She shook her head slowly. "It's like a story out of an old movie."

Dodge glanced at her with a curious grin. "This is the West, Tory. Some things are slow to change."

"So I see," she murmured, thinking her friends in Los Angeles wouldn't believe this when she got back home.

Dodge sensed her reluctance and knew he had to convince her it was okay. "Tory, you realize

116

that Yazzie and Ramona searched for Sharkey together. And when they discovered him at the bottom of the ravine, they brought his body into town. Yazzie was a great help to her."

"Yes, I know about that."

"It'll be okay—believe me."

"I . . . I do." Her eyes met his, and she silently pledged her trust in his instincts. What else could she do?

Yazzie was an enigma from another era. His Indian heritage was blatantly evident in his appearance. His long black hair was tied at the temples by a red bandana, his skin was brown and leathery, his eyes were sharp and black above high cheekbones, and his gait was flawed by a slight limp. His tan twill pants were attached to black suspenders, and heavy work boots, not cowboy boots, were laced up to his calves. Tory stared in amazement at the ageless man who seemed to have stepped off the silver screen at the height of the cowboy-and-Indian movie craze.

"Yazzie, this is Sharkey's daughter, Tory Talbot."

The mountain man gave her a nodding glance, and Tory shuffled from foot to foot, trying to decide whether to extend her hand. She smiled tightly and folded her arms instead. There was something standoffish about him that thwarted any warmth.

Dodge explained their situation and how they needed his help going up the mountain. Could they leave as soon as tomorrow?

Tory held her breath. She could just see them

hanging around this godforsaken place for days waiting on this old man to agree with their plan.

He studied Dodge's proposal for a moment, then spit out his abrupt reply. "Yep."

Tory's head shot up. This was his answer? A simple, short "Yep"? No comments, no questions, no instructions regarding his part in the excursion? Dodge and Tory exchanged surprised glances as the mountain man wheeled around and headed for the corral.

Dodge followed him, recounting the list of supplies they'd brought. Tory let the two men go alone. No one had included her in these negotiations, anyway. She was just a pilgrim on one of the strangest journeys she'd ever undertaken. An adventure . . . to seek the sun. She walked around to the front of the log cabin and perched on a tree trunk in the yard. Her view took in a magnificent stretch of the desert floor several thousand feet below.

Even though she'd spent her life denying him as her father, Sharkey Carsen was now influencing—actually dictating—her actions. His life affected hers far more than she cared to admit, more than she wanted. Was it selfishness driving her to continue on this strange trek, her greed for gold? Or, as she'd told herself a hundred times in the past few weeks, simply what he owed her?

If there were gold, *if* they found it, *if* it were enough to split five ways, she could salvage Tall and Terrific. That was behind it all. She really needed the money to salvage the floundering business she and her mother had started.

After her mother's death, hospital bills compounded her already debt-ridden life. Then her personal grief directly affected her business, and the debts kept piling higher. Tory could only hope that Megan would hold on and keep the shop open until she returned. And she could only pray to return with a bounty of gold that would save everything. It was a dream, perhaps too great.

Damn! Why couldn't Sharkey have died and left her a normal inheritance? A piece of property to sell or a chunk of money lying dormant in a savings account somewhere?

There was only one flaw in her plan to leave as soon as she got her inheritance. Dodge Callahan. It wasn't love, she told herself. In a weak moment, she had succumbed to her natural instincts with the man, merely given in to her own erotic desires.

He was a man like none she'd ever met, a man who obviously could lead her to hell and back and she'd follow willingly. There's what she was doing up here. Trusting a man she barely knew and following an untrustworthy father.

Dodge was different from any man she'd ever known. A rakishly handsome, extremely virile man in whose arms she felt safe and secure. And he had loved her like none other ever had, including the man she'd married.

Love? There was that word again. Was it a word she could use for any part of their relationship? They barely knew each other, yet their loving—their sexual encounters—had been intense and wild and . . . yes, wonderful.

Tory was drawn back to Yazzie's cabin in the

woods by the sound of a Jeep horn and a man's shout. She looked around to see Rex and Ramona climbing from an ancient, well-worn vehicle, Ramona's inheritance from Sharkey.

Determined to make the most of the situation, Tory waved and started walking toward them. Well, the sun seekers had assembled. Tomorrow would find them heading for that elusive gold stuff. And maybe—just maybe—finding it!

That night, Yazzie prepared a fabulous venison stew for supper, accompanied by robust sour-dough biscuits and stout black coffee. Tory insisted on fixing a simple salad of lettuce, tomatoes, and celery. It would be their last fresh vegetables for a while. Soon they would be relegated to eating canned items cooked in a cast-iron pot over an open fire, like the miners of a bygone era.

After eating, they sipped more coffee and ate a chocolate cake Dodge had purchased from a bakery in Sierra Vista.

"Good idea, Dodge," Rex said between bites. "This is a great cake."

"And not a calorie in the whole thing," Tory muttered with an accusing stare at Dodge. Then she took another big bite of the chocolate cake with its double-fudge icing.

Dodge grinned and drawled, "I figured that even though Yazzie is a pretty good camp cook, we wouldn't be getting any special treats like chocolate cake on this trip."

"You figured right," Yazzie commented shortly. The man obviously had no sense of humor. "On the trail, I'll stick to beans, bacon, and biscuits. Gets mighty tiresome, but it'll keep us going."

"How long do you think it'll take us to get to this place, Yazzie?" Rex asked.

"What place is that?"

"Our destination, the lost city of gold."

"There's no gold," Yazzie muttered. "Old Sharkey knew it. I think he's playing a trick on all of you."

"That's not so, Yazzie!" Ramona exclaimed. "You and I both saw—"

"Don't talk about no dead man, Ramona," Yazzie admonished her. "It'll bring us bad luck."

She stood up and shook her finger at the mountain man. "You know as well as I do there's gold up there. And Sharkey must have found it."

"Where?" Yazzie countered. "Courtland? Galeyville? Paradise? They're empty ghost towns. Nothing there but weeds and broken walls. No gold anymore. It's all gone."

"Pyramid's the name of the ghost town Sharkey mentioned in the will," Rex said. "Where's Pyramid? How far from here?"

Yazzie laughed, a rude, cackling sound. "Pyramid? There's nothing at all left of that one. Nobody ever found it again. Maybe it never was there."

"Yazzie," Dodge said, "you sound like you don't want to make this trip. What's wrong with checking out this lost city? You aren't afraid, are you?"

"Afraid? Hell, no! I'll go anywhere as long as you pay me for the use of my mules. It's just a

waste of time because there's no gold out there."
Yazzie stood up and shuffled outside.

The other four gazed bleakly at each other for a moment.

"He's lying," Ramona said finally. "I believe Sharkey, even if the rest of you don't."

Dodge agreed. "We just have to have faith in our old friend."

Ramona nodded, then looked at Tory. "I'm going to put my sleeping bag on the front porch. You want to sleep out there, too?"

Tory nodded and followed Ramona.

Dodge clapped Rex on the shoulder. "And we'll fix our sleeping bags out under the trees, right, Rex?"

"Unless you know of a nearby motel," Rex grumbled.

"Nope," Dodge said, and winked at Tory.

In spite of her sophistication, she blushed at his overture. What was wrong with her, anyway? After all, they had been intimate. She gave him a shy smile, suddenly feeling like a teenager at camp with a crush on the guy in the next tent. Only here, there were no tents.

Rex and Ramona headed for the Jeep to get their sleeping bags while Dodge and Tory went to the Blazer for theirs. Dodge detained Tory with a firmly placed hand on her arm. Taking her hand, he lifted it to his lips for a sensuous series of tiny kisses across her knuckles. "Would you like to take a walk in the moonlight?"

"Gee, Marshal," she drawled in a responding,

affected tone, "I'd love to. You're such a gentleman to suggest it."

"I'll meet you at the tree stump after we've made our beds. And no guarantees about the gentleman part."

"Why, Marshal . . ." She fluttered her eyelids and fanned herself with her hand. "You aren't suggesting—"

He pulled her closer and whispered, "Trouble is, I've already done more than sniff your brandy, Tory. And I feel the need for a little of your fire. I've just got to figure out the logistics of our little problem."

"I think you might as well forget our liaison, Marshal."

"No way, fancy pants. Meet me and we'll discuss the matter in greater depth."

"Dodge, don't you think—"

He pressed his finger to her lips. "I can only think of you sleeping in that tight sleeping bag, all by yourself. And that I'd like to be in there with you, with those long legs of yours wrapped around mine."

"Well, obviously we can't," she murmured breathlessly. The picture he described was enough to set her own imagination into erotic overdrive.

He refused to take her word for it. "By the tree stump. Five minutes. We'll discuss it."

Tory was absolutely shaky with anticipation as she threw her sleeping bag down on the porch beside Ramona's, unfastened the binders, and flopped it open. She fluffed the small pillow and

123

announced in a low voice, "I think I'll take a little walk, Ramona."

"The outhouse is around back. Want me to go out there with you?" Ramona asked politely.

"No, I, uh, Dodge and I are—"

"Oh, of course," Ramona interrupted. "How stupid of me."

Tory turned to go, and Ramona laid a hand on her arm. "Tory? Be careful. Don't go far."

"I told you I'd be with Dodge," Tory snapped. "Don't you think we'll be safe?"

Ramona dropped her hand. "With Dodge, sure. But—"

"But *what?*"

"Oh, nothing. I guess I'm just jumpy after what happened to Sharkey."

"Well, I'm not worried when I'm with Dodge," Tory said to convince herself as much as Ramona. She slipped down the porch steps and met Dodge with an urgency she couldn't hide, even in the darkness.

He pulled her into his arms and greeted her with a silent, hard-pressed kiss, melding their bodies into one shadowed form.

When he finally lifted his head, she murmured, "I think you're right, Dodge. It's going to be a long night without you."

"We could make other sleeping arrangements."

She considered his proposal, then thought of the embarrassing consequences. "No, I don't think we should. Not now, anyway." She grasped his large hand in both of hers and started walking. "How

124

about a walk beneath that beautiful Arizona moon you promised me?"

He scrutinized the somewhat cloudy sky. "Moon's hiding. It'll be out a little later," he promised, directing her to the canopy of a small group of pines. "We'll just have to wait for it to appear. It's waiting for you that's driving me crazy." He stopped on a carpet of pine needles and turned her into his arms. Framing her face with his large hands, he repeatedly murmured her name, kissing her cheeks and eyes and chin.

When his mouth finally merged with hers, she moaned with longing and opened her lips to match his. He kissed her almost savagely, his mouth moving on hers until she slumped against his chest, weak with renewed desire that flooded her body.

His arms held her pressed tightly against him as his tongue caressed the inside of her lips, then probed further. With slow, rhythmic strokes, he dared to sip the honey from the dark depths behind her teeth.

Tory clung to the strength, the sweet-plunging tongue of this man who excited her so wildly and loved her so thoroughly. She felt his aroused maleness and knew she wanted him, too. Now!

"Here, Tory," he murmured, lowering them to their knees on the pine needle cushion. His hands molded around the heaving globes of her breasts, still confined inside her blouse and bra. With a wildness unlike anything she'd ever felt, Tory wanted to rip them away and feel his hands on her bare flesh. God, how she burned for him.

But he left those aching mounds and reached for

the snap on her jeans. Just as his hand slid inside the denim confines, setting her skin ablaze with his touch, she heard a noise. He heard it, too, for he froze.

She quelled a small gasp, and instinctively he covered her mouth with his free hand and dragged her roughly with him behind the nearest tree.

Tory struggled to get free, but he held her firmly against his chest. Her labored breathing blended with his; their hearts pounded together. She strained against him, her eyes wide and puzzled.

"Quiet!" he hissed in her ear.

She nodded frantically, and he slowly released his furious grip. Her lips ached from his overpowering strength, and she wanted to scream at him. But she dared not. Her gaze followed his and detected a figure moving in the pale moonlight.

They watched the dark figure hobble toward the corral, then slip inside and maneuver between the mules. The animals showed no signs of alarm, as they would of a stranger, and soon Dodge realized who the figure was. "It's only Yazzie," he murmured in a barely audible whisper.

Tory matched his sound. "What's he doing messing with the saddlebags?"

"Probably just checking things out."

They watched in silence as the figure moved purposefully to one particular mule, stuffed something into one saddlebag, and left.

"Dodge, he didn't check all the mules. Only one."

"I don't know, Tory. Maybe he was packing more of those god-awful cigars he smokes."

"Why would he hide them?" She shook her head. "Yazzie acts strange to me. Let's go look and see if that's what he put in the saddlebag."

"Why?"

"Don't you want to know what Yazzie was doing over there this time of night?"

"No. They're his mules, Tory, and he can do whatever he wants to with them. What's wrong with you?"

She sighed and leaned her back against a tree trunk, trying to regain her equilibrium after the scare. "Tonight at supper, Yazzie seemed to say everything he could to discourage us going on this search for gold."

"Apparently, he feels it's futile. That doesn't mean anything, though. Lots of people would probably agree with him."

"But, Dodge, you said Yazzie sometimes brings in gold dust for trade. So he must know of gold somewhere up here. Maybe he doesn't want it found."

"That's crazy." The clouds slid aside to reveal a full moon, and Tory could see Dodge's face clearly angry in the pale glow. "What are you getting at, Tory?"

"I don't know . . ."

"Look, Yazzie is just a loner. A solitary mountain man, that's all. Don't try to figure him out, because you never will."

Tory bent her knees up and propped her arms on them. "Dodge, you remember what we talked about on the way up here, about Sharkey being murdered?"

"I said it was possible, not probable. Look, Tory, why don't you just forget that conversation? It wasn't based on fact."

"I can't forget anything that serious, Dodge. As we were sitting around tonight, eating cake and discussing Sharkey's gold, it occurred to me that everyone here has a possible motive for wanting my father dead. And for wanting all his gold."

"That's absolutely ridiculous, Tory! You mean, everyone except you and me, don't you? Or aren't you so sure about me? Is that it?"

She moved forward on her knees and gripped his muscled arms. "No, of course not, Dodge! Not you!"

He tore away from her grasp. "Then don't accuse anyone here of murder, Tory. These people are my friends, even though you think they might be murder suspects. They were Sharkey's friends, too. I'll thank you not to look at us with suspicion."

"Oh, Dodge, I didn't mean to—"

"I know what you meant." He was on his feet and angry. She could tell by his tight, abrupt tone that she'd pushed too hard.

Tory lunged after him. "Please, Dodge, listen to me. What if—"

"I don't want to hear your doubts about my friends."

"But, Dodge, even you said it could happen."

Abruptly, he wheeled around and grabbed her arms with his overwhelming strength. "Listen to me, Tory. As far as we know, Sharkey wasn't murdered. Put that notion out of your head. I don't want to hear any more about it."

She looked at his furious countenance, glowering in the full moonlight. Slowly, she nodded. "Okay, Dodge, I'll forget it." *For now,* she promised silently.

He held her gaze a moment longer, then released her with a jerk. "I think we'd better go to bed now. Alone."

Sadly, she accompanied him back to the porch, longing for his kiss, for his love, yet knowing it would not be hers tonight. She had ignited his fury by revealing her distrust of his friends. And of him, she supposed.

Not you, Dodge, she prayed when he left her in angry silence. Please, not you!

When Tory stumbled to her sleeping bag, Ramona was asleep, or pretended to be. Tory scooted inside the warm folds and lay there a long time, thinking about Yazzie and wondering what he did in the corral tonight. And what connection, if any, he had to Sharkey Carsen's death.

She shifted and snuggled drowsily against the tiny pillow, wishing it were Dodge's substantial shoulder. Her lips still tingled from the strength of his kisses and the power of his hand clamped across them. But her body ached with unsatisfied longing for the cowboy whose loving had become addictive.

And she prayed her suspicions were wrong.

CHAPTER EIGHT

Early the next morning the string of mules headed out single file, taking the sun seekers deep into the Dragoon Mountains of southern Arizona. As they moved further from civilization Tory was engulfed with a feeling of isolation, of being away from any safe, familiar environment. There she was, alone in uncharted territory, perhaps to be a victim of the mountain, as was her father.

Whether or not he was murdered, she couldn't know. Not yet, anyway. However, Sharkey still was a victim of his search for gold. And there she was, searching for that same gold. She could only hope the sheer numbers of the group would keep them safe. But with her new suspicions, could she trust them? Only Dodge . . .

As the day wore on, Tory began to adapt to the slow-plodding surefootedness of the mule she was riding and settled into a comfortable rocking motion. The sights and smells of the wilderness seemed to permeate her, and she grew to enjoy the constant rustle of wind through the pines and take delight in the occasional rabbit they sent scampering.

Yazzie led the way, followed by Rex, Ramona, and Tory. Dodge brought up the rear, adeptly managing three pack mules loaded with picks, camping equipment, and food. His mule carried the Indian jar with Sharkey's ashes. At first the group rode along in relative silence. Perhaps it was because they didn't know—or trust—one another very well. Tory assumed that, like her, each member carried the secret hope that on the return trip they'd be loaded with gold.

Dodge was conspicuously tight-lipped and noncommunicative. He had very little to say to Tory, and she knew she had precipitated his actions. Obviously, he was still angry over her voiced suspicions, and with the alleged suspects in such close proximity, they had no chance to hash it out. Maybe she had been out of line in her doubts. Maybe she was totally wrong.

At any rate, she'd had no opportunity to apologize. But she intended to. She hadn't intended to alienate Dodge, for heaven's sake. Out there, he was her only ally.

Tory and Ramona rode together for most of the day. They talked sporadically about their individual careers and ambitions. Tory learned that Ramona was an avid amateur anthropologist, specializing in the Indian groups that lived in this area of southwestern Arizona. She spent all her spare time in the mountains searching for artifacts and remnants of ancient settlements and had documented many sites that were previously unknown to modern society. Tory found Ramona to be an intelligent, interesting person.

The sun seekers halted for a meager lunch of canned beans and sandwiches. Tory perched beside Ramona on a log. "It's just too good to be true," she muttered.

"What's that?"

"Oh, this crazy mission to find gold way up here."

Ramona smiled knowingly. "It's here, all right. Men have been digging for it—and finding it—for hundreds of years. Now it's just a matter of us discovering the right place."

"You sound like Dodge," Tory chided. "What makes you so sure?"

"I know what I've always heard about these mountains. And I trust Sharkey."

"Well, that's more than I can say," Tory muttered.

"It's too bad you never knew your father. He was a man you could trust, Tory."

"My mother couldn't trust him. Neither could I. But you," she paused, thinking of years of struggling, "you had a different kind of relationship with him, Ramona. Obviously, you made no demands on him, not like a wife and child did."

Ramona lifted her dark head and smiled sadly. She had a certain kind of graceful, proud beauty, with a slight tilt to her brown eyes. "Oh, I tried, but Sharkey was an elusive man. I wanted security as much as any woman does. I loved him and wanted marriage, but Sharkey didn't want that kind of commitment."

Tory looked at Ramona with new respect, and strangely, her heart went out to this "other woman." Ramona was another woman Sharkey had hurt, and Tory couldn't help wondering how many others there were. "How long did you go with my father?"

"You mean, how long were we lovers?" Ramona asked frankly. She gazed into the distance and muttered, "Almost ten years. You'd think in that length of time that a person would know if he loved someone enough to make a commitment."

"Apparently, Sharkey wasn't the type of man who could make a commitment," Tory said with finality as she finished her sandwich. It was more painful than she realized to hear another woman talk about intimacy with her father. Secretly, she had wanted him to be as unhappy and lonely as her mother had been.

She realized that was foolish, the child in her crying out for fairness and revenge. Then it occurred to her that maybe the adult in her wanted a share of fairness and revenge, also. Undoubtedly, she was getting a different picture of Sharkey Carsen and his relationships with women.

After the brief lunch break, the string of mules moved out again, taking the small group higher above the desert floor. As the afternoon heat swelled, dark clouds formed a canopy overhead and a thunderstorm threatened. Finally, Yazzie called a halt. "We'll spread a tarp between those trees until the storm is over."

"Oh, no, not here!" Ramona objected, an unusual shrillness to her voice.

"What's wrong, Ramona?" Tory leaned forward

in her saddle, concerned by the woman's sudden change. She looked visibly upset.

Yazzie answered for her. "Over there," he said, pointing through the trees to an abrupt cliff dangerously close to the path they followed. "That's where we found Sharkey." He slid off his mule and ambled to the edge, motioning to the others. Rex and Dodge quickly joined him, and the three men began discussing the location of Sharkey's demise.

Tory could see that Ramona was distraught and remained with her on the trail. Suddenly, the wind whipped vigorously around them, creating a high whining through the pines. A mournful whine, mourning a place of death.

Ramona reacted hysterically. "I can't go through this again. I have to get out of here!" She dropped the reins of the mule she was riding, slid off its back, and ran distractedly through the woods.

"Hey, Ramona!" Dodge yelled and started after her. "Come back! It's going to rain soon!"

Tory grabbed his arm. "Let me try, Dodge. I think I can talk to her."

"She needs a friend right now," he rebuffed.

Tory considered his curt comment for a moment. "Maybe I can qualify. I think she needs another woman right now."

"You may be right, but hurry. We're going to have a severe storm, and it isn't safe for either of you."

Tory nodded and dashed after Ramona through the pines. Not far away, she found the distraught woman slumped to the ground beneath the shelter of a pine tree.

"Ramona, it's just me," Tory began tentatively. "Are you all right?"

Ramona gazed up, a vacant expression on her still-pale face. "I'm okay, Tory. Just a little shaky, that's all."

The wind whipped around them and whined through the trees. The smell of pending rain was in the air. Tory moved closer. "I know you're upset because of Sharkey. The others are worried about you."

Ramona clamped her arms tightly around her knees and rocked back and forth. "A strange sensation came over me, Tory. I could see him lying down there, just like it were real all over again. Total recall of the sights and feelings. God, it was strange. I wanted to scream and run, anything to get rid of those awful feelings."

"You've been through a lot, Ramona. It was quite a shock. Your feelings for Sharkey run deep —I can see that."

Ramona smiled wanly at Tory. "I was always taught to hide my feelings, not to let them show. To be stoic and strong. And I always have, until now."

"It's okay to let down, Ramona."

"I know. Intellectually, I realize it's good for me. But my heritage teaches me to be strong, especially at times like this."

"You *are* being strong, Ramona. Just returning here shows your strength."

Ramona picked up a small stick and fiddled nervously with it. "I don't feel very strong. I'm feeling pretty guilty right now."

"Guilty? I don't understand."

"Guilty because I pushed him toward this."

"Pushed? You mean encouraged?"

"Yes, I guess." Ramona nodded and gentle tears formed in her dark eyes. "When I was a professor at a junior college in Sierra Vista I met Sharkey. He was a professor at the University of Arizona. But he hated teaching because he felt it was too confining. Besides, he had a dream. He'd always wanted to find gold. I encouraged him to quit his regular job and pursue his dream. But that was selfish. I thought if he could find this damn gold he'd been after all his life, he'd be willing to settle down. With me."

Tory slid her arm around Ramona's shoulders and murmured in a gentle tone, "You can't blame yourself for what happened to Sharkey."

"I'm trying not to, but it's hard when I think of what happened to him—"

"Ramona," Tory said firmly, "surely you realize that Sharkey Carsen had been pursuing that damned gold for years, long before he met you. When he died, he was doing exactly what he wanted to do, and it wasn't your fault at all." Tory couldn't believe what she was saying. She was actually absolving Ramona of guilt for Sharkey's death!

But how could this distraught, heartbroken woman have had anything to do with his death? She loved him.

A wicked flash of lightning zigzagged to the

ground, and thunder exploded from the dark clouds. They had to get back soon or be exposed to the viciousness and danger of the storm.

Tory squeezed Ramona's shoulder. "We'd better go if we don't want to get drenched."

Ramona nodded distractedly, obviously unaware of the pending storm. She stood up. "Tory, thanks. I know this must be difficult for you, too."

"I can see how much you loved my father."

"I can't deny my love for him. But I must admit, I really feel strange telling you these things, Tory. I almost want to apologize, knowing what he did to you and your mother."

"Don't apologize. How can love be bad for anyone? I'm glad"—Tory paused wistfully, then continued firmly—"yes, I'm glad he had such a love as you in his life."

"I hope we can be friends. I think Sharkey has a very special daughter," Ramona said softly with tears still in her voice.

Thunder crackled loudly overhead again, and the two women ran back to the makeshift tent the men had constructed just as huge raindrops started to fall.

Tory concluded that Sharkey had been darned lucky to have had a woman like Ramona.

"You two okay?" Dodge asked, pulling them beneath the meager shelter. "Ramona?"

She lifted her proud head and responded with new-found courage, "I'm all right, Dodge. Tory and I are ready to go on, as soon as you men are."

He looked at Tory curiously. She just smiled proudly and nodded.

After the storm, the mules carried the sun seekers farther along the trail. It was almost dusk when Yazzie stopped to consult with Ramona. "Is the hidden springs somewhere near here?"

Ramona checked the small notebook she carried and pointed. "That way."

"You lead," Yazzie directed. "I don't know of these pictures on rocks where the water runs underground."

Following behind Ramona, the group climbed higher, rounded a bend, and came to a halt near a huge field of weathered boulders. Some were short and looked like stocky stone sentinels; other were large enough to hide men and horses. The place conjured images of renegade Apaches, hiding from the U.S. Army, making their lives in the wilderness.

"There's the overhang where the pictographs are," Ramona announced excitedly.

"I don't see any pictures," Rex commented sourly, dismounting with a loud groan. *"Dios mío,* I hope we're through for the day."

"This should be a good place to stop. It's where we're supposed to find the skull and the other half of the map," Dodge said. "But where's the spring?"

Ramona moved confidently toward the giant boulders. "The pictographs are hidden. You have to lie on your back and scoot under here in order to see them. And while you're there, you can hear the spring rushing." She proceeded to show them how to maneuver under the stone shelf and listen for the hidden water.

Tory watched curiously as Dodge, Yazzie, and finally Rex followed Ramona's lead and scooted under the rock. When Tory's turn came, she went eagerly, intrigued by the ancient drawings that still remained visible and the sounds of rushing waters beneath her body.

She emerged with blue eyes bright and a rush of questions. "Why, the pictures are in color!" she exclaimed, amazed. "How has the paint managed to remain so long? And why are they located here? Did the Indians lie on their backs to draw them? And why is the spring underground?"

Ramona laughed at Tory's eagerness. "I wish all my students had your enthusiasm, Tory. The ancient ones learned to use earth colors, made from clay or dirt or certain plants. And they're permanent, if not damaged or washed away by weather. These were protected by the ledge, so they remained for us to enjoy."

"They're absolutely remarkable! I can recognize bighorn sheep, deer, and lizards."

"This stream once flowed above ground," Ramona went on to explain. "The rock overhang formed a kind of cave. So the ancient artists probably stood upright and drew on the walls. In the years since, the stream went underground and the earth shifted and filled in the vacant area. Now it's almost to the top of the cave walls, so we have to lie down to see inside."

"It's remarkable. How did you find it?"

Ramona smiled and shrugged. "Sharkey and I were digging for gold in this area."

"Speaking of Sharkey," Rex said briskly, glancing around. "Isn't this the area where he hid the map? Under some skull?"

"Yep," Dodge said, pushing his Stetson back and squinting his eyes around the area. "Why don't we spread out and see if we can find it before dark?"

"While you do that," Yazzie said, "I'll make camp. I saw a small stream back at that stand of trees."

"Agreed," Dodge nodded. "I think we've all ridden our limit for today."

"*Dios mío!* I'll second that motion!" Rex agreed, rubbing his backside.

They spread out, searching over rocks and around trees for the acclaimed skull but found nothing. When Yazzie called that supper was ready, they came together wearily. At this point, everyone showed some disappointment, even doubt.

In desperation, they studied their half of the map again to make sure they were in the right area. Four heads, not including Yazzie, hovered over the map, checking the locations and directions.

"I know this is the right place," Ramona said with conviction. "I'm almost positive. Sharkey and I were here on several occasions. We discussed the springs and whether we should try to dig it out."

"According to Sharkey's map, we're in the correct location. Tomorrow we'll have all day of complete light to search. I'm sure we'll find it," Dodge said confidently.

Yazzie eyed them cautiously but didn't join in

the search. He just lighted another of those god-awful cigars and walked away from the camp settlement.

Tory watched him, filled with curiosity and her own personal suspicions. She was tempted to follow him when Rex and Dodge ambled in another direction, each intent in conversation. So whom should she follow? Yazzie, the loner who was strange and secretive? Or Dodge and Rex, Sharkey's former partners who might benefit from his death?

While Tory was considering her options, Ramona approached her. "Let's put our sleeping bags next to the fire for sleeping tonight. It'll be warmer and keep the wild beasties away."

"Don't even tease about that." Tory shivered involuntarily and peered into the darkness surrounding them. "My imagination is already going wild!"

"Don't worry, Tory. The fire will be our best protection."

As she made her bed Tory couldn't help wondering if her suspicions about Sharkey's mysterious death were well founded. And, of course, she couldn't stop worrying that the one responsible for Sharkey's death was in this intimate little gathering of sun seekers. Nothing had actually happened to confirm her suspicions. Perhaps she had jumped to conclusions. It was just a feeling . . .

"Ramona," Tory said, smoothing out her sleeping bag, "is it—is it possible that my father was killed? That his death wasn't an accident?"

Ramona paused and gave Tory a deep, serious

141

look. "Not only is it possible, but I suspect that it's true."

Tory gasped and pressed her hand to her mouth. To have her worst fears confirmed by Ramona was shocking. She expected—wanted—Ramona to dispel her suspicions.

"I've never told anyone that, Tory. I'm sorry if I upset you. But no one ever asked me outright, either. Maybe no one ever suspected it. Or they wanted to deny it. But, sure, I think it's possible."

"Do you think we could be in danger, too?" Tory held her breath, almost afraid to hear the answer.

Ramona sat cross-legged on her spread-out sleeping bag. "It's possible. If Sharkey were killed, his killer is still loose. And the gold is still out there."

"Then you think the gold is the reason?"

Ramona lowered her voice. "I do believe Sharkey discovered a long-lost treasure in these mountains. It's something men have coveted for years, something they've lost their lives over. Some searched but went away disillusioned. Others ran out of money or energy and had to stop looking. But they all believed it's still here. There's a grand mystique to these mountains, from the miners' tales to the Indians' lore."

The two women sat cross-legged on the bedrolls, facing each other, whispering intently.

"And you believe Sharkey found the gold?"

Ramona nodded solemnly. "Yes, I do. He acted a little funny, became very quiet about his mountain treks in the last few weeks before he died.

Maybe he knew about it then but didn't want to say."

"Why wouldn't he tell you his exciting news?"

"Perhaps because he wanted to protect me. If I knew, then I, too, would be in danger."

"So he didn't tell you anything?"

"No, and I didn't see him as much as usual. I think now that he was preparing the maps and getting ready . . . in case anything happened to him."

"Then you think he knew he was in danger?"

Ramona shrugged. "Anyone who has a secret like that knows there's always danger from someone who wants what you have. Or what you know."

"Do you think we're in danger, then? Because of the map?"

"Maybe."

"From whom?"

"I don't know."

"Someone . . . here?"

Ramona laughed quietly. "Maybe someone lurking behind yonder tree."

"I meant, someone in our group?"

"In this group? Heck, no! These people were Sharkey's friends. And you, of course. But you're his daughter, Tory." Ramona fluffed up her pillow and lay back on it.

"Yes, of course," Tory mumbled thoughtfully. "Ramona, why would Sharkey send us on this wild-goose chase if he thought it were dangerous for us?"

"First, it isn't a wild-goose chase. He wouldn't

143

do that to us. Second, he trusted this group of people implicitly. Third, I'm sure he felt that Dodge could take care of anything that came up. And so do I. Go to bed, Tory. As long as Dodge is around, he'll keep the claim jumpers away." Ramona snuggled down between the folds of her sleeping bag and turned on her side, indicating she had finished talking for the night.

"Good night, Ramona." Tory wandered around the camp, putting a couple of fresh logs on the fire, studying the flames and what Ramona had said. About danger. About Sharkey. About his friends that were gathered there. She heard Dodge and Rex talking and ambled toward where they sat on the far edge of the clearing, near the rock overhang and hidden stream.

When she reached them, Rex made an excuse and quickly left them alone. "Is it so obvious," she mused, "that we want to be alone?"

"These people aren't blind."

"But I am. Dodge, I'm sorry about accusing your friends. I'm sorry that I made them look like suspects. I realize now that you are all Sharkey's friends and would never do anything to hurt him."

"Tory," Dodge said quietly, "come here."

She moved beside him in the darkness. "I didn't mean to make you mad. I should never have said anything like—"

"Tory . . . hush." One of his long arms wrapped around her shoulder and he led her farther away from the campsite. "You don't have to apologize. I can understand your concern."

"But, Dodge, I was out of line."

144

"No, not really. Actually, you were quite perceptive to have doubts about his death. Maybe you're right, after all."

"What?"

"This is just between us, you understand."

She nodded anxiously in the darkness.

"After seeing the location of Sharkey's so-called accident, I'm beginning to have suspicions of my own."

"Why, Dodge?"

"Well, according to Yazzie, Sharkey's body was found in a spot that I think was too far away for anyone to have fallen naturally. Sharkey's body should have been more directly beneath where we stood. When I pointed that out to Yazzie, he changed his story. Said that's where Sharkey was found, directly below us."

"What are you saying?" She breathed shallowly, fear creeping up into her throat.

Dodge stopped walking. "I think Sharkey was pushed to the location where he was found. Perhaps he was even killed somewhere else and brought to the rock ledge."

"Oh, my God, Dodge!"

"I want to talk to Ramona about it. She's the only other eyewitness to the location of the body."

"I think you should wait a little while, Dodge. She was quite upset when we went by that cliff today."

"I realize that, but we're talking about something extremely serious here, Tory."

"Oh, my God, and here we are, out here away from police protection and—"

Dodge's arms encased her in the darkness. "We'll be all right."

"But I'm scared, Dodge."

"Don't be." He lifted her chin and whispered, "I'll take care of you, Tory." Then, tenderly, his lips closed over hers.

With him close and holding her in his arms, Tory immediately felt safer. The kiss deepened and the secure swirl of Dodge surrounded her. His strength and warmth reached out to her, and she wrapped her arms around his waist and held him tightly to her. Here was a man to trust, a man who tempted her like none other.

At that moment, the quiet stillness was penetrated by the chilling sound of a scream, a resounding wail that echoed off the boulders and intruded into their safe harbor.

"What th—"

"Was that Ramona?" Tory had never heard such a bloodcurdling yell. She bolted from Dodge's embrace and rushed back toward camp. Nothing, it seemed, was safe and secure. Not even Dodge's arms.

CHAPTER NINE

"Tory, *wait!* It's just—" Dodge lunged for her, but she slipped through his fingers. One minute he was holding her, the next she was gone like a startled doe. Resigned, he raced after her.

"Ramona?" she called as she reached the small gathering huddled around the campfire. She stared at the fire-lit circle, half expecting the three to be embroiled in some fracas. "Ramona, are you all right?"

"Of course." She looked up, her smiling face reflecting softly golden from the flickering flames.

"What was that horrible noise?" Tory gasped between heaving breaths.

"It was just a mountain lion," Ramona said easily.

"A *mountain lion?*"

"Don't worry, Tory," Ramona said from her seat on top of her sleeping bag. "The fire and commotion will keep it away from our camp. Anyway, I'm sure Dodge and Yazzie have guns."

"No—" Tory caught herself before blurting that Dodge's gun had been stolen. Then, in a niggling corner of her mind, it occurred to her that he might have bought another. She'd have to ask him about it later.

"Have a seat, you two," Rex offered with a sweep of his hand. "That is, if you don't mind our humble company. And Yazzie can finish his tale."

Tory glanced at the campfire scene and realized that, indeed, Rex and Ramona were being entertained. Soft-spoken, closemouthed Yazzie was the storyteller. Sighing with relief, she slumped down on a log and Dodge joined her.

Yazzie continued, picking up where he had stopped when interrupted. "So next time that cat screamed, I grabbed my gun and shot into the air. I didn't even aim, only meant to scare her away. But I was a damned lucky cuss. She fell right down into our campsite, shot through the heart. So we skinned her right there on the spot—didn't even have to leave camp. And her hide still warms my bed at night."

Tory shivered at the grisly tale, prompting Dodge to put another log on the fire. He brought them an Indian blanket and draped it around their shoulders. She drew closer to the warmth Dodge provided.

"That's some story, Yazzie," Rex commented, unconsciously peering above them for spreading branches that could harbor some wild creature.

"Would a mountain lion really raid a camp, Yazzie?" Tory asked, fearful of his answer. Yet she had to know about this potential danger.

"Sure. If it's hungry enough, it'll come looking for food, even them dang mules." Yazzie paused to

148

light another cigar and puffed thoughtfully. "But it'd have to be dang-near starving."

"We don't have to worry about that cat coming around us tonight," Dodge advised in a teasing tone. "As long as Yazzie keeps smoking that foul-smelling tobacco, nothing will come near enough to bother us!"

Everyone chuckled and Yazzie took the teasing in his stride. "Reminds me of the pipe-smoking miner from out Denver-way. There were four of them who came down here to the Dragoons a few years back, searching for gold. The leader was a big man, had one of them curving pipes clamped in his teeth all the time, whether he was smoking it or not. Fact is, I believe they were looking for this very town of Pyramid that you folks are after. These fellows heard that there used to be a gold-rush town that was left high and dry, and they wanted to find it again. And get that gold."

Yazzie paused and Rex spoke up. "Then there really is a town by the name of Pyramid?"

"*Was* a town, maybe a hundred years ago." Yazzie folded his legs Indian-style. "Trouble is, those folks from Denver never stopped to find out why Pyramid wasn't a town anymore."

"Well, why?" Tory asked, leaning forward.

"Indians," Yazzie said briefly. "Indians killed the whole town. Twice, they did. Raided the settlement and killed the whole bunch, two different times. After that, everybody with any sense left it alone until those dang fools from Denver came around looking for the gold again."

"What happened to them, Yazzie?" Rex asked warily, a bit of trepidation in his voice.

"They disappeared, just like everybody else who went up there. Nobody ever saw hide nor hair of the four of them again. Years later some hunters found that dang curving pipe, though. Don't know if they fell through an open mine or if a female mountain lion got 'um. Some say there're still bears up there. Or if it was the Indians . . ."

"Nobody could just disappear, with no signs or anything," Rex protested. "I don't believe any Indians are still around here. And if they were, they wouldn't risk something like that."

Yazzie puffed his cigar quietly, letting his story create its own internal havoc. "That's what happened, all right. No sign of them. Until now, nobody has bothered trying to find old Pyramid again."

"Well, we're going to find it, soon as we get that other piece of map," Dodge said firmly, and slapped his thigh. "Since we have a big day tomorrow searching for whatever Sharkey left for us, why don't we turn in?"

"Good idea," Rex agreed. "I'm beat."

Everyone began to move about the camp, making preparations for the night. The men laid out their sleeping bags on one side of the campfire, the two women on the other.

Tory's head was close to Ramona's when they scooted down under cover. The mountain air at night was quite cool, and snuggling into the warm bag felt good. "Ramona?" Tory whispered. "You awake?"

150

The answer was equally quiet. "Yes."

"Do you think this is a wise thing to do, all of us going to sleep with mountain lions and God-knows-what out there? Shouldn't somebody stand guard or something?"

"I'm sure Yazzie would be alert to any dangers approaching during the night. Don't worry about the wild animals, Tory. Or anything else Yazzie says. He's just trying to scare us off."

"Well, he's doing a pretty good job with me. Do you believe Yazzie?"

"Aw, those stories he told tonight are based on ages-old legends, part fact, part vivid imagination."

"Then you've heard of Pyramid? You think it's really there?"

"Yes. I've heard of it. Never knew anyone who'd been there, though."

Tory paused, thinking. "Do you think Sharkey really found Pyramid?"

"Yes."

Tory tried to sleep, but she heard strange noises that kept her eyes peeled through most of the night. At dawn she finally slipped into an exhausted stupor but was awakened within an hour by an animated shout.

"A skull! I found a skull!"

Tory bolted upright in time to see everyone scrambling after the sound. She buried her face in her hands, trying to block out the world. Dear Heavens *What a night!* She could hear everyone's excited exchanges over the discovery. Finally, curiosity forced her to drag her weary body over to the sandy wash where the group stood in a circle. Around the ominous-looking bones. Even Tory could tell it wasn't a cow's elongated skull.

Rex knelt before his find.

"This isn't it!" Tory gasped.

"It's human," Ramona said.

"H—human?" Rex stood up and took a backward step.

"And very old," Ramona continued as she knelt to examine it. "See the discoloration and age lines? Anthropologists will be delighted with this, Rex."

"Anthropologists be damned!" Rex exclaimed, angrily kicking the sandy soil. "I can't believe this isn't the one we're looking for."

"Careful! You might damage it!" Ramona put a calming hand on Rex's arm. "Please, Rex. The anthropology department at school will study this skull later. It's probably an ancient burial place of some remote tribe, and the entire skeleton is somewhere nearby."

"Oh, great," he muttered, glancing around warily.

"Let's leave it as undisturbed as possible so I can bring some experts back up here," Ramona said. "This skull may reveal something about the people who lived in the area. It's an important find."

"Only to you, Ramona," he said furiously. "Where's that damned cow's skull that Sharkey was talking about?"

"You didn't expect to find it right next to the spring, did you?" Ramona snapped.

"Bad sign," Yazzie said shortly.

"What do you mean: 'bad sign'?" Rex asked, his dark eyes sharp.

"If this is burial ground, we have disturbed holy ground. It is forbidden. The ancient ones will be unhappy." Yazzie gave Rex an ominous glare. "You must be very careful."

"Oh, hell!" Rex exclaimed. "This is great. I find the wrong skull, and suddenly I'm in jeopardy with Indian ghosts?"

"No, of course not," Dodge said. "Don't let Yazzie's superstitions scare you."

"Not superstitions. Yazzie knows the secrets of the mountain." The long-haired man pointed to his own chest proudly. "Don't ignore them or you, too, will cause disfavor with the ancients." He moved away, limping.

Tory's blue eyes grew round. Everything that happened or was said only fueled her mounting fears. "Good heavens! I can't believe it!"

"This is ridiculous!" Rex fumed. "How dare Yazzie threaten us like that." He turned around and stomped back to the camp. Ramona followed him, murmuring gentle words of encouragement.

"That's what he's doing, isn't he?" Tory asked quietly, walking away from the area containing the human skull. "Threatening us? Trying to scare us off?"

"Yep," Dodge agreed with a heavy sigh. He stuffed his hands into his back jeans pockets and ambled to the edge of a rocky cliff.

His broad, strong shoulders seemed to sag a little, and suddenly Tory wanted to wrap her arms around him and give him her meager strength. But she'd had her share of misgivings about this trip and felt that all she could do now was give Dodge her support. "We've come this far, Dodge. We can't turn back now because of some old man's crazy ideas."

Dodge squinted at the distant horizon. "Yazzie is a strange man. But don't forget he's from the mountain. I'm sure he feels that we're disturbing some kind of sacred territory."

"Well, that's ridiculous," Tory muttered, perching on a rock. "I don't believe that any more than you do. We have as much right here as anybody. You own the claim, don't you?"

"Of course."

"Then Yazzie has nothing to say about it."

"I don't know, Tory. I'm beginning to think it wasn't such a good idea to bring him along, after all."

"You had your reasons, Dodge. And I think they were valid."

"But I don't want to put our group in danger."

"Danger?" she said with a little laugh. "From whom? Ghosts of the past? You warned me back in Tombstone. I knew what I was getting into and everybody else did, too."

"Tory"—he moved closer and took her hand—"I especially don't want you to be in danger, or hurt in any way." He lifted her hand to his lips and kissed it softly. Then he turned it over and caressed the center of her palm with his lips.

She tried not to react to the sensuous touch of his lips on her skin, but she felt the reaction all the

154

way through. Chuckling, she chided, "Still scared of Sharkey's ghost?"

"No. It has more to do with my own conscience."

She slipped her other hand into his and gave him a confident smile. "I'm not scared off so easily, Dodge Callahan. Anyway, I have you to protect me."

"Protect?" He scoffed.

"Yes, of course." She stood and smiled confidently. "I'm not sorry I came. Even with mountain lions and ghost stories at night and a threatening Indian scout by day."

His brown eyes caressed her and softened as he pulled her into his arms. "Tory, Tory," he murmured and kissed her tousled dark hair, "I don't want you to get hurt. I've never felt so responsible or so concerned for anyone in my life."

"Dodge, I don't have any doubts about what we're doing. We've made it fine this far, and by golly, we'll go all the way." She smiled wistfully. "You know, Ramona and I believe that Sharkey found Pyramid."

"And you see what happened to him?"

"Well, he wasn't careful enough. He should have realized his life was in jeopardy because of what he knew. We're going to be alert and wary."

"For what? Who? The ghosts?" He sighed heavily and she felt his huge body shudder against hers. "Or one of us?"

From the campsite, Yazzie yelled, "Breakfast! Come and get it!"

Dodge lifted her chin and kissed her lips tenderly. "You certainly have changed your battle cry from just a few days ago."

She gave him a shy smile. "You really think so? Maybe I just discovered that I've been a sun seeker all along. You've been showing me how it could be done."

"Well, it isn't going to be a snap. It's risky business."

"Risky business is never easy. Come on. Let's eat. We have the map to find today. And more of a journey ahead of us. To the lost city of Pyramid."

After breakfast the group spread out to search for the hidden skull. Dodge insisted that everyone take along a heavy stick. "Watch for snakes first, the old cow's skull second," he instructed.

Dodge noted that Tory deliberately paired with Rex for the morning's search. The two soon moved out of sight, out of earshot, engrossed in conversation. What would they have to say to each other? Dodge was suddenly filled with the urge to rush after them and grab her . . .

Then he admonished himself. What the hell was wrong with him, anyway? Jealous? Hell, no! Rex was his partner, his friend. He was neither rival nor suspect.

Then *what?* Curious? Maybe. Yes, that was it. Curiosity. So what was Tory trying to find out? He could go crazy trying to figure her out.

Damn it, he hadn't been jealous of a woman in many a year. In fact, he hadn't even been curious. And he sure as hell wouldn't start now with this one. Most of his alliances with women over the past few years had been fleeting at best.

So he and Tory had spent some time together back in Tombstone. So they had been intimate. He supposed this would be another fleeting love affair. God, he hated that word, *affair*. But what else could he call their relationship? Tory would be leaving Tombstone soon. And so would he. They'd probably never see each other again.

Dodge moved swiftly through the scrub oak, his long legs covering giant-sized chunks of land. He winced as the sharp spines of a cat-claw grabbed his sleeve and scratched the flesh beneath. "Dammit!" he muttered under his breath, and stopped long enough to check the damage to his forearm.

He slumped against a rock, letting his mind wander back to Tory and immediately forgetting about the scratch.

How could he stand not seeing those deep blue eyes of hers? He'd never forget them. Never forget how she looked up at him while they were making love, the transformation of her somewhat haughty, mystical expression to one of wild desire.

Chuckling to himself, he recalled how she had marched into the Crystal Palace last week, highly charged with emotion and anger written clearly in those blue eyes. And how she had gentled like a fawn within a few days. Gentled enough to talk about her past, about Sharkey, about the undeniable attraction she felt for Dodge. Then she had allowed something more to develop between them. Something wonderful and intimate . . .

He squeezed both hands into impotent fists. How eagerly she had fallen into his arms. He wanted to hold her now, to kiss her, to reassure her that everything would be all right, that they would be leaving there soon. That they would be successful in finding the gold. But he knew he couldn't promise her anything. Not yet.

Oh, God, how he missed their lovemaking. He was actually beginning to hate this trip because he never had an opportunity to be alone with her. They had barely been alone to talk, with no time for anything more than the briefest kiss. But there she was, right now, off alone somewhere with Rex. What the hell did they have to talk about? Is that all they were doing—talking?

Tory saw this morning's search as the perfect opportunity to talk with Rex. They moved cautiously through thick underbrush, probing each bush with the heavy sticks Dodge had insisted they carry.

"Mind if I join you, Rex?"

His dark eyes darted up, and he welcomed her with an approving nod. "Sure, come on. Two tenderfeet in this wilderness should be better than one."

"We *are* alike in that respect, aren't we?"

"Probably more alike than you realize, Tory. We both have more cultural goals than to tromp around these mountains all our lives. And we just want to take our share of the action and get out."

"You're really only interested in the bottom line, aren't you, Rex? Sounds so materialistic."

"Oh, I don't mean to sound offensive, Tory. But you know I'm looking at this venture strictly from a business aspect."

"But not from a personal aspect?"

He shrugged. "I didn't really know Sharkey that well. But I suspect nobody here did, except maybe Dodge."

"Not even Ramona?" she asked, surprised.

"Sharkey was quite a loner. Didn't spend much time with anyone, even Ramona. Only when he got lonely, I suspect."

"Did he have many friends? Other than those on this trip?"

"Oh, sure, a few buddies in town he played a little poker with from time to time. I guess Dodge was the one who knew him the longest time and knew the most about him. Dodge somehow came up with your address. Maybe it was in Sharkey's trailer. All we knew was that Sharkey's daughter lived in California."

"How did you become involved with him, then, if you didn't know him very well?"

"I had invested in other gold mines in this area. Several went bust, but a couple proved profitable. When Sharkey and Dodge approached me about the Sun Seekers Mining Company, I figured it was a good investment. That's why I'm here today, searching for a damned skull. I don't want to lose my total investment in the company. If there's gold to be found, I want my share. Don't you, Tory? Isn't that why you're here?"

She smiled wryly. "I suppose so. I could use an inheritance right now. Couldn't we all?"

"Financial problems?"

"Oh, just the normal ups and downs of a business. Right now, I have a lot of debts. I guess I figured I deserved some kind of inheritance from Sharkey. But, honestly, when I left L.A., I had no idea I'd be tromping through mountains looking for a skull and map and—" She halted and sighed.

"What's wrong?"

"Oh, this is just not the way I expected to spend my time." She finished weakly, not wanting to tell Rex the alarming things that had happened in Tombstone, about the break-ins and Dodge's gun being taken. She certainly couldn't let Rex know she was trying to figure out if she could trust him.

"What's wrong? This country too rugged for a city girl?"

"Yes, something like that," she admitted ruefully. "Rex? Do you know if my father had any enemies?"

"Now, that's a leading question if I ever heard one." Rex stopped walking and found a seat on a nearby boulder. "Why? Do you think he was murdered?"

She looked at him quickly. Why did he say that? Could he read her mind? Did he know she looked at everyone with suspicion—even him? Maybe she should just be honest, well, partially honest, with him. "I—yes, I think it's possible."

"Hell, that's what I've been saying all along! I tried to tell the sheriff and to get the county coroner to investigate, but everyone said I was jumping to conclusions. They said he'd spent too much time alone in the mountains, and because of his age, it was reasonable to assume he'd had a heart attack."

"Why did you think he might have been murdered?"

"Well, it stands to reason. I always thought Sharkey was a tough old goat. Nobody ever heard of him having heart trouble. And he knew these damn mountains like an Indian. He wouldn't have slipped—it's just too farfetched for me to believe. Besides, he'd discovered gold! Hell, everybody's got a touch of gold fever, whether they'll admit it or not."

She searched his dark face, looking for truth. "Who do you think might have done it?"

"Could be anybody," he said with a shrug.

"Anybody?"

"Everybody. Everybody here." He leaned against a boulder and mopped his brow. "Except you and me, of course. You were an unknown until this week, Tory, so I figure that eliminates you. And I—hell, I couldn't kill anybody, no matter how much gold they had."

"Of course," she murmured, and joined him leaning against the huge rock slab. "Well, tell me, Rex, what are the motives for everyone here?"

"First is Ramona. She wanted Sharkey to marry her, give her some security. But he refused. Instead, he took out a small life insurance policy and made her the beneficiary. Maybe she saw that as her only security from Sharkey."

"I didn't know he had a life insurance policy," Tory said slowly. "But I simply can't believe Ramona would do anything to harm Sharkey. She loved him."

Rex shook his head. "Love does strange things

161

to people, especially unfulfilled love. They say there's a thin line between love and hate."

"What about . . ." She paused, then quickly said, "What about Dodge? Surely you don't think he'd do anything to his own partner." She didn't care what Rex said; she wouldn't believe Dodge could be guilty.

"Dodge Callahan is a man who could be capable of most anything, given the right circumstances. He and Sharkey were friends as well as business partners. All I know is, the Sun Seekers Mining Company was insured, too. Dodge and I will share a small amount, owing to the death of our working partner. Maybe he wanted to take his money and cut out."

"Rex, I can't believe that!"

"Well, you never know. I'm just saying both Dodge and Ramona will benefit from Sharkey's death. Whereas you and I . . ." He shrugged. "You had nothing to gain but the gold. And because of my previous investment, neither do I."

"Oh, I don't know, Rex. Your reasoning is weak. You're forgetting these people cared too much about Sharkey to harm him."

"What about Yazzie? He cares about nobody."

"But what's his motive?"

"He knows about the gold and wants to keep it all to himself."

"But why? He isn't materialistic at all."

"Who knows? Maybe he's never had a chance to be materialistic. He's a strange man, a loner. Who knows what's going on inside his head?"

162

"Why should I think everyone but you could do this, Rex?"

He shrugged. "Trust me, Tory—"

They were interrupted by a loud shout and again the words, "Here it is! I found the skull!"

They rushed toward the sound and found Dodge kneeling beside a cow's bleached white skull. He dug beneath it and pulled out a small metal box, like the ones used as bank lockboxes.

Tory observed the group's reactions to the discovery. Rex and Ramona hovered closely, whereas Yazzie held back and feigned indifference. She couldn't believe he was that uncaring, though. Dodge opened the box and drew out a thick plastic bag, the kind used for freezing food. And inside the freezer bag was the other half of the yellowed map!

Dodge looked up and grinned triumphantly. "Well, folks, here it is. The final directions to Pyramid and the gold!"

"Thank God," Ramona murmured, squeezing her hands together. Her face was aglow with happiness and pride. "It's real. I knew Sharkey wouldn't lie to us."

"Let's get on with it!" Rex exclaimed, rubbing his hands together anxiously. "Old Sharkey knew what he was talking about, after all!"

Yazzie wheeled around and hobbled back to camp. But he spoke loudly enough for them to hear. "It's too late to break camp and travel today. We'll rest this afternoon and spend one more night

163

here. Head out tomorrow morning when we're fresh."

Tory gazed woefully after him. "One more night here? Oh, no."

CHAPTER TEN

"Why are you letting him tell us what to do? We could go on without him," Tory said indignantly to Dodge as she fell into step with him. They were on their way to fish in a small lake a mile or so away. "We're just wasting time. We should be half-way there by now!"

"Tory," he drawled with an admonishing look, "are you prepared to climb farther up this mountain on foot? With everything you need piled on your back?"

"Well, no."

"Then, take it easy. We need Yazzie. But most especially, we need his mules at this point."

"It infuriates me that he's just using another stalling tactic, and you know it."

"Yep."

"Yazzie wants to keep us away from this place. Maybe Rex is right, after all."

He looked at her askance. "What do you mean?"

"Rex thinks Yazzie knows where Sharkey's gold is, and he's trying to keep us from finding it."

"That's possible," Dodge said thoughtfully,

shifting the fishing rods from one broad shoulder to the other. "But why was he willing to go along with us and help find it?"

"I don't know. I'm still working on that one," she replied, grinning self-consciously. "Being a detective isn't exactly my forte, but I'm learning."

"The answer is simple, Sherlock Fancy Pants," Dodge teased. "Yazzie's like the rest of us. He doesn't know where the gold is, but he sure wants a piece of the rock."

"I disagree that Yazzie is like the rest of us," Tory countered as she dropped back and stumbled along behind Dodge on the stony path.

"Hmm, you're right. He isn't exactly like us. Watch your step now." Dodge glanced back to make sure she was okay. "But we all want a piece of the rock, especially if it's a gold one. Some of us, though, want it sooner than the others." He gave her an accusing smile. "Do I detect a rush of eagerness in the newest sun seeker?"

"Well, maybe." Her blue eyes grew intense and sharp. "It's just that we're so close now, Dodge. I can *feel* it! And I want to get there soon!" She knotted one fist and punched the air with enthusiasm.

"It is exciting, isn't it?"

"Then how can you calmly take an extra afternoon and go fishing?"

He shrugged. "Not much choice way up here. No television or old movies to watch. Anyway, wouldn't you like something else for supper besides dried beef?"

"Yes!" she exclaimed, laughing. "I don't see how

Cochise's band survived for nine years on this stuff."

"Oh, the Indians hunted for fresh meat. We could look for wild boar or deer. Maybe even a mountain lion. Some say there are still black bears left up here. How does a thick, juicy bear steak sound?"

"Thanks, but no thanks," she murmured sourly. "We'll just go fishing." She continued behind him in studied silence.

Dodge's strides were long and even, the gait of a man who enjoyed the wilds and seemed to belong. *Really* belong.

Tory, on the other hand, viewed each bush and tree as an alien being, unusual plants growing in a wilderness amidst dangerous rock cliffs, strange ghost towns, and wild animals. The terrain was rugged, fit only for the heartiest of souls like Sharkey or Yazzie or even Dodge. But not her. She was a city person, only here temporarily.

Then what would happen to her relationship with Dodge? Would they part and never see each other again? It seemed inevitable.

Dodge was so natural and at ease in this country, and he exuded an indomitable spirit, not unlike the early miners or explorers who traversed this uncivilized land.

Although Tory enjoyed the untamed beauty around her and the absolute tranquility of the wind in the trees, she knew she couldn't last long. She belonged in the city where she could wear her fancy pants. She would only stay until they found gold. Then she would have to go back home, to her business.

The thought of leaving Dodge tore at her heart, and she wondered if she could endure it. Even more important, she wondered how he felt about it. They were doomed to part, and the knowledge saddened her.

Soon they arrived at the banks of a small turquoise-colored lake, hidden deep in the Dragoon Mountains. Large water oaks and giant buff-colored boulders surrounded the water, making it a bastion from the civilized world. Visions of Native Americans from past aeons inhabited Tory's imagination, and she could see them bathing and washing clothes and swimming in the cool waters. Laughing, loving, living in untamed freedom.

"It's beautiful," she murmured in a low tone as her gaze swept over the remote site. "Are you sure this pond has fish, Dodge?"

"Absolutely. Blue gill, bass, and catfish."

"How did fish get way up here?"

"Farmers down in the valley stocked it years ago to keep it clean for the wildlife. They didn't want it lying foul, breeding mosquitoes and other problems. Occasional fishermen hike up this far and keep the fish population under control."

"Whether or not we catch any fish, I won't mind spending a few hours in such a lovely place." She followed Dodge to a little rocky niche between two huge boulders. They settled down and shared some water from the canteen, then Dodge threaded their fishing lines. Tory dropped her line in the water and settled in, absently watching her red and white float bob on the crystalline water. "What will you do when this is all over, Dodge?"

"You mean this trek for gold? Well, if I'm not a millionaire, I'll go back to work."

"Where? Cochise College? The University of Arizona?"

"No. I've applied at the University of Nevada in Reno. I think I'd like to work out there for a change."

"What if we struck gold? Lots of it? And you became very wealthy?"

"What would I do if I struck it rich?" He reclined lazily and studied the puffy white clouds floating in a sphere of blue. "First thing I'd do is pay off some debts. Then, buy a yacht and sail around the world. There are a million places I'd like to see, a thousand things I still want to do. And you? What if you strike it rich, Tory?"

"I'd pay my bills, too." She gave an embarrassed laugh. "I have a ton of debts. There might not be anything left after that."

"Hospital bills from your mother's illness?"

"Yes. And I let things fall behind at the shop during her illness and after . . ." She paused, sadly remembering how deeply the loss of her mother had affected her. And how she'd let everything go for months. "Mismanagement, as much as anything. I just couldn't seem to get it all together. Thank God for Megan."

"Megan? Who's she?"

"She's been my manager and right-hand person for several years now. Steady, honest, and a great friend. She stood by me during the roughest of times and is handling the shop right now."

"Sounds like you're lucky to have her."

"I am. And when I get back, I intend to give Megan a special bonus if I have the money. She certainly deserves it."

"I'd say she's lucky to have you as a boss, too."

"Maybe."

"So after you pay off your bills and give Megan her well-deserved bonus, then what? What will you buy? What will you do with the money?"

"You're mighty confident there'll be an abundance of money to pass around."

"Just 'what if?'"

Tory gazed at Dodge with a sparkle in her eyes. "Do you know what I've always wanted?"

He shook his head.

"A house."

"A *what?*" He leaned up on one elbow.

"After Sharkey left, we never had a house. We moved from one rental to another. Never had anything to call our own. Even now, I still rent an apartment. And I want a home, a place to sink some roots. A little house with shutters and a picket fence." She laughed. "Oh, God, that's crazy! But it's what I want."

His voice was low and gentle. "It isn't crazy if it's what you really want."

She turned her face toward his. "But it's the furthest thing from what you want, Dodge. You want freedom. I need security. We're . . . so different."

"Does that matter to you, Tory?"

"Sometimes. I wish . . ."

"What?"

"Oh, nothing. It's just that you're a perennial sun seeker. And I'm looking for a chance to place some roots."

Dodge pursed his lips. "Is that what you think, Tory?"

"Yes." She nodded soberly.

"Sharkey was the only perennial sun seeker I ever knew. The rest of us were just part-timers. We shared the desire with him." He glanced over at her. "But so do you, Tory, or you wouldn't be here."

"Like father, like daughter, huh?" She smiled reluctantly and leaned back on the rock. "It's been quite an experience. I'm glad I came. I'm glad I met you, Dodge," she whispered softly. "Even if there is no gold and we never get rich."

He leaned forward and kissed her moist, inviting lips. "Is this the same fancy pants lady who castigated me for not hurrying off to find the city of gold less than an hour ago?" He kissed her again, lingering on the sides of her mouth, tasting the tangy-sweet flavor of her skin.

"Hmm," she said between kisses. "But I'm beginning to think you had the right idea, after all. Fishing at the old water hole . . ."

His lips smothered hers, blocking out all sound, save a tiny purring, as they dominated and molded to her heart-shaped lips. He laid aside his fishing rod so he could hold her with both hands. He couldn't stop touching her, couldn't resist the tempting thrust of one rounded breast. "Fishing

171

can wait," he muttered raggedly as one palm flattened against that gentle mound. Encircled and gently massaged. "We can't . . . Oh, God, I can't."

"Yes, Dodge. I've wanted to be alone with you a million times during this whole trip. But it's been impossible." She breathed quickly as his thumb caressed the budding nipple beneath her blouse.

"Not half as badly as I've wanted you. I lie awake every night for hours thinking of you alone in that sleeping bag only a few feet away." He caressed her other breast, gently squeezing the tip to firmly pronounced perfection.

"I wanted you to keep me warm every night." Her hand eagerly reached out to the sturdy wall of his chest. She tingled all over from the mere feel of his hard-muscled body beneath her fingertips. He was a bulwark, an indomitable man who could overpower her with one look, one touch. And she was malleable in his hands.

"Warm . . . God, could I ever keep you warm," he whispered huskily, and shifted until they were as close as possible. "You're beautiful, my little fancy pants."

Warm air swirled around them and fell hot on her face as his lips forced hers open for the intrusion of his tongue. A sweet heat radiated through her as he plunged rhythmically into the dark, honeyed depths behind her teeth.

She formed a welcoming sheath to receive his deeply thrusting tongue, then teasingly parried hers against his. At this point, it was a game they played, an adult game of sensual promises that they both could win. But neither knew if it would last beyond the moment. Although unspoken, they realized they were gamblers, playing a game of chance. But they willingly took the risk.

Tory's blue eyes closed in ecstasy, for she had no desire to end the pleasure of Dodge's exquisite lovemaking. She raised her head to the muscular pillow of his arm, reclining against his strength.

Dodge tucked her closer to his lean, trim body, shielding her from the intense sun. He was like an invincible fortress, a masculine stronghold, and Tory relished the glory of being in his arms again.

She dropped her own fishing rod and entwined her fingers in his hair, pulling his head closer to hers, letting him know the desperation of her desire. "Oh, Dodge, love me."

"I couldn't stand another minute without you," he told her passionately and kissed her soundly again.

Her passion matched his as they scooted into a crevasse between the rocks that was just big enough for the two of them. She could feel the magnificence of his arousal through their clothes and knew the days and nights alone had created the same yearning in him. And she wanted him, too.

"Unbutton your shirt," she said urgently. "I need to feel your skin next to mine."

She opened her blouse and pressed her bare breasts to the heated wall of his chest. The mingling of their fire, of warm flesh to warm flesh, set the smoldering coals within them aflame. Fervently, he kissed her face and lips and neck. Then, lowering his head to her breasts, he caressed them with eager forays, careful to lave each nipple with his moist tongue.

She arched to meet him, moaning softly with the renewed pleasure as he buried kisses in her soft breasts and along the heated valley between them.

With a ragged sigh, he shifted away long enough to discard his jeans and briefs, then helped strip off her panties. Tory watched him in frank admiration and welcomed him to her arms. He was gorgeous and she could hardly wait for him.

Together they sought the balm of complete fulfillment. His large body flattened hers as he lowered over her, molding his maleness to her soft femininity. With a muffled gasp, she opened to receive him.

He withdrew immediately at her raspy sounds and propped himself up on elbows, his face above hers. "I want you with a desire hard to control, Tory. I don't want to ravage you. This should be good for both of us."

" 'Good' is an understatement," she admitted frankly. She gazed at him with clear blue eyes, her blatant admiration obvious. "Come on now, don't tease. Love me, please, Dodge. Love me and don't stop." Her hands spread wide on his sinewed back and demandingly pressed him to her.

He caressed her body with searching hands, trailing his fiery touch past her waist and the gentle curve of her hips. Then he reached the moist petals of her desire and stroked the folds, finally opening them to probe gently.

"Ohh, Dodge . . ." She was an undulating bundle of energy beneath him, unable to lie still any longer.

Realizing she was dangerously close to the brink of her endurance, he slid his hand between her thighs and pushed them wide enough for his slim hips. She welcomed him, urging his rhythm even before he was fully inside her. Raising her hips higher, he drove completely into the heated heart of her.

Tory couldn't subdue the hidden passions that filled her with joy, spilling over with love. Dodge brought forth feelings she'd never before experienced. Even as his body physically overwhelmed hers, she knew that what she felt for this man was love. Love, sharp and driving. Love, shadowy and strong. And she prayed theirs would be a love, long lasting and shared. Whimpering softly, she lost a little control and scraped her fingernails down the length of his bare back.

She matched his fierceness with a fervor of her own, and they hurled together to an exhausting climax. Time after time, she shuddered as passion vibrated through her body. Endless passion, endless love. Full and resonant, resounding against the deaf ears of a wilderness. Whispered words of love kept her going and let her down easy. Panting, sighing, lamenting breezes cooled their moist bodies and whined through the pines.

Dodge hovered over her, watching the expression on her face change from intensity to contentment. There were times when he was afraid he was too strong for her, too wild, too uncontrolled. Even if he tried, he couldn't hold back once he was

175

inside her. He had to admit, this time Tory had been like a raging storm engulfing him, a wildly impassioned woman. Wind and fire and rain all at once. Just for him. He smiled with the remembrance.

But his feelings for this woman clinging to him were deeper and more passionate than mere desire. He wanted to possess her, not just sexually but completely. He wanted to hold her and caress her daily. He wanted to reassure her, to be with her. But even as they lay there, yielding to each other, he knew it wasn't to be. Not the forever part.

He bent and tenderly kissed her earlobe. "Tory, my sweet Tory, I want you with me always." How can I ever let you go?

She smiled and snuggled contentedly against him. His kisses continued until the high mountain breezes had cooled their passion-raked nude bodies.

"Tory, I'm getting a sunburn on my buns. I think it's time."

"Time? There's no time schedule out here. We're in the wild."

"We're in the nude and we need to go fishing. The others are depending on us to catch supper."

"What are we going to do about tonight, Dodge? I want to sleep with you."

"I don't know. I'm still working on that."

"Maybe we can go fishing every day."

He laughed, a deep, rumbling laugh from his chest that reverberated through her. Then he moved his heated body away from hers. "Let's get dressed."

*   *   *

There was no chance to be alone together that night, and Tory and Dodge climbed into separate sleeping bags, exchanging glances of sad defeat. The next day, there was no time for fishing.

They rode the mules for hours, Yazzie plodding ahead, stopping frequently to study the yellowed map Sharkey left for them. He definitely lacked enthusiasm, almost as if he were now reluctant to make this last leg of the journey. The terrain was steep and rugged and slow going. They rode in silence, each member of the party lost in his or her own thoughts. To find the gold was foremost in everyone's mind, however.

Finally, Yazzie halted the line of mules and shifted around in the saddle. Pointing to a valley between two mountains, he announced, "There's the lost city—Pyramid."

The electricity that ran through the group was almost tangible as they rushed forward to see. Tory wasn't sure what to expect. Certainly she knew there wouldn't be gold-glittered houses, as the early Spaniards claimed, or streets paved with gold, as the old miners bragged. But she expected —perhaps wanted—the place to be distinctive.

But Pyramid was not distinctive.

It was practically invisible. Which was one reason it had remained lost in time all these years. Tory had to strain hard to discern anything substantial past the sea of weeds, thick bushes, and small trees that nearly obliterated the crumbling adobe walls of the old buildings.

Ramona was the first to speak. "It's kind of sad

but also lovely. Like viewing a piece of history, minus the people."

"This is a forbidden place," Yazzie muttered. "Bad spirits live here."

"Bad spirits?" Rex scoffed. "Bunk! It's picked clean, that's all. I just hope there's still gold left beneath that old mine shaft." He pointed to a tall hill beyond the small town where the remains of a wooden mine shaft lay in ruins.

"So that's where Pyramid got its name. The mine is located on a pyramid-shaped hill above the city," Dodge observed. "Not much of a city, is it? Single street and a few buildings on both sides."

"It has a cemetery," Tory said as a chilling breeze sent shivers down her spine. "It's an eerie place, isn't it?" She rubbed one arm nervously.

"All ghost towns feel this way," Ramona said with a nod. "They have a certain aura, an energy. Some good, some not so good."

"This one is not so good," Yazzie confirmed with narrowed eyes.

Dodge slapped his mule's flank. "Shall we go down and take a look, folks? We traveled long and hard to get to this place, and I don't intend to stay up here on this hill overlooking it."

Dodge led the way this time, and Yazzie brought up the rear. By mule, they traversed the short length of the town, which consisted of a single narrow street flanked by the hulls of six or seven remaining buildings. Lost in weeds were the meager foundations of several other houses that hadn't withstood the ravages of time. Only one rectangular building remained in reasonably good condition. Although the roof was completely gone, partial adobe walls divided the interior into separate rooms.

They ended up tying the mules to the still-sturdy hitching post in front of what they decided was a boardinghouse, where many miners had probably lived.

"Let's look around a little before we make camp," Dodge suggested.

"I'm for that," Rex agreed. "I want to see if that old mine has anything of value left in it."

"Not this evening, Rex," Dodge warned. "We'll examine the mine tomorrow when the light is better. It's almost dark now, and that's a dangerous area. Anyway, I know it doesn't look far, but it's quite a climb up to the location."

Rex shaded his eyes and gazed toward the mine, which was perched on a triangular-shaped mound above town. "Yeah, I guess you're right. But I'd sure like to know what's under that ground."

"Be patient, my friend," Dodge said with a chuckle. "We all want to know. And we will, in due time. What's one more night?"

"The ghosts, too, have one more night," Yazzie said with a snort. He looked around in disdain. "I can *feel* the bad spirits. They are disturbed and unhappy with us." He limped off alone, leaving the others to shift around uncomfortably.

"Spirits? Ha!" Rex laughed. "I'd look out for snakes if I were you, Yazzie!" He turned to Ramona. "Come on, let's tour the place."

She slid off her mule. "Sure, I'll go with you,

Rex. I want to examine that small building down by the jail. I think it may have been an infirmary."

"Don't go far," Dodge called in warning as everyone scattered. "We really should stick together until we know more about the place."

"Bad vibes, Dodge?" Tory asked teasingly.

"No," he denied stoutly. "I just think this is a dangerous area, that's all. We need to take every precaution."

"From what? Ghosts?"

"No, Tory. Certainly not ghosts. Wild animals, for one thing. They're accustomed to this town being empty. Who knows if a black bear has made a home around here? Abandoned mine shafts are another, perhaps worse danger. Some of them are completely open and quite deep."

"But that wouldn't matter around here in town, would it?"

"You never know where an old mine shaft might be. That's why I want us to wait until the sun's bright and we can see exactly where we're going. State law dictates that abandoned mines be fenced nowadays. But there's no one in a place like this to follow the law. Or enforce it."

"Well, after the warning, I'll definitely watch my step. What do you think this building was?" she asked as they approached freestanding adobe walls.

"Don't know. Let's go inside."

The roofs were completely gone from all the buildings, assuring that anything left inside would be exposed to the elements. Floors were gone, too, leaving bare earth to sprout new growth of weeds and bushes.

"Why, Dodge," Tory said excitedly, lifting a broken whiskey bottle from a pile of glass in the corner, "I'll bet this was the saloon."

He joined her and agreed. "Yep. The saloon was always one of the first buildings to go up in these old towns. The men worked hard and played rough. And drank like fish."

Tory walked to the far end of the room and stopped before the yawning doorway. The perpetually open space framed a view of another adobe ruin. And in another direction, yet another ruin. "Looks like Yazzie found the jail," she said, motioning toward the long-haired man.

Yazzie walked around the corner of the square building and halted abruptly. He looked up with foreboding at the single window, still filled with steel bars. The jail. He ambled around front, leaned his back against the sturdy wall beside the solid metal front door, and pulled out a smoke.

He stood there, the crippled knee bent and foot propped on the wall, surveying the small valley with its sparse buildings and gold mine entrenched in the triangular hillside. They were completely surrounded by mountains. No wonder it had been so hard to find. It was practically hidden. But no more. Now five people knew about it.

Ramona walked slowly, stopping occasionally to pick up some forgotten object that once belonged to someone who lived there. She pulled absently at weeds, gingerly touched the adobe bricks, and finally found a seat on a staircase leading nowhere.

When did Sharkey discover this beautiful place? Why didn't he tell her about it? How much time did he spend there? He must have known she would love this old town. Did he plan to bring her back if he hadn't died? Oh, how she would have loved coming here with him. But then, he was so damned independent, maybe he didn't plan to bring her there at all. Maybe he intended to enjoy it alone, as he did so much of his life.

When Ramona sat down on the steps with a dreamy expression, Rex headed across the street. As he tromped through the weeds, he nearly tripped over an old piece of a blackboard. He realized that must be the school. Kicking around the place soon left him bored, and he ambled out the back way. There was a rickety little building perched halfway up the hill toward the mine. Like a curious young boy, he headed for that shack. He'd just check it out before heading back to the group, he told himself. It would be dark soon, anyway.

"We'd better fix our camp for the night," Dodge said, and steered Tory out of the saloon, "before it gets dark."

"Where?"

"I think the best place for us to bed down is in what appears to be the boardinghouse. We'll have to clear out the weeds and scrub oaks, but those adobe partitions will provide a little privacy. Espe-

182

cially if everyone wants a semiprivate room of their own."

"Count me in," Tory replied, grinning.

"Besides, if we play our cards right, you and I might get a partitioned section all to ourselves."

"I knew you had an ulterior motive there."

"Of course," he admitted frankly. "I'd put the rest of them in another building altogether if I thought I could get away with it. But we probably ought to stick close together until this expedition is over." He draped his arm over her shoulder, and Tory slipped her arm around his waist. Alone in their own little loving world, they went back to the boardinghouse ruins.

"Which room do you want, fancy pants? Since we're the first ones here, we get our choice."

Tory chose a corner room. "This one. What a mess!"

"After we clear out a few of these weeds, we'll level the earth so our beds will be comfortable."

"Oh, what a dreamer you are!" She laughed. "Whoever said sleeping on the ground is comfortable?"

He paused and gave her a special look. "I'll see that you are entirely comfy tonight, Miss Fancy Pants."

"What? You found a motel nearby?" she teased.

He rolled his eyes. "You and Rex! Two of the tenderest of tenderfeet!"

Using a few of the digging tools packed on the mules, Dodge and Tory began the necessary cleanup. They were in high spirits, joking and laughing while they worked. But everything halted abruptly when they heard a scream.

Tory bolted upright, her wide eyes flying to Dodge's face. "That was definitely not a mountain lion. That was Ramona!"

"You're right, Tory!" Dodge headed to the open doorway and looked in every direction. The sun was setting over the western mountain range. Soon they would be in complete darkness. "Where the hell are they?"

Ramona's call could be heard again.

"Damn! What in the hell are they doing way up there?" Dodge lunged forward. "At the explosives shack! Come on!"

Tory followed close on his heels as they ran toward the frantic sounds.

By then Ramona's voice was a wail. "Oh, my God! Come quick, Dodge! Please help!"

CHAPTER ELEVEN

Tory rushed up the hill behind Dodge. She felt the tug of a prickly pear cactus on her jeans and the sting on her legs as a few stickers penetrated the denim and tore at her flesh. She rushed on heedlessly, spurred by Ramona's panicky voice.

"It's Rex! He's down there somewhere!" Ramona's usually tanned face was drawn and pale. She clutched at the front of Dodge's shirt, her strong fingers white knuckled and demanding.

Panting, Tory halted beside Dodge. She was suddenly a participant in a real-life horror story. Ramona, panicky and near tears. Rex, disappeared into an open pit. Dodge, the only one in control of his emotions, even if not of the situation.

He gripped Ramona's arms and shook her roughly. "Calm down, Ramona. Tell me exactly what happened."

Ramona took several sobbing breaths and tried to retrace her steps. And Rex's. "I don't know, exactly. We were wandering around the infirmary. I sat down on a step, and the next thing I knew, Rex had gone off by himself. I saw him walking up here, toward this little shack."

"And you followed him right away?"

She nodded. "And by the time I got here"—she reached for the yawning black hole with outstretched hands—"he'd disappeared in there!"

Dodge knelt beside the abyss. "My God, it looks deep. What the hell was he doing way up here, anyway?" His voice was gruff, edged with the aimless anger that frustration brings.

Tory watched the angled planes of Dodge's face, dark and prominent in the twilight. His lips pressed together tightly, and a muscle in his jaw twitched. He was, at that moment, a strong man with no power.

"He doesn't answer, Dodge," Ramona whispered. "Do you think he could be—"

"No! He's down there and we're going to get him out, that's all!"

Tory stared helplessly at the two of them, appalled at the possibility of such a tragedy. A chill swept through her as she tried to gain some sense of the reality.

Ramona wrung her hands. "Rex was—is—so curious about that gold mine. He could hardly wait for tomorrow when we could go up there."

"Yeah, see what curiosity got him?" Dodged grumbled low.

Ramona shook her head hopelessly. "I'm scared, Dodge."

"We'll work something out, Ramona." Dodge looked around and began to scout the area. Like the other abandoned houses, this one was a roofless frame.

Ramona knelt down and called again. "Rex?

186

Rex, can you hear me? Answer me, Rex! Oh, please, say something!"

The three paused to listen. Silence greeted them.

Dodge rushed over and shouted again, not willing to accept the fact that his partner was so badly injured he couldn't answer. Or that he could be dead. "Rex! Hey, Rex! Can you hear us? We're going to get you out!"

Still nothing.

Tory finally found her voice. "The fall could have knocked him out temporarily."

Dodge muttered, "Yeah. But it doesn't look good. No telling how deep this shaft is."

"My God, I can't believe this has happened," Tory moaned. "It's like a nightmare, something you read about in western novels, not experienced in real life."

"For years I've heard about people falling into these abandoned mines, but I've never known anyone who did," Ramona murmured.

Dodge grabbed Ramona's arm to hush her. "Listen!"

They leaned toward the hole, silently willing the sounds they wanted to hear. And indeed, they did hear something. A scraping, like shoes scooting in loose gravel. And a man's groaning.

"He's alive!" Ramona mouthed excitedly, defusing their worst fears.

"Rex! Hey, Rex!" Dodge yelled, then paused and called again, loudly. "We hear you, Rex! How are you, ole' buddy? Come on, Rex. Answer!" He ended with an almost demanding tone, inspired by fear and desperation.

Faintly, they heard another groan. "Aaggg . . . ohh, my head."

At the sound of the misery-laden but distinguishable words, the three hovering outside the abandoned mine pit cheered aloud. Ramona excitedly clapped Dodge on the back, then turned to hug Tory.

"Okay, we have to get busy if we're going to get him out before dark," Dodge said, noting the sun receding behind the mountain. "I'd say we have less than an hour."

"How?" Tory asked hopelessly. "We don't even know how deep he is."

Dodge ignored her questions. "We'll need rope, lots of it. And a couple of mules. The strongest ones. Let's hurry." He placed a gentling hand on Ramona's shoulder. "You stay here and talk to him, Ramona. See if you can determine how badly he's hurt. And keep his spirits up. We'll be back as soon as possible."

Tory and Dodge hurried down the hill to get the necessary tools and mules. Yazzie was nowhere in sight, so they grabbed what they needed and quickly rushed back up the hill to the disaster site.

"Have you been talking to him?" Dodge asked Ramona. "Keeping him awake and alert? Is he hurt?"

"He's alert enough to be complaining. He hit his head when he fell. As Tory said, that probably knocked him out temporarily. He's complaining about pains in his head, his chest, and his arm."

"He could easily have cracked a few ribs in the fall. They're damned painful, too. And it's entirely

188

possible he broke his arm." Dodge knelt beside the ever-blackening hole. "Rex, you still with us?" While he was talking, Dodge skillfully knotted the ropes together.

"Where the hell would I go?"

"Yes, he seems okay," Dodge said over his shoulder to the women. "Same belligerent Rex." Then he talked again to Rex. "Tell me where you're hurt, Rex. We're working on a way to get you out."

"Well, what the hell are you waiting for?"

"Can you help yourself, or do you need me to come down on a pulley and get you?"

"Lower a rope. I can do it."

"Can you hold on? What about your arm?"

"Hurts like hell."

"Are you sure you can hold on while we pull you out?"

"Better make it a sling."

"Okay, we're working as fast as we can. Don't move around. I'm going to lower the rope to you, and I want you to sit still and wait until it reaches you. Don't go fumbling around searching for it. Tell me when you get it."

"He sounds pretty strong," Tory said with growing enthusiasm.

Dodge began feeding the rope down the black hole and looked up at Tory and Ramona. "The best I can figure from the sound of his voice, he's about fifty feet down. This should be enough rope. When he gets it, we're going to tie the ends to those two mules. Then I'll stay here and keep it steady and help Rex over the ledge while you two lead the mules away. Walk slowly but keep them steady and the ropes taut."

Tory and Ramona nodded seriously, feeling the tension mount. Rex's life depended on everything and everyone working together, including the sometimes unpredictable mules.

"I have it!" Rex shouted. "I have the rope!"

Dodge gave Rex terse instructions for getting into the makeshift seat, then secured the ropes to the two mules. With a quick nod, he motioned for Tory and Ramona to proceed forward, continuing to feed Rex constant reassurance. "Hold the rope with your good arm. Brace your body against the rope. Walk up the walls. You can do it, Rex! Come on . . ."

Tory's palms were hot and sweaty as she clutched her mule's bridle. The rescue seemed to take forever. She could hear Rex's agonized voice as he moved along.

"Oh, my ribs! Oh, my arm! Oh, damn, it hurts to breathe! How much farther?"

Dodge kept up his verbal encouragement. "You're doing fine, Rex. Come on up. Almost here."

When Rex's head appeared over the edge, time accelerated. Suddenly everything erupted into a melee of loud congratulations and hugging. The shadowed figures seemed to huddle together, out-lined against the deep purple of the surrounding mountains. One of their party had survived a near-tragedy, but they couldn't avoid the unspoken fear —*would they be so lucky next time?*

Tory and Ramona went ahead while Dodge

brought Rex on one of the mules. They found Yazzie stirring a pot of stew over a glowing campfire. Relief flooded Tory, leaving her shaky.

Ramona's emotions were closer to the surface, and she lashed out at the cook, who seemed so safe and unshaken. "Where have you been all this time, Yazzie? Rex's life was in danger and you were no help."

The long-haired man looked at her steadily. "Did you need me?"

"No. We managed to get him out of that abandoned mine. He's all right, if you care to know."

"I knew Dodge could handle it. My job's cookin', not rescuin'. I figure if Dodge wants my help, he can call for it. Don't you want some hot coffee and stew?"

Ramona looked at him askance. "How can you think of food at a time like this?"

Tory interrupted. "Come on, Ramona. Don't take your frustrations out on him. Everything's all right now. And we do need food, at least Rex does."

Ramona turned on Tory. "Just who does Yazzie think he is, not being a part of this group, not helping when someone's life is in danger?"

"Let's get the beds fixed," Tory said, changing the subject. "Rex will need a comfortable place to lie down. And a little supper. We don't want him to go into shock."

"You're excusing Yazzie for doing nothing?"

"No," Tory said. "I just don't see any sense in placing blame at this point. Come on, we have work to do. It's been a long day. We're all tired and uptight." She placed an encouraging arm around Ramona's quivering shoulders and steered her away.

Ramona let Tory lead her away. They prepared Rex's sleeping bag and searched out whatever medical supplies they'd brought along.

Finally, Ramona admitted, "I'm sorry for my outburst, Tory. That was dumb, to verbally attack Yazzie, but he makes me so damn mad."

"I know, Ramona. You were scared and frustrated. We all were. And you took it out on the one person who didn't seem to risk anything, the one who doesn't seem to have our same fears."

Ramona ran a nervous hand over her forehead and smoothed back her jet black hair. "When I realized Rex's life was at stake, all the horror of Sharkey's death came back to haunt me. And I think, more than ever, that your suspicions are right."

"You mean about Sharkey—" Tory halted abruptly.

Ramona shrugged silently, and her eyes met Tory's with unspoken fear.

When Dodge arrived in camp with the shaken and injured Rex, everyone began working to make him comfortable for the night. Rex was unusually reticent, quietly letting them patch his wounds.

Dodge confirmed the fear that Rex's arm was broken and helped Ramona wrap it. Tory brought him a small bowl of stew and a cup of steaming coffee. The others gathered around the campfire to eat, and Rex motioned to Tory. "I've got to talk to you."

She sat on a large round stone and hugged her knees against the night coolness. "You okay now, Rex?"

"As well as can be expected, considering I'm wrapped up like a damned mummy." He touched the bandage around his head.

"You gave us quite a scare, you know. Dodge's right. Those open-pit mines are—"

"Listen, Tory," he interrupted, motioning her closer, "we're in big trouble up here, and I mean *big trouble*. You and I never should have come along on this trip. We're too inexperienced. I mean, they all have a great advantage over us."

"I know it can be dangerous up here."

"We're still in danger."

"You're just upset because of this accident, Rex. But we've all been upset by it. I'm really sorry about your injuries, but you know they could have been much worse."

"What I'm trying to say is"—his dark eyes grew intense and hard—"I don't think this was an accident."

"What?"

"Shh. Not so loud. Keep it down."

"Rex, don't make any rash accusations. You'll just upset everyone."

"Tory, I think I was pushed."

"Pushed? Oh, no! You couldn't have been."

"No"—he waggled his hand—"I take that back. I know I was pushed. I *know* it! As I think back on it, the whole series of events is coming back to me. I was climbing up the hill to see that little hut. When I got there, I walked around back and found

193

a mound of earth. I thought it was probably an open mine pit, so I approached it with utmost care. Honest to God, I did."

"Rex, that earth was loose. It would have been easy to fall down and slide out of control. And there's nothing for you to grab or to break the fall."

"Only the bottom of the pit."

"You were lucky to land on that ledge."

"I was unlucky to be pushed!"

"Don't say that." Tory lifted her hand to her own lips in a motion to silence him. "Oh, Rex, I—I don't know what to believe. Who would do such a thing? And why?"

"Obviously, I was getting too close to the gold. Maybe it's in that very pit!"

She shook her head. "I doubt it. Dodge says it's old, probably the first mine dug around here. And probably depleted of all metals."

"Dodge says? Do you realize the nice share of insurance he'd have if I weren't around?"

"Don't you dare accuse Dodge of anything like this. Anyway . . . anyway, he was with me the whole time." She admitted it reluctantly because she realized she was looking for an alibi for Dodge. "Dodge wouldn't do anything like that, Rex. He saved your life. How could you possibly think that he—"

Rex touched her hand with his unbandaged one. "Take it easy, Tory. Okay, okay. I'm not blaming him. I'm just saying he has reasons to want to be rid of me. With Sharkey gone, he has to share everything with me. With me gone, he could have it all to himself."

"Oh, no. I won't believe it." But in the back of her mind Tory remembered how she and Dodge had daydreamed yesterday by the lake and mused about how they'd spend the money if they struck it rich. Dodge definitely had thought about it.

But then, so had she.

Rex sipped his black coffee and continued. "Of course, Ramona was right behind me. I heard her scrambling up the hill. Pushing someone into a hole is certainly easy enough for a woman to do . . ."

"No! I will not listen to another moment of this trash!" Tory said in an angry whisper. "It wasn't Ramona."

"How do you know? Was she with you, too?"

"No, but—"

"Then why are you defending her? I'm just telling you what *could* have happened."

"No, you're telling me someone around here attempted murder."

"Look, you were the one who first suggested this, Tory. Remember your doubts about Sharkey's so-called accidental demise? Well, they make more sense now. I'm afraid the violence was aimed at me tonight. But who knows who's next?"

"P—please don't say that. Eat your stew, Rex. You need to get some rest. I know you'll feel better in the morning." She moved the bowl closer. "Want me to feed you?"

"No, I do not want you to feed me. I want you to heed my warning. And believe me. Who made

195

this stew? Yazzie?" He looked at the bowl as if he had spotted a six-legged creature floating on top.

"Who else? Of course Yazzie made it. He's our cook, isn't he?"

Rex shoved the bowl of untouched stew toward her. "Thanks, but I'm not hungry."

"Rex, this is preposterous. You need the energy."

He crooked a finger and motioned her closer. "Look, I think you're absolutely right. Somebody did away with Sharkey. And now he—or she—is starting on us."

"Good heavens, Rex, you are absolutely paranoid. It's just all you've been through. You'll feel better tomorrow."

Glancing surreptitiously at the others eating beside the campfire, Rex muttered under his breath, "Who better than Yazzie to do away with the whole lot of us with one pot of stew?"

Tory shivered. Rex must be hallucinating after the fall, and she was victim of his paranoid ramblings. Now what she had to do was calm his fears.

"That's impossible. Yazzie's eating out of the same pot, himself."

Now was not the time to get hysterical. And there—in the lost town of Pyramid—was definitely not the place. They had to see it through, get back down the mountain together, and then look around at the situation. So far, her suspicions about Sharkey had been circumstantial. But coupled with what had happened to Rex tonight, it was enough to keep her awake at night.

Finally, Dodge called to her. "Tory, your stew's getting cold."

She helped Rex slide down into the sleeping bag. "Please try to get some sleep, Rex. You'll feel better and things will look different in the light of day." Fervently, she hoped so.

Tory ate quietly, mulling over what Rex had said, and while trying to dismiss it as postconcussion paranoia, she had to admit that there was a trace of logic to his conclusions. But only a trace.

Yazzie collected everybody's bowls and grumbled over Rex's untouched food.

"He didn't feel like eating. Shock, I guess," Tory explained simply, trying to make it sound normal.

Ramona yawned and claimed exhaustion. Everyone agreed and proceeded to drag out their sleeping bags.

Tory agreed and headed for the corner 'room' she and Dodge had chosen with such delight. But the excitement of having some privacy was gone. Now the area seemed dark and ominous, especially after Rex's ramblings that somebody was out to get them. She took a cupful of water and brushed her teeth near an empty window frame.

After stopping to check on Rex, Dodge joined her. "Rex is sleeping like a baby. Thank God he made it through with nothing more than a broken arm and a few busted ribs."

"Uh-huh," she replied quietly, hoping Dodge had no idea what kind of thoughts were roaming through his partner's head. Or hers!

"He was damned lucky."

"Yes, he was."

"I've always had that fear, that someone would fall into one of those pits," he said reflectively.

"Guess I'd better watch my step from now on."

"Absolutely!" Dodge bent over their sleeping bags and became very busy rearranging and manipulating. "That's why I've always warned everyone. And why I wanted to wait until tomorrow when the light was better. My God, do you realize we could have lost him!"

Tory gazed intently at Dodge, unconsciously judging his reactions. "It was a close call. But are you sure it was an accident, Dodge? Rex isn't."

"Of course . . . Well, what do you mean? What does he think?" Dodge sat on top of the sleeping bags and began peeling off his boots.

She took a deep breath and knelt beside him. Should she share her burden with Dodge? But if not with him—if she couldn't trust *him*—who could she trust? She had to believe that he was innocent of Rex's accusations. And she had to be truthful with him. If Rex were right, they all should know. Tory lowered her voice. "Rex says he was pushed over the edge of that mine."

"What?" Dodge frowned. "That's ridiculous."

"He claims he would not have gotten that close to the edge, that he knows the inherent dangers, that he was shoved from behind."

"So he thinks someone tried to kill him? Who, for God's sake?"

She took another deep breath. Was it obvious that Rex doubted everyone, even his only remaining business partner? "That's why he wouldn't eat Yazzie's stew tonight."

"He suspects Yazzie? Hell, we were all eating that stew, including Yazzie."

"I know. And I tried to tell him that, but he wouldn't listen. He was still quite upset about what happened, as you can imagine."

"Obviously," Dodge agreed with a slow nod. "What made Rex think someone pushed him? Did he hear anyone behind him or have any other proof?"

"I don't know. I tried to dismiss his accusations as ramblings after the accident. And possibly his head injury. But maybe he has a point, Dodge. Maybe somebody is after all of us because of the gold."

"Yazzie?"

"Not necessarily."

"Then *who*? Ramona? Or me?" Dodge's eyes grew sharp and hard in the darkness.

"Well, no, not really." She hesitated. "I don't agree with him, but Rex thinks insurance payouts could be incentives."

"Then he's accusing me," Dodge breathed through his teeth.

"Not exactly." She rushed on. "Of course, I denied that either you or Ramona could have had anything to do with this. And I . . . I really believe that. I trust you both, completely." She paused and touched his arm. "Dodge, listen. Hear that?"

They looked around in the dark. Then Dodge said, "That's just Yazzie, walking around somewhere. He's restless, as usual."

"What if he falls in an open-pit mine? Or what if

he's the one who—" She pressed her fingers to her mouth, keeping the fears from surfacing. "Oh, God, Dodge, I'm scared."

"Tory, Tory, with Rex's help, you've worked yourself into a real lather over this. Don't pay any attention to what Rex said. Try to forget it." He took her hand and gently pulled her down into the comforting cradle of his arms.

She rested her head against his chest and smothered a quivering sigh against the hair she could feel beneath his shirt. "Hold me, Dodge. I'm so scared. This whole thing has me puzzled. I don't know what to think."

"Yes, honey, I know." His words were soothing, his body comforting and strong. This was what she needed. *He* was what she needed and Tory went eagerly to him.

Her tormented soul exulted as his renewing energy swept around her, engulfing her with masculine warmth and power. His lips were gentle and comforting on her hair, then seeking and hungry on her face and throat. Then he found her lips, and his kiss answered all her questions and removed whatever doubts she had . . . for the present.

Dodge was honest and innocent and *hers.* Tonight they would cling to each other with trust and understanding. Tomorrow would be another day of doubt and worry, but tonight they had each other. And she was safe and secure in his arms.

A force greater than either of them drew them together. As Tory relinquished to his passion, she knew this was the way it was meant to be. She and Dodge belonged together.

Dodge practically ripped off his shirt, discarding it and ignoring the cool night air. His powerful shoulders reflected the moonlight and presented a human fortress for her shelter. With an impatient ruggedness, he pulled her shirt from her waistband and helped her unbutton it. Then, with an admiring gaze, he wrapped his arms around her, forging their heated bodies together.

She melted with him, praying this moment of shared love would never end. That they would never have to part. Yet knowing they would.

They struggled to remove tight jeans, then squeezed into the sleeping bags, which Dodge had made into one. Instantly, they arched to mold and match, two bodies needing each other, desiring to be one.

She had known his male strength and yearned again for his pleasures. Her body flared with passion that matched his, and begged for his fulfillment, for the satisfaction that only Dodge could give her. She felt his male need rising against her thigh and writhed sensuously beneath him. She was on fire for him. Erotically, she touched him, stroking with an urgent need of her own.

He pulled her close and, with a quick thrust, slid into her softness. Tory knew completeness with him, loving the fortress of his body as it dominated hers. She undulated with him, her desire building with each thrust, hotter and higher. The pleasure was intolerable, the sensations wild and tempestuous. The climax came in ripples, endless waves of rapture unlike any others.

Dodge held off as long as he could, until the

heat inside him expanded to the point of explosion. He rose faster and faster, pounding his strength into her, reaching the ultimate with a force that shuddered through him and left him depleted of strength. And desire. And still, for minutes or hours—for endless time—they clung to each other.

Finally, Tory stirred. "Dodge . . ."

He kissed her. "I know . . ."

She turned her head away. "No, listen. I hear something—"

"Not again."

"Someone's coming, Dodge!"

They froze, their arms still locked around each other.

"Dodge, Tory?" The small voice in the night was Ramona's.

Dodge managed, "Yes, Ramona? What is it?"

"I'm sorry to intrude into your privacy. But do you mind if I stay here in your section? I'm—I hate to admit it, but I'm scared. Too much has happened lately. And Yazzie is still gone. Where could he be at this hour?"

"He probably made his bed out near the mules. You know how private he is," Dodge explained, trying to regain his self-control after the throes of passion that had so recently engulfed him.

"Of course you can stay here, Ramona," Tory said generously. "Dodge will protect us."

"Thank you." Ramona hauled her sleeping bag into their little private adobe "room" and settled down for the night.

Dodge rolled over and whispered in Tory's ear.

"How am I supposed to protect the two of you? I don't even have my pants on!"

"Don't worry, my brave hero. You'll manage something." Tory snuggled down with a smile, resting her head on his arm.

"It'll be a struggle," he grumbled.

Dodge lay awake, long after everyone else was breathing softly in sleep. In the soft moonlight, he could see the relaxed expression on Tory's face and knew she felt safe and secure with him. So did Ramona, lying nearby. He found himself straining for unusual sounds and didn't sleep very much during the night. The responsibility was too great.

CHAPTER TWELVE

"Is this it? This hazardous hole in the ground is what Sharkey sent us after?" Rex, his head and arm bandaged, perched astride a mule and fumed angrily.

The rest of the sun seekers stood around and gaped at the abandoned gold mine atop the pyramid-shaped hill.

"Obviously, the digging will have to take place below the surface. Which is what we all expected, I think," Dodge observed. He kicked the rickety old mine frame. "This can't be trusted. Nor the elevator. We'll have to lower ourselves into the mine using the pulleys we brought along. Yazzie, want to go down with me to explore the place first?"

Yazzie nodded and helped Dodge rig the pulleys with a seat. Tory watched anxiously as the two men disappeared into the bowels of the mine pit, and she realized, perhaps for the first time, that the actual digging could be quite dangerous. A hundred things could go wrong, and there they were, aeons away from the real world and help. Twenty minutes later the men returned, excited about their findings and eager to get started.

"This is it," Dodge said with a firm finality. "It's going to take some hard work, but the gold's there. And we're going to get it out!"

They worked out an equitable schedule alternating work and rest periods. A water barrel was brought up to the mine as well as all the lighting and digging equipment. Tory and Ramona also joined in the effort, agreeing that they had come this far and wouldn't be denied the opportunity to dig for the gold, no matter how rough it was. By noon, Tory realized she'd taken on more than she bargained for, but it was too late to back out. She noted Ramona's large, capable hands, then her own scraped, raw fingers with nails chipped and broken. Her hands were too delicate and weak for this kind of work.

At lunchtime, everyone was hot, sweaty, and already tired, but the conversation was animated. The morning's dig hadn't been very fruitful, but spirits and hopes were still high. They all voiced expectations to find the treasure soon. *Gold!*

However, by nightfall they had extracted only a few buckets of low-grade ore, not worth very much. While Rex rested, the four workers hovered beside the campfire, exhausted and frustrated.

Yazzie seemed to be the only one with high spirits. "You didn't think it would be easy to get the gold, did you? What'd you expect, pots of it sitting around at the end of a rainbow?" He began dishing up supper and passing heaping plates of meat and potatoes around the quiet circle.

Dodge was at the end of the line and accepted the plate passed to him. "Nobody expected it to be easy, Yazzie, but we didn't expect to come up empty-handed, either."

"Well, we did get a few rocks with a little value," Ramona admitted, taking an unenthusiastic bite of the hash on her plate.

"*Very* little," scoffed Rex. "So far, our findings haven't been worth my trip. And my injuries."

"How are you feeling tonight, Rex?" Tory asked. Even though the man had a broken arm, they hadn't considered sending him back. And he hadn't suggested it, either. The urge for gold was too strong. She couldn't help wondering if this gold fever that seemed to inflict them all was too strong for their ultimate well-being. But it was too late to question that now.

"Aw, I'm as well as can be expected," he grumbled, then turned to Dodge. "Let me see that map again. Maybe we aren't in the right area."

"We're right, I tell you," Yazzie said firmly. "This is exactly where the map directed. Now, if it isn't here, he was wrong. It's possible, you know. Sharkey may have been mistaken."

"I don't think so," Ramona objected. "He got us this far, didn't he?"

"Let me see for myself," Rex insisted, stretching out his one good hand.

"There's no use," Yazzie stated. "We're digging exactly where he directed. Dodge and I double-checked."

"*Dios mío,* man! I just want to see the map!"

Dodge shuffled over with the yellow sheet. "Here, Rex. What's the big fuss? Take a look for yourself."

Rex studied the page quietly for a while, then returned it with a low grunt. "Okay, okay, I'm satisfied. This is it."

Tory looked at Rex with great concern. "Do you think you'll be all right without medical care for a few more days? We don't want your arm healing crooked."

"Damned if I know," he mumbled. "The pain's still there, a dull ache unless I move it wrong. Then it shoots up my arm. Otherwise, I'm just sore. And I understand there's nothing much to do about these damned ribs except wrap them and try not to move. They only hurt when I breathe."

She brought him a coffee refill. "I'm sorry you've been injured, Rex. You know, maybe we should go back and take care of you."

"Go back?" Ramona and Dodge chorused together.

Rex gave Tory a grateful glance. "Sometimes this lady speaks with great insight. I wouldn't be opposed to it. I don't see anything that proves Sharkey found gold, just a few glittering rocks. Hell, that won't even pay my medical bills."

"See?" Tory said. "Rex needs help. And I . . . I'm sorry, but I agree with him about the gold. So far, we haven't seen anything positive enough to risk staying much longer."

"I can't believe you're saying this," Ramona implored. "You know it's here. Sharkey said so."

"No, I don't know it," Tory said, shaking her head. She sat down again and examined her own chipped nails and battered hands. "This is not what I expected, I'll admit. I guess I was thinking

207

of something more like buried treasure, as Yazzie said, with all of it piled in a hidden trunk or something. I didn't realize we'd have to work so hard for it. Maybe I'm just too soft, but I can't see going on much longer."

"She's right," Yazzie spoke up. "It looks hopeless to me. We haven't seen anything yet, and we should have. We could be here for years, chipping away at a stone wall. I vote with Rex and Sharkey's daughter. We ought to pack up and leave."

Dodge shifted and dropped his hands between widespread knees. "Maybe we could speed the process up if we blasted—"

"That's too dangerous!" Yazzie interjected quickly. "No blasting. There's no need for it, anyway."

"Why not? You brought some dynamite along, didn't you?" Dodge gave him a darkly accusing stare.

Yazzie narrowed his black eyes. "I don't know if there's any dynamite in the supplies or not. I didn't pack 'em."

"But you brought some in your own saddlebag, Yazzie," Dodge said firmly. "I saw it."

"Well, if so, it's not enough for anything. I don't want to have anything to do with blasting up here. Too dangerous."

"I assumed that's what it's for. We can't chip away all day and come up with nothing. We need some help speeding up the process."

Yazzie stood up, and his voice reached a voluminous pitch. "Hell, no! You don't know all the dangers, Dodge. I won't allow any blasting around here! Do you want the entire mine to cave in on us?"

"No, of course not. I realize it must be done carefully."

Swiftly, Yazzie set his coffee cup down near the fire. "I said no blasting. That's final." He wheeled around and stalked away into the darkness. "Somebody else might get hurt."

Everyone stared curiously at the blackness where their Indian guide disappeared.

"What the hell was that all about?" Rex grumbled.

"Why did that comment about somebody else getting hurt sound so ominous? Almost like a threat!" Ramona countered with a frightened glint in her dark eyes.

Dodge observed a distant tiny glow on the hillside and knew that Yazzie was lighting a cigar. "Sounds like Yazzie doesn't want to rush this job with a little blasting."

"Is he right?" Tory asked. "Is it really that dangerous to blast?"

"Sure, there's danger. You have to know what you're doing," Dodge said. "I've worked around it a little. And I know Yazzie has. He would know how to do it safely. But obviously, he has a major objection to using explosives at this site. I don't understand why, though."

"It's because he doesn't want us to find anything," Rex grumbled.

"Could be," Dodge mused, stroking his mustache thoughtfully.

Ramona gazed up the hill where Yazzie sat

smoking and rubbed her arms warily. "I wish I knew what was going on inside his head. He makes me nervous."

"Me, too," Tory agreed, tightlipped.

"Well, I say we should give it one more day," Dodge proposed. "Let's see what we can discover tomorrow. If nothing that glitters shows up, I'll consider returning. We do need to get Rex back to medical care. What do you think, Ramona?"

She nodded reluctantly. "Something inside me says we're pushing it. One more day and that's it."

"Rex? Tory? You two agree?"

Everyone nodded affirmatively, and they rose to get ready for bed.

"Uh, Dodge . . ." Ramona approached him almost shyly. But she didn't have to ask, for he understood.

"Sure, Ramona. Come on and stay with us," he said.

"Yes," Tory agreed with a smile, and fell into step with Ramona. "Like Dodge said earlier, we need to stick together."

"And trust one another," Ramona said with a grateful smile.

"In fact, everyone's so uneasy tonight," Dodge said softly, "I think I'll keep watch for a while. Just to make sure nothing unusual happens."

"I'd feel better if you did, Dodge," Ramona agreed. "The way things have been going lately, you can't tell what'll happen next."

Tory wasn't sure if she felt safer with Dodge on watch or with his arms wrapped around her all night. The thought that they needed a watchman was unnerving. A brief smile aimed at him revealed a twinge of regret that they wouldn't be lying together.

While Dodge made more coffee, the women quietly fixed their sleeping bags and slipped into them. It was a strange combination of circumstances that had drawn Sharkey's daughter and his lover together. What had started out as a natural antagonistic relationship between the two women had become a warm alliance.

"G'night, Tory. I've never been so tired," Ramona said. "I ache all over."

"Me, too. I've never worked so hard. Good night, Ramona."

From his vacant window ledge seat, Dodge watched over the small sleeping group. He sipped black coffee and leaned back against the sturdy wall. The old adobe bricks were still warm from the day's heat, and he absorbed it gratefully into the deep aching muscles of his back. Aching from only one day of the backbreaking labor of trying to find that elusive gold.

Dodge knew that some men did this for years. Some for a lifetime. Some, like Sharkey, never found it. Or when they did, it was too late. Meanwhile, Sharkey, like many of the others, lost everything and everyone who ever loved him. Was it worth the losses? Sharkey lost his wife and daughter. Oh, he always said if he ever struck it rich, they would get a large share. *If.* Of course, for him it never happened.

Dodge couldn't help wondering if that's where

he was heading. In the same direction as Sharkey, looking for something so elusive that it was impossible to find? And losing everything and everyone valuable along the way.

So far, there was nothing of value in his life. He'd carefully avoided any lasting relationships, had skipped out on a few situations that looked too promising, too long lasting. In his fleeting relationships with women, Dodge was known as a heartbreaker, but that didn't bother him. Until now.

His dark gaze swept over the two bedrolls that cocooned Ramona and Tory. He was proud of them. The two women had worked hard today and complained little. Now they both slept, completely trusting his ability to keep them safe from harm.

Trusting. That's the way Tory had come into his arms. Fully trusting him, completely willing to be his lover. What did she think would happen to them? Did she want it to continue, after they were through here?

Dodge sat bolt upright. *Did he?*

Right now, he couldn't answer that. He didn't know his own mind, his heart. What did his heart tell him? That she was in love with him? Her blue eyes confirmed it when she looked at him. But did he love her? He only knew that he would do anything in his power to keep her from being hurt.

He'd always prided himself that he'd never let any woman "catch" him, had never been "trapped" by affairs of the heart. He'd always admired Sharkey for living the kind of life he wanted to, without the impediment of a family, even the remote one in California. Now, though, he'd met a member of that small family and could see the years of pain and sadness and trouble Sharkey had caused by his irresponsibility.

Now the whole situation took on a different tone. He saw Sharkey as a selfish man, willing to sacrifice anything or anyone for his own personal interests. Interests that at one time had seemed the same as Dodge's. But now, he wasn't sure.

Oh, he still wanted to find the gold. But even for that he was unwilling to risk the lives of his friends. And nothing—nothing—was worth risking harm to Tory.

The sun seekers had a job to do tomorrow. And only one day to do it. After that, if they didn't strike it rich, all of them would go back to their own lives. Yazzie could go back to being the remote mountain man, renting mules to occasional mountain expeditions. Rex could continue his business successes, making a name for himself in the community. Ramona could be the quiet, intelligent college professor who documented Indian pictographs. Tory could return to L.A. and her retail business.

And himself? Teaching? Not much hope in that. Oh, he could continue being a drifter, a sun seeker. Not a very promising future. But it seemed to be all he knew.

As the pink shafts of dawn colored the sky above the eastern slopes of the Dragoon Mountains, Dodge was boiling coffee to a rich black brew. Yazzie joined him, and slowly the others began to wake.

They ate a meager breakfast of pan toast with honey and canned fruit before heading up to the mine, leaving the breakfast cleanup to Rex. He tackled the job willingly, for it gave him something to do. Even though his culinary efforts were one-handed and clumsy, he could make a contribution to the expedition.

Meanwhile, the others sweated and chipped away at the hard rock that concealed the elusive gold without the convenience of dynamite.

It was midmorning when Rex heard the shout that sent his heart racing.

"Gold! We found gold!"

Rex shaded his eyes toward the mine. Ramona waved excitedly at him. "Come on up and see it, Rex! Gold!"

He waved in return and hurriedly made his way up the hill, leading a pack mule as he had been instructed. The mule would haul the gold back. Oh, they were well prepared for the bonanza! Rex clucked and pulled on the mule's bridle. By the time they reached the mine, Rex was bathed in perspiration from the rising heat, and the mule was covered in a thin, foamy lather.

The heat only increased his disappointment at the meager gold. "This is *it?*"

They gathered around the little pile of rocks. It took a trained eye to determine that there was gold somewhere in that yellowish stone. And Rex's eye was far from trained. He—as well as the others— expected glittering hunks.

Yazzie's fiendish laughter cackled at Rex's reaction. "Yep, that's about it. Hardly worth a broken arm and cracked ribs, is it?"

Rex bent to handle the rocks and let the smaller pieces tumble through his fingers. "How do you know it's gold? It isn't gold colored. It's . . . it's ugly!"

Ramona knelt beside Rex and pointed out several discolored trails through the rocks. "There. And there. Dodge says it is. Even Yazzie admitted it was gold."

"Of course, we have to have it assayed to determine its value," Dodge explained.

Yazzie laughed again. "Right now we hardly have enough to pay for the supplies and food for this trip. Haven't gotten to your doctor bills yet, Rex."

"Come on, Yazzie," Dodge said. "This is just the beginning. It merely proves there's gold down there. All we have to do is get to work and find it."

"And haul it out," Ramona added soberly. She, too, was disappointed in the quantity. She could only hope the quality was high.

"Hell, all we have to do is chip this whole mountain away!" Yazzie exploded. "And all Rex has to do is wait for us to do the work. Then he can be rich."

Rex stood and faced Yazzie angrily. "Look, you jerk. Who do you suppose put the money up for this little exploration in the first place? I funded everything Sharkey did, and I'm still putting out the bucks! So far, all I've gotten in return is a broken arm, cracked ribs, and a lot of flack from the likes of you!"

Dodge stepped between them. "Take it easy, you two. Everybody's hot and tired today. Yazzie, he's right. Rex's investment comes off the top of our find."

"Not mine," Yazzie said stoutly.

"Let's work this out later," Ramona said. "Time's passing and it's getting hotter. Come on. We have work to do. It's our turn to go down, Yazzie. Let's go. They can load what we have here." She took Yazzie's arm and led him away from the confrontation.

"What's *wrong* with him?" Rex moaned as he opened one of the saddlebags for Dodge to load their small prize.

"Beats me. We're all tired, though. Two nights with practically no sleep have left me nearly exhausted. I guess Yazzie is in about the same shape."

"Why don't you go take a little siesta, Dodge?" Rex suggested.

Tory agreed. "Yes. This will be a good time while Yazzie and Ramona are down in the mine. After they've had their turn, we'll all take a lunch break."

"Actually, we should all take a little siesta until this heat has eased up a little," Rex said.

"Sounds too good to refuse," Dodge replied, shaking his head. "Okay. Just a couple of hours, though. Wake me." He left the mule for Tory to lead and accompanied Rex back down the small mountain to camp.

As Dodge heaved himself down in the shade of a large mesquite tree, he muttered, "Just a few hours

216

of shut-eye, Rex. Then I want to go after the mining again."

Rex prepared sandwiches for lunch, and afterward, everyone willingly agreed to take a break from the extreme heat. And still Dodge slept.

"He didn't even wake for lunch. He must have been exhausted," Ramona commented.

"I think so," Tory agreed, her gentle gaze caressing Dodge's long, lean frame stretched out under the tree. His Stetson shaded his face from the midday sun, and his hands lay relaxed below his belt buckle. His jean-clad legs sprawled apart, and Tory averted her eyes from his erotic position. She joined Ramona, sipping another cup of cool mountain-water tea and pulled out her fingernail clippers. "My hands are a mess and my nails will never be the same," she grumbled.

Ramona shifted restlessly and finally said, "You know, Tory, this will probably be my last chance to explore this area, especially if we head back tomorrow. How would you like to go with me to look for Indian pictographs?"

Tory considered the offer for a moment, then nodded. "Sure, Ramona. I'd love to go. It sounds interesting."

"I think it is. You never know what you'll find." Ramona's eyes lighted up with the prospect of introducing Tory to her special hobby. "Sharkey used to go with me. It wasn't his thing, but he did share some of my enthusiasm. And he helped with some interesting finds."

The two women started off together, hiking around the base of the pyramid-shaped mountain.

They found a few pot shards, broken remnants of the lives of ancient people who lived in the area hundreds of years ago. Spurred on by the interesting items, they started to climb toward the huge boulders on the far side of the pyramid.

"We're in luck, Tory. Here's something that's very old." Ramona picked up a smooth gray stone large enough to fill her palm and held it out. "The Indians used this against another stone to grind corn into meal. It's called a mano. The other part is a bowl-shaped stone and called a metate. It might be around here, too. Let's try to find it."

The women searched intently for the other part of the ancient kitchen utensil.

"Ramona, this looks like a small stairway, carved right into the rocks." Tory pointed to the shallow grooves pockmarking a sheer rock, leading upward. "Do we dare follow it?"

Ramona examined the area. "It leads up to that ledge. Are you afraid to climb up there?"

"After the climbing we've done in that gold mine?" Tory laughed. "Heavens no! This is a breeze. Let's go. I'm curious."

"At the very least, we'll have a great view of the whole valley from up there," Ramona said, and led the way. Carefully, she placed each foot into one carved step at a time. She grasped the steps above her for balance.

Tory watched the process and followed suit. When they reached the ledge, they found that it was a sort of staircase landing in the rocks. The stairs continued. So the women proceeded farther.

At the next landing, the path led to a low, narrow opening between two huge boulders.

"Shall we go on?" Tory eagerly went ahead. "This is fascinating, Ramona. Do you think ancient people actually lived here?"

"Oh, yes. It's a secure area, with an excellent view of the valley for protection. The warriors could sit here and see for miles. Imagine the Indian woman climbing this with a baby strapped to her back."

"I'll bet it made them think twice before they said, 'I'm going for a walk,'" Tory said, chuckling. "Or told the kids to go out and play." But her laughter dwindled as she squeezed through the doorway and turned the corner that led into a cavelike room. And stepped back in time.

She drew in a gasp and stared in silent amazement, awestruck by the ancient trappings surrounding her. The room looked as if it had just been abandoned by the near Stone Age family who lived in it.

Ramona stepped into the cave and stood beside Tory in silence. Finally, she murmured, "Oh, my God, I can't . . . believe it." Her voice cracked with emotion as she realized just exactly what they'd found. "This is a chance of a lifetime, Tory. It's an anthropologist's dream, like a real-life museum, left intact for the future generations to find. Usually, all we have to work with are bits and pieces. But it's all here together. I still can't believe it's never been found."

Tory began to walk around, curiously picking at a few things. "This must have been the kitchen," she said, an unconscious reverence in her voice. Charcoal sticks lay in a circular pile on the floor, and soot marred the ceiling above it. A huge clay pot, the bottom blackened from cooking, waited for the next meal. Though undecorated, the pot was complete and unchipped, a rare relic, even for museums.

Pots and bowls crudely decorated in black and white were stacked along one wall, waiting for the next meal.

"Everything for their daily lives is here," Ramona said, moving through the room. "The kitchen, with their crude utensils. They must have slept over here. Look, Tory, a turkey-feather blanket. I've seen a couple in museums, but most haven't survived—they're so fragile. And look at this, a wooden toy. And this . . ." Ramona went around the room, exclaiming over each discovery, explaining them all to Tory with pure, exhilarated enthusiasm.

Tory appreciated the rarity of the articles, but as Ramona continued to talk, she began to realize the academic significance of the find. Ramona would receive tremendous credit and accolades in her field of work. It would provide great opportunities. No wonder Ramona was so excited.

Ramona picked up a crudely woven basket. "This might be two hundred years old, Tory! I just can't believe it!"

"It's amazing to think they've lasted that long."

"Pueblo Bonito, in New Mexico, was like this. And Mesa Verde in Colorado. The cowboys who found them sold the items to other states, even other countries. But this one—Pyramid—will remain here, in tact, for extensive study. Future generations can learn firsthand how the people lived in those years. Oh, Tory!" Ramona turned around, tears of joy filling her eyes. "I'm so glad you were here with me today."

"So am I. Look!" Tory reached down. "Could this be an ancient spear—"

"Do not touch it!" a loud voice demanded.

Startled, both women looked up.

Yazzie stood by the doorway, a gun in his hand. "I said, don't touch a thing in here. It is a holy place."

"Why, Yazzie, surely you know we would never damage anything here. It's amazing, isn't it?" Tory took a step toward him.

"Hold it right there," he warned, and lifted the weapon a little higher. "Do not move from that spot."

"Yazzie . . ." Tory's eyes riveted to the gun. And the inlaid turquoise star on the barrel. *Dodge's gun—the one stolen from the trailer.*

CHAPTER THIRTEEN

"You!" Tory gasped. "You're the one!"

"Shut up!" Yazzie demanded, the gun in his hand wavering slightly.

Ramona took a step forward and muttered, "Put that stupid gun away, Yazzie. We aren't—"

"Don't make a move! Stand still, Ramona!"

Instinctively, Tory reached for Ramona's arm. "Do as he says, Ramona. I'm afraid he means business."

"Huh? Yazzie?"

Tory looked accusingly at the man with the gun. "You broke into my motel room, didn't you? And when you didn't find the map, you broke into Sharkey's old trailer where Dodge was living."

"He did *what?*" Ramona looked at Tory as if she had lost her mind.

"We didn't mention the break-ins," Tory explained. "Mainly because we didn't want to alarm anyone. Plus we didn't know who did it and wanted to see if the person would show his hand. And sure enough"—she narrowed her eyes at Yazzie—"you did. You scum! You took Dodge's gun! Did you also have anything to do with Rex's fall?"

222

"You can't prove anything."

"Oh, yes, I can. Dodge's gun has a mark. The star on the barrel. I remember it. Anyway, it's registered. And numbers don't lie."

"No, but I do," Yazzie sneered. "And you poor, dear ladies won't live to tell anybody otherwise."

"You can't shoot us! Dodge and Rex will hear gunshots and know who did it." Tory folded her arms defiantly. Her brave facade was just a masquerade, but with her arms clinched tightly, no one could see her hands shaking.

"Not if I shoot them first."

"Shoot them?" Ramona gasped. "But why? What is this all about, Yazzie?"

He began pulling a thin rope from his hip pocket. "I have to keep them from finding this treasure. This is holy ground, the place where spirits live. It is unfortunate that you two found it. Now you must die."

"That's ridiculous, Yazzie," Tory objected. "Yes, this place is a treasure, but it's a national treasure that belongs to everyone. It's a wonderful discovery."

"It must never be discovered again. The spirits must be allowed to rest here alone." He began walking slowly toward them.

"That's crazy!" Tory said. "We aren't going to destroy it—"

This time Ramona hushed Tory with a squeeze of her arm. "Don't anger him anymore, Tory. This is what he's been after all along. Not necessarily the gold, but the Indian treasures here. The part about the spirits is folly. I don't believe that at all.

You want to sell these artifacts, don't you, Yaz-zie?"

Yazzie's mouth spread into a sinister grin. "The cowboys discovered that these old things are worth a fortune on the foreign and black markets. They're worth nothing here. But I will sell them only when I'm ready. And I will not share the profits with four. I discovered them, and I will be the one to gain."

"Then you knew that Sharkey had found this place, too. You followed him here. You—"

"Sharkey got in the way!" Yazzie said angrily. "He was stupid, only caring about the gold. There isn't enough gold here to buy a broken-down mule! But these"—he waved the gun in an arc—"these are centuries-old artifacts that are worth thousands. Many thousands!"

Ramona's face paled and became drawn as the awful realization settled in. "You—oh, God, you killed him!"

In one catlike motion, she lunged for Yazzie. He tried to avoid her and stepped back quickly, stumbling in the process. He landed on the floor, in a seated position, looking up at Ramona. With both hands, he raised the gun to aim directly at her stomach and pulled back the hammer.

"Don't come any closer, or I'll shoot you now," he commanded coldly.

Frantic, Tory grabbed her friend in a bear hug from behind and held as tightly as she could.

Ramona was hysterical, sobbing and screaming, "*You* killed him! *You* killed him! How could you do that to your friend? I hate you!"

Tory had no time to react to the news, for she could only think that she had to keep Ramona from getting shot by the crazed Yazzie. She held on as tightly as she ever had, using strength drawn from an inner power she didn't know existed. But she held on. "Ramona, please, don't! You have to keep your head right now. Don't make it harder on me."

Yazzie was on his feet in an instant. He tossed one length of rope to Tory and barked, "Use one end and tie her up. Make it tight, because I'm going to check it. Hands behind her back. Leave the other end for her ankles. Don't try any tricks."

Tory began clumsily wrapping the hemp rope around Ramona's wrists. By now, Ramona had stopped struggling. She was limp and weak as tears streamed down her face. Tears of hatred and of sorrow.

When Tory finished her unpleasant job, Ramona stood erect and faced her lover's killer with a defiant gleam in her dark eyes. "You'll get yours, you bastard," she muttered. "I'll see to it! You'll never get away with this."

He laughed defiantly. "Not from you, Ramona. No one will see or hear from you again. The facts will die with you. Now, sit over there against the wall." He shoved her and she fell clumsily to the spot he indicated. To Tory, he barked, "Tie her feet with the other end of that rope."

Tory did as she was told. There was nothing else to do with a cocked gun pointed at them.

"Now, you turn around," he said gruffly. "Hands behind your back."

She did and with some relief heard the thirty-eight's hammer released. Yazzie tied her hands so tightly that she could feel her fingers tingling even before he finished. Then he pushed her down and tied her feet.

"When they find you two, you'll look like that skeleton we left in the wash halfway down the mountain." He laughed evilly as he backed out of the room. "You'll never get out of here, so don't even try."

Tory lay very still, hoping, praying he would leave them unharmed for now. She could hear certain strange noises, but when all was quiet, she whispered to Ramona, "What was he doing?"

"Beats me. I think he's gone."

They waited a while longer, but as soon as they were sure he was gone, they began struggling to release their bonds.

After a few minutes, Ramona stopped struggling. "Now, wait a minute. This is not working. We can't untie them, obviously, so they have to be cut or burned or broken in some way."

"Well, just whip out your trusty pocket knife and cut them," Tory muttered dryly.

"I usually do carry a pocket knife, so don't laugh."

"Then get it! I'm not laughing."

"It's in my saddlebag at camp."

Tory groaned. "Good place. At least it's safe."

"Maybe there's something around here we can use," Ramona mused, rolling to her side so she could look around the room.

"Even I know the Indians didn't have pocket knives in those days."

"No, but they did have spears. You almost picked one up."

"Ramona, dear, I'm sure that after two hundred years or so, that spear has lost its edge."

"Well, there must be something that will clip these ropes."

"Clip? Yeah, clip!" Tory said with mounting excitement. "Clippers! I've got some fingernail clippers in my jeans pocket. I had to trim another broken fingernail just before we left, and I stuffed the clippers into my pocket. Now, if I could only reach it . . ."

"Roll over here. I'll see if I can get it out," Ramona said quietly. "I'll back up to you, and you scoot around until my hand can reach into your pocket."

It took them almost half an hour of wriggling and wrenching, but the clippers were finally captured and the ropes were cut, bit by tiny bit. Finally, when the last string was snipped, they both expelled a whoop of joy and, in a spontaneous moment, hugged each other. Then they dashed for the narrow exit.

"Dammit! He blocked it!" Tory grasped futilely at the huge stone Yazzie had wedged between the two boulders that formed the small entrance to the cave.

"So that's what he was doing! I could hear him grunting but couldn't imagine what he was doing. Maybe we can move it." Ramona pounded impotently on the stone with both knotted fists. "Oh, how I hate that man! We can't let him continue with his evil deeds. We just can't!"

Unwilling to accept defeat, they pushed and shoved and heaved at the immovable force until they slumped on the floor in exhaustion.

"Now what?" Tory moaned. "We have to warn Dodge and Rex. If not, it'll be disastrous for all of us."

"Maybe there's another way out of here." Ramona hopped to her feet.

"I never thought of that." Tory followed closely behind her.

Ramona pointed out a sliver of light between several rocks. "I'm sure this served as a window for the ancient ones who lived here."

Tory squinted closely at the window, which was located high above their heads. "If I could somehow boost you up there, Ramona, do you think you could slip through?"

Ramona gazed skeptically at the slit. "No way. I'm not *that* thin. But we can yell and try to attract attention."

Eagerly, they yelled at Dodge and Rex until they were hoarse, but no one answered their calls. And they weren't sure anyone even heard them. In frustration, they explored the room again.

Ramona ran her large hands along the walls. "See if you can find any breaks or hidden entrances."

Suddenly, Tory felt the stone beneath her fingers shift. Excitedly, she cried out. "Look, Ramona! A hole!"

They discovered a narrow tunnel, a passageway

to another area. Eagerly, on hands and knees, they followed it. At the end was another room, this one much smaller and completely empty. There was no exit there.

"What was this room used for, Ramona? It looks strange to be so empty when the other one is so full of interesting items."

"Yes," Ramona said as she walked around the small area, rubbing the walls with curious finger-tips. "It's depleted." She stopped short and looked up at Tory. "Depleted . . . Oh, God, Tory. That's it! Yazzie has already stripped this one and sold some artifacts. It makes me sick to think of it."

"I'll bet he loads them on the mules and hauls them out of the mountains," Tory said. "That might explain what he's been doing every night when he goes off by himself. Loading his saddle-bags with artifacts."

"Yes, that's it! I'm sure of it! And he probably intends to lock us in here so he can unload that other room. Nobody would ever find us here."

"Especially if he dynamited the hallway leading to this room."

"Dynamite? Then he has some explosives, after all."

Tory nodded. "Dodge and I saw him load something on his mule before we left his cabin. Then Dodge figured out it was dynamite to blast for the gold."

"Well, obviously it wasn't for the gold mine. In fact, the best I can figure it, this cave backs up to the mine on the other side of the mountain. Their

229

rear walls probably meet. So if we used dynamite in the mine, we'd risk tearing this place apart. That's why Yazzie didn't want Dodge using it."

"Of course! Oh, he is a devil, that Yazzie! Is there no way out of here, Ramona? We've got to warn Dodge!" Tory swallowed hard and discovered she was near tears. They'd really gotten themselves into a terribly dangerous mess. And she was scared—more scared than she'd ever been. Not only was her own life in jeopardy, but those of her friends. And Dodge. What could happen to him frightened her more than anything. She couldn't stand the thought of Dodge getting hurt. Or of losing him now.

"It looks like a dead end," Ramona said, turning back to the wall and pressing and scraping with her fingers. A loose stone came off into her hand, and she smashed it in frustration against the wall.

The stone broke into several pieces and fell to the floor, as did several chunks of the wall. Ramona stared, then picked up another stone and banged it against the same spot. Breathing rapidly, she picked up another. And another.

"Ramona, I know you're upset, but this won't help," Tory said. "Anyway, you might hurt your hand . . ."

"Tory!" Ramona ran her hand along a discolored strip on the rock wall. "Tory, look at this!"

"Ramona, please stop before you—"

"Do you see that I've uncovered a vein of placer gold?"

"What?"

Ramona turned an excited face to Tory. "This is it! This is what Sharkey sent us after! The gold is here!"

Tory peered dubiously at the discolored vein. It was hard to see in the cave's semidarkness, and this wasn't exactly what she had in mind for the big gold discovery. However, if Ramona said this was gold, she guessed it was. "Fat lot of good a gold discovery does us now. Look what a mess we're in!"

Ramona sighed. "You're right. We have to get out of here and warn the others."

In desperation, they went back to the tiny window and yelled some more. Finally, with backs pressed against the wall, they sat on the cold rock floor.

"It's getting dark," Tory murmured sadly.

"Yeah."

"Damn! I wish I knew what Yazzie was doing. What's happening down there?"

Sudden gunshots penetrated the heavy silence. Two of them. Then more silence.

Tory grabbed Ramona's hand and fought back tears. She'd never been so afraid in all her life. Afraid for the man she loved. She squeezed her eyes shut and prayed silently. It just couldn't be Dodge. But her imagination went berserk and she saw Dodge writhing in the dust, clutching his chest. Her eyes flew open. "Oh, my God, Ramona. I can't stand this!"

"Tory, listen to me," Ramona began gently. "If . . . if Rex and Dodge are, uh, hurt, Yazzie will be back to take care of us. We have to be ready."

"Ready? What do you mean? I—I couldn't stand it if Dodge were hurt. Oh, Ramona, I love—"

"Listen to me, Tory." Ramona's voice was sharp and commanding. "We can't just sit here and let Yazzie decide our fate. We have to be prepared to defend ourselves."

"Defend? How? There's nothing here."

"I'll show you . . ." Ramona scrambled into the artifact room and Tory followed.

CHAPTER FOURTEEN

Tory and Ramona awaited their evil captor, armed to the teeth with Stone Age weapons, the only things available to the lost-in-time room.

"They might not be very sharp, but remember, Tory, we'll have the element of surprise."

"I'm so nervous, Ramona, I'm shaking all over. I'm not sure I can do this. What if—"

"Don't entertain thoughts of defeat. Imagine success. Picture us wrestling Yazzie to the floor and me holding a gun on him while you tie him up. We can do it! Didn't you ever watch western movies when you were a kid?"

Tory perked up. "I saw *Butch Cassidy and the Sundance Kid.* But they lost in the end . . ."

Ramona groaned softly. "Forget that one. Think about John Wayne and . . . and Harrison Ford. We're going to escape by our wits, just like they did in *Temple of Doom!* Now, listen carefully. Yazzie has to bend over to enter this small doorway. That's when we jump him, while he's off balance. It's our only chance. The minute he appears through those rocks, you lunge for his back and hang on for dear life. That'll give me time to knock his gun away. We can do it, Tory. We have to."

"I've never done anything like this before, Ramona." Tory spoke with hesitancy.

"That's because your life has never been threatened. Just stay calm and it'll work."

"But, what if—"

Ramona raised a warning finger to her lips. "Shh, I hear someone coming."

The two women raised their weapons, poised for battle. The sight was almost ludicrous, but Tory knew their lives could depend on their ability to get the upper hand over Yazzie.

The noise outside the cave's entrance increased, then they heard a man's groan. Someone was definitely trying to come into their little prison. It was time for the showdown, and Tory gripped her ancient club with sweaty palms.

They held their breath in the tomblike silence until a familiar baritone voice roared on the other side of the rocks.

"Tory! Tory? Ramona? Are you in there? Are you okay?"

The shocking—wonderful—sound of Dodge outside the cave was met with wild jubilation. The women dropped their crude weapons and raced to the doorway, both shouting and cheering at the same time. "Yes! *Yes!* We're all right, Dodge! Are you?" They pushed from the inside while Dodge shoved from the outside until the boulder shifted enough to admit him.

Tory flung herself into Dodge's arms. She

needed to feel him warm and solid inside her embrace.

Dodge lifted her off the ground, his arms wrapped securely around her. He repeatedly murmured, "Oh, God . . . Oh, God! Tory . . . Tory!"

Finally, they tore apart and included Ramona in a clumsy, three-way embrace. In their emotional release, the women were laughing and crying and nearly hysterical with happiness and relief. Then Dodge hugged Tory again and kissed her briefly on the lips.

Ramona watched unembarrassed with a grateful smile on her face. Their love was obvious but so beautiful, and her heart swelled with joy that something good had come from all the tragedy surrounding Sharkey's death.

Tory refused to completely release Dodge and stood next to him with her arm curled around his ribcage. It was a good, secure feeling to know they were both safe in each other's arms. With Dodge close, she remembered to ask about the others. "Where is Yazzie? And Rex? Is anybody hurt? Tell us what happened."

Dodge shook his big shaggy head. "Everybody's fine. Except for Yazzie."

"Did you shoot him?" Ramona asked, a vicious gleam in her dark eyes. Her absolute hatred for Yazzie was obvious. "He deserves the worst."

"He's injured slightly, Ramona. In the shoulder."

"Where is he now?" Tory asked.

"In jail."

"Jail? Already?" She gave him a curious, unbelieving look. "How? Did the sheriff's patrol arrive already?"

"Nope. We did it. The self-appointed sheriff of Pyramid and his self-appointed deputy." Dodge patted his chest mockingly. "The town jail still works, so we locked Yazzie inside one of the cells. Deputy Fierro is the official jailer until we head back down the mountain."

"In jail?" Tory repeated, laughing with hysterical relief. "How did you lock the door?"

Dodge shrugged his broad shoulders. "The walls are solid and iron bars block the windows. We just wired the locks together. Of course, the deputy is there, keeping watch."

"Rex?" Ramona smiled, in spite of herself. "I can't believe it."

"He's in his element." Dodge grinned. "You should see him perched on the jail steps with a six-shooter in his one good hand!"

They all shared a good chuckle as Dodge finished the story. Then he gazed around the room for the first time. "What have you two found here? Looks like Indian ruins."

"Yes," Ramona said, smiling proudly. "It's grand, isn't it?" She showed him around the room, briefly explaining a few of the rare items. "Of course, Yazzie knew the value of all this. That's why he wanted us out of the picture. So he could sell it off for profit. His exclusive profit."

"He wanted more than the gold. He wanted it all," Dodge said bitterly.

Ramona nodded. Her voice grew hoarse as she

continued. "We also found out that Yazzie killed Sharkey."

"I'll be damned," Dodge muttered through his teeth. "If I'd known that, I might have aimed lower than his shoulder. The bastard! All for this! Sharkey lost his life for this—and we lost Sharkey!" He tore from Tory's grasp and stalked around the room, venting his anger in loud expletives.

That's when she noticed the blood on his jeans, just above his left knee. "Dodge! What's that?"

He shrugged off her concern. "It's just a nick."

"Yazzie shot you?" Her voice rose shrilly.

"I told you, it's nothing. Just a graze."

She folded her arms. "What happened?"

"He shot at me. I shot back."

Tory glared at him. "I thought he had your gun?"

"I bought another before we left town."

"Why?"

"You can't travel in this country without some sort of weapon. There're snakes and mountain lions and . . . you never know what! Thank God I had it."

She glared at him for a moment longer, then sighed. Where would they all be right now if Dodge hadn't been able to defend himself? If he hadn't been alert and able to use a gun? It was just like in the old wild West days when the six-shooter was the law of the land. She didn't like it, but she had to admit its value right now. "I guess so."

"How did you find us here, Dodge?" Ramona asked.

"Yazzie said something about you being locked in a cave. I just started searching for it. The most likely place seemed to be up around these rocks. Come on. It'll be dark soon and I think we'd better go see how the deputy is doing with his prisoner."

"We have something else to show you, Dodge," Ramona said, leading the way to the hidden room. "Sharkey's gold."

They crawled through the narrow passageway, and Dodge examined the discolored vein in the wall. "Well, I'll be damned. A treasure to cherish." He beamed at them, his dark eyes aglow. "Ole' Sharkey knew what he was talking about, after all."

Around the campfire that night, they discussed everything fully with Rex. The four of them were partners, shareholders in a bizarre and dangerous search for gold. And now, for the first time since the journey began, the four looked at each other with complete trust.

Rex surprised them by pulling out a bottle of chardonnay. "I'd say this occasion deserves a little celebration," he said, pouring the wine into styrofoam cups and distributing them.

"Thanks, Rex." Ramona accepted her cup. "How thoughtful of you."

"My pleasure," he said, handing the next one to Tory.

She smiled. "Ever the gentleman, even in the wilderness and with your arm hurt."

"Someone has to keep us from becoming complete barbarians," he answered, winking. He handed Dodge a cup. "Here you go, partner. No more doubts about who our real friends are."

"You bet," Dodge agreed. Lifting his cup high, he said, "I'd like to propose a toast. To Sharkey's real friends, the remaining sun seekers who are gathered tonight around this campfire."

"To the sun seekers," they all chorused, touching cups.

"Now," Dodge sighed, settling down on a crude log bench, "what we have to decide is what to do about the gold."

"It's what we came after," Rex said. "Why don't we take an extra day or so and load it up."

"Well, it won't be quite that easy," Dodge told him. "In fact, it'll be real tough hauling it down from that cave."

"I'm willing, if the rest of you are," Ramona said. "How do you feel, Rex? Do you think you could wait a few more days before getting medical care?"

"It isn't so bad that I couldn't wait a little longer." He grinned devilishly. "Anyway, with the golden opportunity at hand, how could I refuse?"

Tory sat beside Dodge. "What about Yazzie's injury? Can he wait?"

"I think he'll be okay, especially if we douse his wound with plenty of antiseptic," Dodge said. "I don't think a day or two will hurt him."

"Then let's try," Tory responded with a little smile.

"Everybody in agreement?" Dodge asked.

They nodded, their eager faces glowing in the firelight.

"All right, sun seekers"—Dodge stood up— "we're going for it!"

Everyone shook hands and clapped each other on the back and ended up hugging each other.

"It'll be a long, hard day tomorrow. We'd better hit the sack," Dodge advised.

Ramona touched his arm. "Rex and I will sleep here, close to the fire. You two go on over there by yourselves."

Dodge smiled gratefully. "I think you'll be safe now, with Yazzie in jail." Wrapping an arm around Tory, they ambled over to the makeshift room they had cleared for themselves the first night they arrived. For the first time, they were alone. Sort of.

As they snuggled down into the sleeping bag together, Dodge pulled Tory to him with a fierceness he couldn't hide. Kissing her long and hard, he finally lifted his face to murmur, "I can't believe I almost lost you today."

"I had the same feelings, Dodge. It was so scary to be locked up there and hear gunshots. And not know what happened."

"I was frantic to find you, Tory."

"Dodge, did it matter that much to you?"

He framed her face and kissed it all over. "You matter that much to me. More than any woman ever has. More than anything."

"Oh, Dodge . . ." She succumbed to the delight of being in his arms.

And he held her close to his lean, hard body and allowed their natural responses to take over, capturing them both. Desire slipped in, creating a beautiful magic between them, leading them to love. Love . . . implied and sensitive. Love . . . seeking and touching. Love . . . encircling and encompassing and . . . overwhelming.

She lay very still beside him, her nude body seeking his warmth. He radiated heated energy, a relentless source of power and strength. She arched to pair with him, to taunt him with her smooth skin. She rubbed her hard-tipped breasts against his chest and heard his quick intake of air. It was a satisfying sound, and she grew bolder, undulating and using her body to caress his.

She felt his hand between them, stroking her belly, spreading his fingers lower. Instinctively, she moved back to allow him more freedom, while at the same time going crazy with his erotic touches. Then he slid his hand between her legs and touched her sweet inner core.

He muffled her soft moan with a kiss and kept his lips pressed to hers while his hand continued to work wonders with her moist, pliant body.

They were quiet, oh, so quiet, in their little love cocoon, and Tory didn't know when she'd known such torture. For fear of alerting the others to their intimacy, she couldn't say anything, couldn't tell him how good he made her feel, how she loved his touch. She had to silently endure when she wanted to cry out with joy.

She imagined them floating in sensuous silence through cottonlike clouds that muffled all sound. They couldn't speak, couldn't hear. Only touch could speak for them. And they covered each other with gentle touches, with lips that kissed se-

241

cret places, but didn't speak of love. The love codes came through their touches. But the message they communicated was loud and clear.

I love you . . . love you, she willed her body to say. And she hoped his was answering the same.

Possessively, protectively, Dodge hauled himself over her and held her in his arms . . . safe and secure. And kissed her again and again. When she thought she couldn't endure another moment, he slid between her thighs and they blended into one. With thunderous, earthshaking thrusts, they spiraled upward to sensations of the highest order, and Tory wanted to scream—wanted to shout about the glory of knowing and loving together. But she was silent.

Yet she knew she had never been so filled with love . . .

They took an extra day to mine the small placer vein. No one could be sure about its value until it was assayed, but it was definitely gold. Sharkey's gold. And they decided to take as much as they could and still leave the Indian ruins intact.

As Dodge had predicted, it was quite a difficult job hauling the diggings down from the cliff cave. But the four of them managed. When sunset colored the surrounding mountains deep purple that evening, they had loaded the saddlebags as full as possible.

By the fireside that night, the four partners agreed it was time to leave.

* * *

At the next dawn, the sun seekers gathered on the side of the triangular hill overlooking the lost city of Pyramid. Streaks of pink and pale orange heralded a glorious sunrise, another sun-filled day. In the distance loomed the ripple of mountains they must cross before returning to civilization. Their journey was not yet ended.

But now they had to finish the unpleasant task that brought them there.

The group was serious. Rex cradled his injured arm against his chest. Dodge held the brightly painted Indian pot. For the first time, he looked uncomfortable holding the container. Ramona was tight-lipped and somber, staring with sad dark eyes at the horizon. Tory stood back a little, the years of hating a father she never knew finally erased from her expression.

Dodge stumbled over his words. "I, uh, I'm not sure how to do this. I've never conducted a funeral before."

"Well, neither have we," Rex assured him. "Just say a little something."

"Like a eulogy?" he asked dubiously.

"Like a message," Ramona said softly. "To him."

"Oh." Dodge looked around at the others, then took a step forward. "Well . . . hey, Sharkey, if you're listening, I want to thank you. For introducing me to this beautiful territory and for the privilege of knowing you. For the friends around us. For your little girl, Tory." His voice grew thick and raspy. "For giving us the chance to be sun seekers with you for a brief time. And for, uh, the touch of gold we have with us."

Rex stepped forward. "You were right all along, Sharkey. Thanks to you, we're all going to make it. Thanks for the gold."

Tears coursed down Ramona's cheeks. "Thanks for everything, Sharkey . . . the laughter, the fun . . . and the love."

Tory unashamedly wiped away a tear, but her eyes filled with tears again and spilled over her cheeks as Dodge cracked the colorful Indian pot on a rock. The contents spilled over the rocks and caught the wind and drifted over Pyramid.

Tory knew that because of this trip, and because of Sharkey Carsen, her life would be forever changed. She certainly thought of her father differently now, and that was better than carrying hatred around for the rest of her life. She gazed at Dodge Callahan's broad shoulders and knew he would make the biggest difference of all. Without him, what would her life be? How empty.

And suddenly, she knew she couldn't bear leaving Dodge. She wanted to be with him, to follow him, to love him the rest of her life.

She slipped her hand into his and squeezed. "You gave him a very nice tribute, Dodge."

He squeezed her hand back and brought it up to his lips for a lingering kiss. Hand in hand, they followed Ramona and Rex down the mountain. Tory was filled with complete contentment. She would be forever grateful to Sharkey for sending her to Dodge so they could meet. And love.

The two men arranged the injured Yazzie on one

of the mules. His shoulder and one arm were wrapped rather crudely, and one foot was tied to the stirrup. If he should attempt escape, he would be dangling by one foot.

"I know this sounds strange coming from me, but I'm almost sorry to leave," Tory said as they lined up the mules for the long trek back.

Ramona's gaze swept across the ghost town. "Maybe we can return someday."

"Not me," Rex said with a groan as he swung a leg over his mule.

"Nope," Dodge muttered, "I don't think we'll ever ride this way again." He paused for one last look over the tiny valley, then motioned with one arm. "Let's head 'em out."

They rode silently, Dodge in the lead, followed by Yazzie, then Rex. Tory and Ramona plodded behind, sharing control of the three pack animals loaded with their gold. They had all been changed by the journey into the Dragoons. They were linked by a bond of shared secrets and struggles for life. From these, relationships had been sealed.

And perhaps . . . they were a little wealthier.

CHAPTER FIFTEEN

On the afternoon they arrived back in Tombstone, it poured, transforming the desert into a cool, fragrant haven. They had pushed themselves to return in less than three days, considering they were accompanied by two injured men.

Ramona transported Rex to the nearest hospital and took their precious gold treasure to the assayer's office. Dodge and Tory delivered Yazzie to the authorities, filed their complaints ranging from assault with a deadly weapon to Sharkey's murder, and made their statements to the district attorney. Then they headed for the trailer, mentally and physically exhausted—and soaking wet.

"This isn't a rain," Tory complained as they watched the moisture sheet the Blazer's windshield. "It's a torrent, a cloudburst, a gully washer!"

"A squall, a real toad strangler," Dodge added, pulling to a stop in the driveway. "But that's the way we get our moisture around here. It's all or nothing."

"That's the way of many things in life, I guess," Tory said sadly, thinking that "all or nothing" related to more than she cared to admit. Like her relationship with Dodge. What would happen now?

"I'll go unlock the door," he said, getting his key out. "And you follow."

"How gallant of you, sir, now that I'm already soaked to the bone."

"Can't help it. Justice must be served. I must admit, I'll rest better knowing Yazzie is behind bars in a real jail, not a hundred-year-old ruin."

"I'll bet Yazzie is already dry and has had supper by now."

"But he can't run out and play in the rain if he wants to. And we can."

She eyed him closely. "I do not want to run out and play in the rain. I'm wet and tired. And anyway, this rain's cold. I want to take a shower and get warm."

"Hmm, I should be able to manage that," he assured her with a devilish smile.

She nodded and smiled graciously. "And I'm hungry!"

"Hungry, huh? Why, I think we may have a few cans of dried beef or chicken chunks left."

"No! No! Please, not canned chicken chunks!" she exclaimed, beating him on the shoulder with a teasing fist. "And if I never—ever—see another stringy slab of dried beef, I'll be content! Now, go! And have my shower running when I get there!"

"Ah, yes, your highness!" Dodge said laughingly, and dashed through the rain.

Tory followed closely, and soon they were scrubbing each other's backs in a hot shower. And still later, sipping hot tea and eating Ritz crackers and peanut butter in bed. In the nude.

"So this is your idea of an instant meal?" She teased and poked a peanut-buttered cracker into his mouth for a bite. Then she popped the remaining cracker into her own mouth.

He chewed and rolled his eyes as if it were the best meal in the world. "Why not? Peanut butter has held me together, body and soul, through all my bachelor years. It's life sustaining. Great on toast and English muffins and even, may my Jewish uncle forgive me, on bagels. Great on bagels, in fact! And for those watching their lovely waistlines"—he paused to caress her slender bare arm—"spread it on celery. It does everything!"

"Everything?" She gasped just before his lips claimed hers in a demanding, long kiss.

"Ah, yes, my favorite fragrance—peanut butter breath!" And he kissed her again to prove he wasn't lying.

"Hmm, everything . . ." she murmured happily. "Just like you, Dodge. You do everything for me." She turned her face up to his as they scooted down between the cracker box and peanut butter jar.

Gray clouds shrouded the small trailer, giving its occupants the illusion of darkness. And they sought comfort from each other.

His lean tanned body was a brown shadow in the bed beside her, and she ran her hand over every masculine inch, luxuriating in the feel of him. She felt the contours of his face, stroking his cheeks and nose. Her tongue edged his lips, teasing and tasting. "Hmm," she murmured softly, letting her hands move over the muscles of his chest.

Her head moved over his chest, her tongue tasting the beadlike nipples and making a hot, moist trail down his middle. She followed the tanned hair trail, dipping her tongue into his navel, then caressing his hips with curious hands. Daring, probing fingers slid over him, down to his thighs, then up again. Tormenting and teasing, the passion in her body was expressed by her hands as she showed him how much she wanted him.

Lightning streaked across the sky, blazing jagged electrical currents from the storm-darkened clouds to the earth, sending flashes of light on the enraptured couple in the small trailer.

Tory watched Dodge's body react to her every touch and felt her own blazing response to his closeness. She knew that she loved him. She wanted him inside her, branding her with his own fire, giving her all his strength. And she wanted him now and always.

Instinctively, as she continued spreading her fingers over him, she felt this would be the last time they made love. She would make it good. Better than good—fantastic, bells ringing, wonderful, greater than great! She would make him want her love forever. She would love him like he'd never been loved. It was quite a challenge—but the thought of leaving Dodge after knowing him like this was torturous.

Thunderous explosions rumbled continually overhead, sounding like a never-ending freight train. The noise was so abrupt and ominous that instinctively she ducked her head as if the roof were about to fall in on them.

Laughingly, he pushed her down on the bed and began to kiss her all over. "Don't worry, my sweet little fancy pants. I'll take care of you." He engulfed both breasts with his large hands and kissed each one tenderly, finally burying his face in their softness.

"It sounded so close," she said.

"It was close," he answered, his words muffled against her silky skin.

"But what if the roof caves in?"

"Then we go together. But in ecstasy!" He laughed raucously and kissed her navel and the flat stomach between her hip bones.

"Wait!" She protested suddenly as his kisses came closer to the crest of her femininity. "I was going to do that!"

He raised his head. "This?"

"Well, no, I wanted to kiss you!" She giggled embarrassedly as he molded his body to hers and slithered up until their lips were close to matching.

"Do what to me?"

"Love you. Until you couldn't stand it without me."

"I already can't."

"No, I mean, *really!*"

"I'm crazy for you, *really!*" He kissed her and, at the same time, rolled her over on top of him. "Now . . . that better?"

Tory grinned and wriggled over her victim. "Yes, that's better." She felt his hard arousal firmly assailing and probing, searching for her warmth. And she wanted him inside her. But he would have to wait. *Until he was crazy for her!*

She kissed him all over, making love to him with all of her body as he had done to her. Her lips tasted him, her tongue drew moist circles over his aroused body until he begged for her. And she knew she had him! She had accomplished what she'd set out to do—drive him crazy for her. It was a heady feeling, this power she held over the big, brawny Dodge Callahan.

The wind howled around the corners and found tiny cracks in the trailer to whistle through, making a high, wailing noise that accompanied the lower, more ominous sounds.

"Tory, Tory . . ." he moaned softly, "come to me."

She wasn't sure who was crazy for whom in the end. She wanted to feel his power, wanted him inside her more than she ever had before. This time her desperation was born of love and fueled by fear. A deep, abiding love for a man who was entirely different from her and fear that she was losing him.

Her knees straddled his hips, and she pressed herself to him, rocking to adjust to the power she sought. He moved beneath her hands, writhing and moaning as her warmth enfolded him.

The wild wind stalked outside the windows, shaking them as if trying to enter, to interrupt the happenings inside the trailer. In futility, the wind grabbed the small metal building and shook it hard.

She gasped and shuddered as the force of his

throbbing manhood filled her completely. Arching her back, she clasped herself tightly around him, seeking the satisfaction only he could give.

"Slowly," he instructed hoarsely, his hands guiding her undulating hips. "Take it easy, ea–sy . . ."

Moving ever so gently above him, she obeyed. Weaving and sliding, making sure they stayed together, yet allowing the heat to build naturally between them.

His chest heaved as he tried to control his raging passion, tried to control them both. Tiny beads of perspiration glistened on his curly hair. "Oh, yes, my sweet little fancy pants . . ."

She pushed herself upright and dug her fingers into his chest. Joy erupted within her, and she stifled a cry as she began to move out of control, faster and faster, rotating, swaying, circling.

He met her wild passion by thrusting upward, hard, again and again. She rode with him, clinging and grasping, never letting go, never stopping, all the way to the summit.

Lightening flickered and their bodies glowed with a love sheen.

In an overwhelming burst of delight, they shuddered together and rose in a wild frenzy that left them both weak and trembling. When they were still at last, she slumped over him, letting her heart beat against his.

In time, their breathing became more normal and their heartbeats slowed. Gently, he cradled her in his arms. "Are you warm now?"

She snuggled against him. "Hmm. The warmest."

His lips brushed her cheek. "God, you make me crazy, Tory."

"Yes." She smiled. "You, too."

The rain plunked rhythmically on the trailer's tin roof, lulling its occupants to sleep. And they slept around the clock, dreaming of this ecstasy in each other's arms lasting forever.

But when they awoke the next day, they knew it couldn't last forever. It was a feeling in the air, more than anything said.

Dodge woke first and was fixing coffee when Tory staggered in, wearing a man's flannel shirt she found in the closet.

"Do you mind?" She lifted one arm.

He shook his head. "It isn't mine. Sharkey's."

"Oh." She looked at the blue plaid curiously. "Well, then, I suppose it's okay. From what I've learned about my father, he seemed like the sort of man to give you the shirt off his back."

"Oh, yes, he was," Dodge said smiling, and poured them both a cup of coffee.

Her face was tight and serious. "We've got to talk, Dodge."

"I know."

They sat at the tiny table. Tory remembered the time, not very long ago, when they sat across from each other at this very table as strangers. Perfect strangers. Now they were perfect lovers. She smiled hopefully at him, thinking how her life would change with a man to love. It was exciting, for this man was different from any she had ever known. And she loved him so . . .

"When do you have to go back?" he asked, interrupting her thoughts.

"I need to get back as soon as possible. I've already left the shop with Megan in charge longer than I planned. But maybe we could wait a few more days—"

"We?"

"Yes. If you need a few days to close out your business here. Or if you need a little more time getting rid of Sharkey's stuff, you could join me later."

"Join you?" He winced and narrowed one brown eye at her.

"Yes. I understand this kind of thing takes time. Plus we have to get the gold situation settled."

"That may take weeks to finalize, but we should know something about the value today when we meet with Ramona." He paused to thoughtfully sip his coffee.

"Good." She reached over to pat his hand. "Of course we'll probably have to return here for Yazzie's trial, but that'll be just a pleasure trip. In the meantime, though, we can get settled in L.A. I have a small apartment, just big enough for one, so we'll want to get a larger one. And we have to find you a job—"

"Hold it, Tory!" His face was a dark scowl. "What are you talking about? I'm not coming to live in L.A."

"You aren't?" She straightened against the back

of the booth. "Well, what do you expect me to do? Transfer my dress shop to Tombstone?"

"Expect you to do?" He shrugged. "Why, nothing."

"Wait a minute, Dodge. What are you planning to do?"

"I think I'll go check out Reno and the University of Nevada. I told you I applied for a job there. Maybe I'll work in Nevada for a while."

"Maybe . . . *Maybe?*" She looked at him wildly. "I don't think you understand any of this. Or maybe I don't. I—I love you, Dodge Callahan. And somehow in the last few days, I figured you felt the same. What do you say about that?"

He ran his hand over his face, his fingers lingering to stroke his mustache. "Frankly, it scares the hell out of me."

"What?" She wanted to jump up and scream. "After all we've been through together, all we've done. After sleeping together . . . Doesn't that mean anything to you?"

His dark eyes clouded. "Of course. It's just that suddenly you're sounding like someone taking charge of my life, tying me up to convention."

"Oh, no, I wouldn't do that. But, Dodge, we could make a good team. You could help me get the shop straight, help me keep it solvent."

"I've never done that kind of work in my life, Tory. I don't know anything about retailing."

"But you could learn. We'll work together on it. After we're married—"

"Hold it, Tory." He stood up abruptly. "I don't know if I'm ready for that."

"What does it take?"

"For me? Time. And, uh, oh, God, Tory. I think we both need time here."

"I only know one thing. That I love you, Dodge Callahan. And you're refusing my love."

He faced her, his dark expression frantic. "If it means I have to conform to your standards, I guess so. Don't you know me well enough to realize I can't live like that? Oh, Tory, don't you see? I need space. And I need a little time to figure out what all this means."

"What—what about us?" She felt as though someone had socked her in the stomach.

"I don't know yet. I have to think. We both do. We'll work something out to be together, Tory."

"Sounds like a long-distance love affair is what you want."

"No, I want us to be together, but—"

"You know what I think?" She ran a hand through her short dark hair, mussing it even more. "I think this is a repeat of history."

"What?"

She folded her arms. "Only I was lucky enough to find out about it sooner than my mother did."

"Tory, what are you talking about?"

"Oh, Dodge Callahan," she muttered, shaking her head slowly, "you're just like my father. You can't make a commitment."

"No, you're wrong, Tory. I'm different from Sharkey. I want you with me. I just haven't figured out how to keep you yet. But I will."

"Well, when you do, let me know what you've decided!" She bolted from the room and slammed the bedroom door. Her frantic gaze fell on the rumpled bed where they'd made love, where they couldn't bear to be apart, where they were crazy for each other. Her eyes filled with tears, fogging the view. Furiously, she threw her suitcases on the bed and began piling her clothes into them.

This was it—the end! They'd been lovers . . . perfect lovers. But nothing more than perfect lovers. She couldn't believe her plan hadn't worked, her plan to make him love her. She'd wanted Dodge so badly. And she thought he wanted her. But, obviously not.

His voice sounded strained as he called through the closed door. "Tory, we're supposed to meet Ramona and Rex at noon at the Crystal Palace."

"I remember. I'll be ready." *And then I'm leaving.* Her heart was heavy with sadness as she finished packing.

In a spontaneous moment, she removed Sharkey's plaid shirt and stuffed it into a corner of her bag. Dodge wouldn't want it, and she would value it as a small memento of her father. Suddenly, her eyes filled with tears as she realized she regretted never knowing him. And that meant more to her than any inheritance he could have left for her.

The Crystal Palace was crowded with tourists. Tory and Dodge were there first. They sat in the back near the framed antique roulette wheels in strained silence. Heck, the bartender, brought them cold drinks while they waited. Tory stared at the huge mahogany bar that covered one long wall, wondering how many lovers' quarrels it had witnessed. Or how many lovers had parted from there, heading for separate futures. Like her and Dodge.

Well, she'd come to Tombstone and stepped back in time, far enough to fall in love with a man very much like her father. Far enough to leave herself aching and brokenhearted, like her mother had been.

It would end between her and Dodge today. She had no illusions about them getting together again. That was a dream with no hope of coming true. They had loved, and now they would part, never to be together again.

"There she comes," Dodge said quietly, nodding toward Ramona entering the front door. "But Rex isn't with her. Wonder if he's all right?"

Tory watched Ramona's confident demeanor as she walked across the crowded room, slipping between the tourists who came to admire the antique bar and review times past. She recalled the first time she had seen Ramona and how she felt when she discovered Ramona was her father's lover. It was something close to hate. But then, she disliked a lot of people that day. Sharkey included.

Now that she had gotten to know Ramona, they had become good friends. And it was a friendship that would last, bonded by mutual respect and the crises they'd overcome.

Tory met her with a hug and a smile. "Okay, what gives? You look like you swallowed a canary!"

"Have I got some great news for you!" Ramona kissed Dodge's cheek, then sat opposite them.

"Where's Rex?" Dodge asked first.

"He's still in the hospital. They had to do a little corrective surgery on his arm, but he's going to be out and fine in a few days. I stopped by to see him this morning to give him the news, and he was sitting up in bed, letting a blond nurse feed him."

"Leave it to good ole' Rex to find the prettiest woman, even in a hospital," Dodge said, chuckling. "I guess keeping him from medical attention those extra days didn't hurt him much. What about his other injuries?"

"Mostly minor." Ramona's dark eyes twinkled. "But still he was talking about needing special round-the-clock nursing care when I left."

Dodge rested his large hands on the table. "Tell us, Ramona, did we dig up enough gold to pay his hospital bills?"

Ramona couldn't keep from smiling and opened a couple of forms from her purse. "I think so. Here, these belong to you. They give an accounting of the assayist's preliminary evaluation. It'll be a few weeks before we know how much, and before any money is forthcoming, but it looks good."

Tory reached for the paper and scanned the confusing columns. "How good?"

"Oh, perhaps ten thousand or more. Each."

"Ten? Ten thousand?" Tory couldn't contain her joy and jumped up to hug Ramona. "This is fantastic! Just great! Better than I ever dreamed."

"Me, too." Ramona nodded happily. "It'll mean I can start the Center for Southwestern Studies, something I've always wanted to do. We'll document and investigate every pictograph I've re-

259

corded. And we'll be able to study that ancient skull we found in the wash."

"You could have a whole new career, Ramona," Dodge said.

She nodded proudly. "All because of Sharkey."

"What about the cave room full of Indian artifacts?" Tory asked. "What will happen to those?"

"That entire area will be federally protected and preserved in its present state. The college will administer to its protection and be permitted to study the ghost town. The Indian ruins are at least two hundred years old, maybe more. It's all very exciting and will improve our academic standings in archeologic study."

"And yours as a professor?" Dodge added.

"Yes," she admitted with a shy grin. "I don't think I'll have any trouble getting my book on Indian pictographs published now. And I have ideas for about three others!"

"That's fantastic, Ramona," Tory said with enthusiasm. "I'm so proud of you! Now you have to promise you'll come to visit me in L.A. when your first book is published. I'll give you a big autographing party. Oh, we'll have a wonderful time together."

"So you're going back to L.A.?" Ramona looked pointedly at her, then to Dodge. He remained impassive.

Tory answered quickly. "Oh, yes, I have to get back to my business. Been gone too long now."

"What will you do with your money, Tory?"

"Well, although it's very nice, ten thousand won't make any of us qualify for *Lifestyles of the*

260

Rich and Famous, but it will allow me to pay off my debts. Then, I don't know. Maybe I'll give the shop a little facelift to improve business." Tory shifted and looked at Dodge. "What about you, Dodge? What will you do? It isn't quite enough to buy that cruiser and sail around the world."

"No, there won't be any cruises." He sighed with a shrug of his broad shoulders. "You're right, it isn't enough to make dreams come true, although it sounds like Ramona is coming pretty close."

She smiled sadly. "There is one dream I'll never see come true because Sharkey is gone."

"I think losing Sharkey was a great loss for all of us," Tory said.

Dodge and Ramona looked at her curiously. "Even for you, Tory?" Ramona asked softly.

"Especially me," Tory admitted painfully. "I came here, not as his daughter but as a stranger, angry about my past. Through all of you, I've been able to learn about my father and to get to know him a little bit. That knowledge has given me a connection with the past so I can understand myself better. I want to thank both of you for enduring me when I was so overbearing at first."

Ramona reached for Tory's hand. "Actually, we're the ones who have benefited the most, to get to know Sharkey's little girl."

"Thank you," Tory murmured shyly. "Well, it's time for me to leave. I have a plane to catch."

"I hate to see you go," Ramona admitted. "But that's selfish of me. I know you have other things to do." She looked at Dodge. "What about you? Are you going to stay here with your old job?"

"Teaching at the University of Nevada in Reno. It's time I settled down to a regular job and lived a regular life for a change."

Tory's hands knotted in her lap, but she said nothing. They'd be parting soon, her to go back to her old life, Dodge to live a "regular life." Why couldn't he live that regular life with her? There was only one reason, and it broke her heart to acknowledge it.

"A regular life for you sounds dull, Dodge," Ramona said with a little laugh. "Somehow I can't imagine that."

"Well, you never know. I may find another gold mine to explore."

Ramona folded her assay slip with her large hands and stuffed it into her purse. "Sharkey's mine will be closed forever. Fenced and boarded. What we got out of it will be the final digs because the mine backs up to the protected Indian ruins. If anyone should dig much further, or use explosives like we discussed, the whole thing could be ruined. They don't want to chance it, so I guess this is it."

"I'm happy with it," Dodge said.

"Me, too," Tory agreed. "Actually, it's more than I expected."

"That's because you expected nothing," Dodge mumbled.

"But I got a lot," Tory admitted. "I hope you'll all come to see me in L.A. Crazy as this sounds, I do appreciate the experience of going into the mountains. It was beautiful in many ways. It opened me up to another way of life that is totally different and even better in some ways than the city life I've always known."

Ramona stood and hugged Tory long and hard. "Meeting you has been a highlight, Tory. I wish you didn't have to go so soon."

"I know, but we'll probably see each other in a few months when they have Yazzie's trial. I'm definitely coming back for that," she promised. Slowly, she turned to Dodge.

He was already standing, and his hands went around her naturally.

She felt so clumsy with him. Why, just last night they'd made love. *For the last time!* Now she couldn't decide whether to hug him or shake his hand. She didn't think she could touch him casually, so she tried not to touch him at all. Like a dope, she leaned her cheek forward for a pecking kiss.

Refusing to settle for such, Dodge cupped her chin in one hand and lifted her face to his. The kiss was breathtaking and hard and far too long. They broke away to applause and turned to see that every tourist in the place was watching them.

Tory was embarrassed and somewhat flustered. Grasping her purse, she hurried out amid a sprinkling of oohs and ahs from the audience.

Dodge watched her disappear, even listened for her footsteps on the wooden sidewalk. Then they, too, were gone. Even though the Crystal Palace was full, his life was now empty. He knew it and couldn't do a thing about it. In his cowboy style, he ambled over to the huge dark bar and ordered.

"Heck, give me a Scotch and water. No, make that a double."

Heck didn't raise an eyebrow. He just filled the glass with amber liquid and slid it in front of Dodge, then moved away.

Ramona walked over to the bar and stood next to Dodge. She was quiet for a moment, then looked up at him. She smiled sweetly, although her dark eyes were cold. "You know, Dodge, you always were a lot like Sharkey. Sometimes that's pretty good, sometimes not. Right now, I think you're the biggest damn fool I've ever known, except for Sharkey. That woman loves you. And from that stupid expression on your face, you love her. But you're too big a fool to know it. Or to know what to do about it."

She wheeled around and walked out of the Crystal Palace.

Dodge just stared at her, then he turned back to his Scotch. But it didn't help.

CHAPTER SIXTEEN

"Tory! There's been a big mistake!"

"Huh?" Tory whirled her chair back around to the desk. Daydreaming out the office window held more interest for her than the piles of rubble on her desk. Somewhere in that rat's nest was Cliff Snyder's letter stating that Yazzie's trial was set for September. She and the others would be subpoenaed, so she should make the appropriate arrangements to take a short leave from work. She and the other sun seekers would be there, including Dodge.

Dodge's note was there on her desk, too. But she knew exactly where it was. She had hidden it beneath the right corner of the large flat calendar.

Megan, Tory's assistant, strode into the office waving a pink order blank. "This just can't be right." She jerked open a drawer of the gray metal cabinet and began leafing furiously through the files.

"What's wrong?" Lethargically, Tory watched as Megan flipped back her straight blond hair and mumbled to herself as she searched the files. Tall, statuesque Megan was a natural with sales at Tall and Terrific. She was also a natural with the book-keeping. And the ordering.

Megan didn't halt her search but said over her shoulder, "I'm positive we only ordered thirty, but they've delivered three hundred! Now what are we going to do with three hundred alpaca vests? Aha! Here it is!" She pulled out a corresponding sheet and studied it with pursed lips.

"What does it say?"

"Says here three hundred." Megan looked at Tory. "Your initials."

Tory's blue eyes widened. "Oh, good heavens! Did I do that? I'm so sorry . . ."

Megan shook her head. "Don't apologize, Tory. I'll see what I can do about rectifying it."

"Maybe I should go talk to him since it's my mistake."

"No, let me." Megan paused and looked at her boss. "It's probably none of my business, Tory, but you're just not with it. You haven't been since you returned from Tombstone. I don't understand. It's like you just don't care anymore."

"But I do care. It's just a simple mistake." She ran her fingers through her hair. "I know, I know. No mistake is simple."

"Maybe I should do all the ordering to prevent this from happening again."

Tory nodded weakly and watched rather help-lessly as her capable assistant whirled out of the room. She tapped her glossy fingernails on a tiny cleared spot on the desk and listened as Megan explained the mistake to the delivery man. What *was* wrong with her? In her heart, she knew. She had fallen helplessly, hopelessly, in love with a rake and a rambler named Dodge Callahan. *And he was not in love with her.*

She looked down and studied the mess on her desk. She really should get this stuff organized. Tomorrow. She'd do it tomorrow.

Megan's pleading voice hushed, and Tory waited expectantly.

It was a few minutes before Megan reappeared, a cup of hot tea in each hand. With her elbow, she cleared a corner of the desk and set the cups down. "Hope you have lots of friends who'd like alpaca vests for birthday and Christmas presents for the next ten years. We're stuck with them."

"Oh, no!"

"Oh, *yes.* Signed and sealed. A deal is a deal." Megan posed with a finger alongside her cheek. "Maybe we can come up with some crazy promotion and give them away."

"It's a thought."

Megan laughed off Tory's seriousness and reached into the bottom drawer for a small brown bag. "I've closed the shop so we can take a lunch break. We'll discuss vest gimmicks later. Right now, there's something else."

Tory smiled and sipped her tea. "Okay, what's on your mind?"

"Look, I don't know what's bugging you, Tory, but I feel we should talk about it. We've been friends as well as coworkers for a long time, and I wish you'd share it with me. Maybe you're worried about the upcoming trial with all the negative ramifications it might have."

"No, I feel very positive about that. It's the one thing I can do for my father. Our only link. I'm looking forward to testifying against the bastard who killed him."

Megan nodded silently and studied Tory's intent expression. "Well, if not the trial, what is it then?"

"Oh, Megan, I haven't meant to exclude you," Tory said earnestly. "But you're right. I've had a lot on my mind lately, and I haven't been very alert to the business at hand. Actually, I've been thinking seriously about selling the shop."

Megan's eyes flew wide open at Tory's bombshell. "What?"

"Don't worry, I intended all along to offer it to you first. In fact, I want you to have it so much that I'm willing to work with you on the finances. You *do* want it, don't you?"

"Yes, but it comes as a shock! You've never even mentioned selling out completely. I had no idea you were thinking about this."

"I know. I just came up with the idea recently." Tory played with her cup nervously. "It was a hard decision to make. There are lots of memories around here."

Megan smiled gently. "Tall and Terrific was your mother's pride and joy."

"That's just it," Tory agreed. "The shop was Mama's, not mine. I merely helped her run it and evolved into being the manager when she was sick. Of course, when I inherited it, I tried to carry on. But it just wasn't the same without her around. And I just don't have the enthusiasm for this type of business."

"I can see that."

"But you, Megan . . . Why, right from the start, you had a way with the customers and a feel for the business. That's why you're just the right person to run it, and I'd feel good about selling to you, whereas to a stranger . . ." Tory's voice dwindled to nothing, and Megan filled in the silent gap.

"I do love this type of work. And this shop. I love the idea of me owning Tall and Terrific." She looked sharply at Tory. "Are you sure this is what you want to do?"

Tory's smile was sad but firm. "Yes."

"But what will you do?"

"I honestly don't know yet. I haven't given it much thought."

Megan looked closely at her friend. "You haven't thought about the future? Maybe you should wait a little while before making a final decision. I don't mind, honestly."

"No, I've decided for sure. I'm going to sell it to you, Megan."

The two looked at each other for a moment, then fell into a warm embrace.

"I can't believe this is happening to me," Megan said happily, and opened her lunch bag.

"Maybe we should go out to lunch and have some wine to celebrate," Tory suggested.

Megan shook her head. "This may not be very appropriate, but it'll have to do. I think we both need to save our money." She pulled out several small packages and lined them up on the desk. "Take your pick. Boiled egg. Ritz crackers and—"

Tory gasped audibly. "Not Ritz crackers and peanut butter!" Surely she didn't have Ritz crackers and peanut butter, Dodge's old standby.

"No, but that's another favorite." Megan chuckled. "This is almost as bad. Ritz and cheddar cheese. You like it?"

Tory sighed with crazy relief. "Yes, cheese on a Ritz is fine." She had to stop doing this, letting her mind go berserk, letting everything remind her of *him*. Why, cheese and peanut butter were common foods, not restricted to a rangy cowboy named Dodge Callahan. Still, her hands fluttered, and she fumbled the small cracker sandwich and dropped it right into her tea cup. "Oh, drat! Look what a mess I've made! How awkward of me!" She took the cup into the adjoining bathroom and dumped it into the toilet.

"Tory, are you all right?"

"Yes, sure. Just a little flighty today." She emerged with a fake smile.

"Shall I fix you more tea?"

"No—uh—yes. No, you stay there, Megan. I'll do it. I can certainly fix myself a cup of tea."

Curiously, Megan watched Tory's nervous antics. Finally, Tory sat down again, with fresh tea and another Ritz with cheese. "It's that man, isn't it?" she asked quietly.

Tory's blue eyes shot open, then dropped just as quickly. "What make you say that?"

"Just a feeling I have. It's that man you met in Tombstone. Dodge Callahan. Wonderful name, Dodge Callahan," she murmured dreamily. "Have you heard from him?"

Tory swallowed hard and decided to try to talk about him. If she couldn't tell her closest friend, who could she tell? Anyway, maybe talking about it might relieve this tremendous pain deep inside her. "Actually, yes. I got a note from him just this week inviting me up to see him in Reno."

"Great! Then that's why you're so nervous."

"No, I don't think so." Tory kept her eyes averted and tried to convince herself it didn't matter.

"Well, what is it? You're going, of course." Megan popped a cracker into her mouth with a satisfied smile. "A trip to Reno to see Dodge Callahan should settle you down."

"I don't know if I'm going." Tory folded a tissue neatly in her lap and stroked it as one would a cat. "I haven't decided."

"Don't you want to see him again?"

"Well, it isn't that simple. Of course I'd like to see him . . . Well, what I mean is, it would be nice—"

" 'Nice'?" Megan repeated shrilly. "I think you might just crack into a million pieces if you *don't* see him. That's more than 'nice.' "

"Now, Megan, you don't understand everything."

"What's to understand? Do you like him?"

Tory pressed her lips together and nodded.

"Love him?"

"It doesn't matter what I feel. That feeling isn't mutual."

"Has he said so?"

"It's what he hasn't said that counts."

271

"I see. Well, I wonder if he's as miserable as you are?"

Tory smiled weakly. "I don't know."

"Then why don't you go find out?"

"I . . . well, maybe I should . . ." Tory's eyes clouded as she thought of the rugged, broad-shouldered man she'd loved so quickly. And left. But there was good reason. They weren't well suited for each other. They were as different as night and day. The man was too much like her father. A rake and a rambler. A sun seeker.

"Tory, I'm no great voice of experience, but I am your friend. I hate to see you going through such pain. And as much as I want to buy this shop, I'd also hate to see you do anything drastic, like selling out because of this unappreciative man."

"Oh, I'm not selling because of him. It's because of me."

"Don't ruin your life over a man, Tory."

"You're a good friend, Megan, and I appreciate your concern. But selling the shop is the only thing I'm sure of. In my heart, I know it's right for me. Somehow, I just know it." She lifted her chin and smiled firmly.

"Before you make a final decision, go visit Dodge Callahan. See for yourself if it's over between you. The fact that he invited you to see him indicates something, doesn't it?"

Tory raised her eyes. "I . . . I suppose it does. Yes, maybe I should go see him." She began to smile, and a devilish gleam lighted her blue eyes. "I'll have a showdown with the town marshal!"

"The *what?*" Megan laughed.

"Dodge played the rough and tough town marshal in the streets of Tombstone the first day I arrived. He gunned all the bad guys down in a blaze of glory. Maybe I should see how tough he is under fire of a different sort."

Megan grinned and punched her fist through the air. "All right! You *show* him, Tory!"

But by the time Tory's plane landed in Reno, her fire had dwindled somewhat. During the flight, she was as nervous as a cat on a hot tin roof. Then she saw Dodge standing in the waiting room, head and shoulders over everyone else. Her heart soared with joy. He looked the same: white Stetson, western shirt, well-worn jeans and boots. And he looked wonderful!

Dodge spotted Tory right away. He smiled. A lady of five feet nine stood out in any crowd. She looked fantastic in a classy jade green blouse and Levis. Absolutely beautiful! Her blue eyes glistened happily as she approached him. He wondered if she were really as glad to see him as she appeared to be.

He met her with a big bear hug and a quick kiss right on the lips. Then he laughed and grabbed her again, swinging her up in his arms and around in a circle. "Tory, you look great!"

She smiled up at him, and all her reservations about seeing him again flew out the window. His strong arms swept around her, and she knew this was where she belonged. She embraced his neck and encouraged him to kiss her again. He obliged, this time long and hard. By the time they came up for air, most of the crowd had cleared.

One elderly lady scuffled past them and winked at Tory. "Atta girl! Go after 'im! The bigger they are, the harder they fall!"

Tory smiled at the spicy lady. "Not this one." She didn't think Dodge had fallen at all. Certainly not for her, it seemed. Although his welcoming kiss was nice. Very nice.

His arm tightened around her ribs. "What do you know?"

She looked up at him curiously. "I know you, Dodge. You're your own person. Independent and restless. You're not going to fall for anyone."

"I'm not like that anymore. I've changed."

"Changed? How?"

"You'll see." He gave her a smug look and ushered her through the airport and into his waiting car.

She slid into the new-smelling leather interior of a blue sedan. "Very nice. Is it new?"

He nodded proudly. "Traded the Blazer for it. I knew you'd like this better."

"But what do you use for going up into the mountains?"

"Don't do that anymore. Don't need to. Too busy doing other things."

"Oh." She rested her hands in her lap. "Busy doing what?"

While he drove through town, Dodge explained about his job and all that had kept him busy during the past weeks. "I'm the assistant geology professor in charge of Mineral Deposits on the Western Slopes, and that title puts me in line for tenure. Plus I've published a position paper on gold deposits in the Dragoons. That gave me instant peer recognition and influence with the administration."

She listened, wondering if this was the same Dodge Callahan she'd left in Tombstone. "Do you mean you haven't been to Lovelock or Rebel Creek or Midas?"

He breathed through his teeth. "Why would I want to go to those places?"

"Gold, of course." She gazed at him with clear blue eyes. "I'd hoped you could show me some of your favorite haunts around here. I brought my softest jeans and my mountain boots."

He pursed his lips. "I—uh—don't have any favorite places to look for gold because I don't do that anymore, Tory."

"Hmm, funny. I thought you'd never quit. Sharkey didn't."

"Well, I'm not Sharkey."

"No, but you're a lot like him."

"I don't think so."

Oh, yes, you are, Dodge Callahan, she thought with a smug smile. She leaned back on the seat and tried to relax. They drove along in relative silence, exchanging bits of information about the weather and saying life in general was "just fine." Both of them were lying, and strangely enough, both sensed it. But neither commented on it.

Dodge's house was on a hill with a curving driveway. When they halted in front, Tory gaped in awe. "A house? I thought you'd have an apartment." The place was lovely.

275

"How do you like it?"

"Beautiful, of course! Are you renting?"

"No, it's mine. Bought it last month. I thought you'd like it."

"This is what you did with your share of the gold? You didn't buy a new four-by-four or a swank cruiser to take you around the world?"

"Naw. Don't need them." His brown eyes were alight with a special glow. "Come on, I want you to see the living room."

"What's in the living room?" She grabbed her purse and small overnighter and followed him up the stairs. The multilevel house was built into the hillside and sported blue shutters on the front windows. Tory wondered if it had a neat little picket fence, too.

Dodge dropped her bags in the foyer and led her into the sunken living room. She gazed in awe at the stone fireplace that covered one end of the room and the potted fir tree in the other. "How interesting," she commented with a curious glance at him. "It's like having your own Christmas tree growing right in the house."

"I thought you'd like it." He beamed proudly. "Want to see the pool? How about a drink first? Perrier, isn't it?"

She nodded and followed him into the spacious kitchen. "Sounds great." The kitchen was gorgeous, with every modern convenience and wooden cabinets and long stretches of countertops. She waited while he poured her sparkling water, then popped a beer for himself. "Thanks."

"My pleasure. Want to continue the tour on the patio?"

They stepped out onto the brick patio that surrounded the blue-tiled pool. She walked around a little, admiring everything. Finally, she turned to face him. Was this the same Dodge with whom she'd fallen in love? Maybe she didn't remember him right. Maybe she never knew him at all. She took a deep breath and felt the uneasiness in the air.

"Well, you've certainly been busy, Dodge. Going after tenure, writing articles, getting them published, buying a house . . . changing."

"Yep. Changes for the better, I hope." He propped a booted foot up on a brick step. "It feels good to put down roots. I'm steadier now and—"

"Duller."

He chuckled uneasily. "Well, maybe. Certainly more secure. And that's important. Isn't it important to you, Tory?"

"I suppose . . ." She used to think that. So what was wrong with her?

He slapped his knee. "Enough about me. What about you, Tory? What have you been doing since we last met?"

"Just working."

"At your shop?"

"The shop was my mother's, you know. I just inherited it."

"Like you inherited the debts? I'm assuming those are all paid off now. How's business?"

"Matter of fact, I'm in the process of selling it."

"Selling the shop? Why?"

She lifted her blue eyes imploringly. Would she be able to make Dodge understand? He, of all people, should. "Because I realized the shop wasn't for me anymore. It was never mine from the beginning. It was my mother's idea, her project, her life. Not mine."

He looked at her with a puzzled expression. "I'm not sure I understand. It's a business, and a good one. Most people would give their eye teeth for something like that."

"I know." She sighed. He did not understand her. Why did she think he would? "But I'm not a retailer. After Mama died last year, I tried to carry on, but it's been a disaster. Without Megan, my manager, I would have been bankrupt long ago."

He shook his head. "I thought you liked it?"

"I tried to like it. I wanted to. After all, that was the normal thing to do. But I've discovered that it just holds me down. A business is too confining for me. I want to be freer, I guess. Surely you, of all people, understand that, Dodge."

He ran a large hand through his unruly hair, messing it even more. When he didn't answer, she continued trying to explain. "So I've decided to sell the business to Megan. That's a safe bet, you know. She loves that shop, and actually, she'll do a better job of running it than I did."

"I see." He ambled around the pool, pausing to gulp the beer, then continuing to walk. "What are you going to do with yourself after you sell?"

"I don't know. Haven't decided yet. I thought" —she chuckled self-consciously and followed him —"I thought that it might be interesting to invest some of my money into a capitalistic venture. Like maybe . . . gold mining."

He looked up quickly, then away. "Yeah, well, I don't know how profitable those are."

"If you trust the company, it isn't so risky."

"I don't know of any around that can be trusted."

"Perhaps you're interested in forming another Sun Seekers Mining Company, Dodge."

"Naw. Too busy."

"Too busy writing articles and—"

"Too busy putting down roots."

"Oh." She sighed deeply. "Well, I know this all sounds sort of bizarre and unconventional."

"For you, Tory, it does. It doesn't sound like you at all."

She confronted him. "Does it sound like something Sharkey Carsen's daughter might do?"

He glared at her, his mouth working silently beneath that wonderful shaggy mustache. "Yes, maybe it does."

"Then what's wrong with it?"

"Nothing . . ." There was another moment of tense silence.

Then she spoke in a strained voice. "This whole thing is really crazy, Dodge. Seems like you've been busy buying property and putting down roots. And I've been busy selling everything I own and pulling up roots."

"Looks like we've both been busy changing."

"Yes, I'm afraid so." She turned and walked slowly back inside, placing her glass on a kitchen counter.

He followed her, saying nothing.

She halted before her bags in the foyer. Inside her chest was a knot that threatened to choke her. Things were not right here, not the same, not what she expected. And obviously, not what Dodge expected. All Tory could think of was that she did not belong in this house.

Dodge stopped in the doorway, almost filling the space with his large frame. "I'm still the same, Tory. Just in different surroundings."

"No, Dodge, you're different. I don't know what happened to us. Maybe we're both different. But I don't think this is right. I don't belong here."

"Don't you see, Tory? I did all this for you."

She clutched her bosom. "For *me?* Why—"

"Because you wanted a place of your own. And roots. And because . . . I love you."

She gasped and for a moment she couldn't move. Slowly, she turned around.

His face was filled with love. "I could never say it before. I was scared of what it would mean, how it would change everything for both of us. But I found that my love for you would not go away. So I tried to become what I thought you wanted in a man."

"But, Dodge, I never wanted anyone but you. Just the way you were. I fell in love with Dodge Callahan, the rough and ready cowboy, the sun seeker."

"I thought you wanted someone steady, someone who could offer security and roots because that's what you never had."

"So that's why you bought this house instead of a cruiser? And traded the Blazer for a sedan?"

He shrugged and laughed. "I never really considered a cruiser. I'm not a sailor. I'm a . . . gold digger."

"I suppose unconsciously I tried to become what I thought you wanted in a woman. Someone who could ride into the mountains with the best of them."

"I fell in love with a classy woman with the longest legs in the world and the most beautiful eyes I'd ever seen. Especially when I made love to you. And I don't give a damn about how well you ride a mule into the mountains. Now, after seeing you again, I love you even more."

"Dodge . . ."

There was no more hesitation. She flew into his arms, and he lifted her off her feet. She squeezed him tightly, as if to make sure they never let go. And he held her securely, pressing their bodies and hearts together. For a wildly happy moment, Tory thought she might cry and buried her face against his neck. "Dodge, oh, Dodge, what have we done?"

His lips caressed her bare neck. "We almost lost something very, very wonderful."

She leaned her head back and allowed his kisses to trail around her neck, to the sensitive areas of her skin. "I missed you, missed what you do to me." He loosened his hold on her, and she slid sensuously down his unyielding body, down just far enough for their lips to meet. Then, lips still locking, he slowly lowered her further until her feet touched the floor.

His kiss practically took her breath away, a reminder of what they'd missed, a preview of things to come. It was wonderful and wild, and she could hardly believe they'd held back all this time. All the love they had stored away and held dormant in their hearts flowed to the surface. And bubbled over.

When they finally came up for air, he looked slightly dazed. "God, I thought I'd never get to see you again, or kiss you."

She took a deep breath. "Wow, what we've missed."

"And we nearly ruined everything by changing."

"Don't ever change, Dodge. I love you, Dodge —just the way you are."

His kiss smothered her lips as he lifted her up in his strong arms. "Tory, my darling fancy pants, I love everything about you. Every inch . . ."

"Show me."

"Thank heaven you haven't lost your loving spirit, Tory Talbot!" He chuckled throatily as he whisked her into his bedroom.

"Thank heaven you haven't lost your desire for me, Dodge Callahan."

"Never, my love." He laid her on the bed and began stripping off his shirt and jeans. His feverish hands couldn't work fast enough, and by the time he'd discarded everything, his lean, muscular body glistened with the heat of anticipation. He was aroused and ready for her.

She watched him with delight and wriggled around on the bed to remove her own clothes. He stood there, waiting impatiently for her to finish, his eyes darting over her pale nudity. She smiled seductively, as if she even needed to entice him, and traced the feminine shape of her body with her hands.

When she reached her hips, he took up the game. His large hands outlined her, tracing her silken torso, then widespread fingertips grazed her breasts, sending shooting stars through every inch of her. "Come on," she whispered, and opened her arms to him.

They came together, nude and ready for love, yet only holding each other close for a long time.

"I thought I'd never get to hold you again, Tory. Never get to touch you . . ." He bent his head to kiss her breasts.

She wanted him with a desire she never thought possible. "Oh, Dodge, oh! I thought you'd never touch me there again. Or there!" She arched against his roving hand, and they rolled together on his bed, joyous in their sex play.

"Tell me," he demanded, "do you like this? And this?"

"Yes! Oh, God, yes!"

Tory's joyous laughter danced through the rambling house, beneath the Christmas tree and up the spacious fireplace in the living room, out onto the brick patio and around the tiled pool.

Then the house was quiet, save for low murmurs of love. Brief, sexy words punctuated the hush. They came together and merged with a clashing of cymbals, a ringing of bells, a pounding of drums. The world celebrated in imaginary noisemaking, wild and unrestrained, while they made love. And they rose to the highest of timbres . . . to the ecstasy of love.

Again, all was quiet. Tears of joy fell from her beautiful blue eyes. Dodge murmured soothing words and stroked her back.

And she said, "It's all right. I just love you so much. Hold me, and never let go."

"You will always be here, near my heart."

Later they stirred.

"Tory, my sweet beauty, we haven't lost a thing. If possible, my feelings of love are stronger than ever. It scares the hell out of me to think I almost lost you."

"You'll never lose me because I belong right here in your arms, Dodge."

"There's only one way this can work, you know. I want you to be my wife."

"Is that a proposal?" She laughed aloud. "Oh, I get it! A professor working toward tenure can't have a live-in lover."

"It has nothing to do with tenure," he objected gruffly. "A man who loves and desires only one woman in the entire world wants to make doubly sure of the commitment. And I know for sure, Tory, I want you forever."

She ran her fingers through his hair, tousling it even more. "I love it when you insist on having your way."

He kissed the soft throbbing spot on her neck. "I hope my way is your way."

"This time it is," she murmured, lifting her chin for his further meanderings along her willing body. "I think we're more alike than either of us was ever willing to admit. Actually, I like the idea of putting down roots in this house."

"You do?"

"Of course. It's a lovely house, as houses go. But I honestly can't believe you'll be willing to give up completely on finding the mother lode."

"I would do it for you."

"Oh, Dodge, I won't let you!" She raised up on one elbow. "The way I see it, you're a sun seeker by desire, but I come by it naturally. I have the blood of Sharkey Carsen in my veins, and my legacy calls me to the mountains in search of that glimmer of sun caught in the rocks. We were successful once, and I'll bet we can do it again. I'm willing to take a chance on a couple of gold diggers that show promise for success. We could find Callahan's gold this time."

He threw his head back and laughed. " 'Callahan's gold,' huh? Sounds good to me."

"We could try."

"We could," he agreed. "But no promises on the gold. The only promise I can make is that I love you, Tory, with all my heart and soul. I love you now and forever." He sealed the pledge with a kiss.

She snuggled into the cradle of his arms. "That's a good, solid promise. It's all I need."

"You're all I need . . ."

And Tory smiled, content in the knowledge that she would lie in Dodge's arms . . . and make love forever.

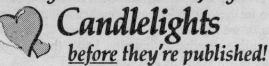